GROWLERS

Screaming, Piotr pointed his Uzi straight at the thing and blasted it with a hail of lead, oblivious to the bullets that were also pulping his own foot. Alexi brought his own weapon to bear—and only under the combined firepower of assault rifle and submachine gun did the thing finally release its hold. It scuttled away under a bank of cryotanks, leaving a smear of steaming ichor on the floor. Four of the glass-walled cryotanks cracked open at once, spilling infant growlers onto the floor. Landing on their apelike feet, they immediately bounded for Piotr. Three of them sank slavering teeth into the wounded soldier, chewing gaping holes in his sides. The fourth clamped its jaws onto Piotr's face, cutting off his scream.

Alexi's mind was filled with a single thought that kept repeating itself.

Not again. Oh Christ, not again . . .

VOR: THE MAELSTROM

Novels available from Warner Aspect

Vor: Into the Maelstrom
by Loren L. Coleman

THE PLAYBACK WAR

LISA SMEDMAN

ASPECT®

WARNER BOOKS

A Time Warner Company

WARNER BOOKS EDITION

Copyright © 2000 by FASA Corporation
All rights reserved. No part of this book may be reproduced in any form or by any electronic or mechanical means, including information storage and retrieval systems, without permission in writing from the publisher, except by a reviewer who may quote brief passages in a review.

Aspect® name and logo are registered trademarks of Warner Books, Inc.

VOR: The Maelstrom and all related characters, slogans, and indicia are trademarks of FASA Corporation.

Cover design by Don Puckey
Cover illustration by Donato
Cover logo design by Jim Nelson

Warner Books, Inc.
1271 Avenue of the Americas
New York, NY 10020

Visit our Web site at
www.twbookmark.com

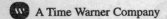 A Time Warner Company

Printed in the United States of America

First Printing: January 2000

10 9 8 7 6 5 4 3 2 1

THE PLAYBACK WAR

1

On the evening that time started to unravel, Alexi had already made up his mind to die.

But he wanted to find his glasses first.

Alexi crept through the rubble on hands and knees, patting the ground, his weapon dragging behind him by its shoulder strap. Bullets tore through the air overhead, occasionally sending a spray of cement chips pattering down on the back of his armored vest. Explosions rocked the streets outside the ruined building where Alexi had taken shelter, making the ground tremble. The air was thick with the smells of smoke, dust, and ruptured sewer lines.

For three days, the Union's heavy-assault suits had been chewing their way through Alexi's battalion. The under-equipped Neo-Soviet infantry troops were being decimated. They'd fought and died valiantly, but there was really no point in going on; there were simply too many of the Union juggernauts. And after three days without much sleep, Alexi was simply too exhausted to care whether a bullet found him. He decided to stop trying so hard to survive. Let death come if that was his fate. He had nothing left to lose.

Another explosion rattled the cement under Alexi's

knees and hands. Outside the ruined building, the battle for Vladivostok was raging. Alexi no longer cared who won the battle. But perversely, he cared about finding his glasses. Ironic, that a man who was ready to give up on life wasn't ready to give up on his eyesight.

Alexi patted the rubble he knelt on, hands blindly searching. He couldn't see a thing. At about the distance of an outstretched arm, everything became a blur.

"Hey, Alexi."

That was Boris's voice, somewhere just ahead. Alexi squinted, and the voice resolved itself into a dim blur that was hunkered down beside a brighter patch that must have been a hole in the ruined wall.

"Boris!" Alexi called back. "I can't find my glasses. Can you see them anywhere?"

Alexi gently patted the uneven mound of broken concrete and twisted rebar on which he crouched, praying that the glasses hadn't slipped down into a void in the two-meter-deep pile of rubble that used to be the building's first floor. His helmet visor was stuck in an up position; if he'd only been able to close it, his glasses wouldn't have flown off his face when he tripped. The speaker built into his helmet next to his right ear hissed on and off, giving him static-obscured bursts of panicked voices. The rest of the squad was pinned down by something—probably one of the heavy-assault suits that were chewing their way through the underequipped battalions that had been hastily assigned to defend the city. And as usual, *Leitenant* Soldatenkof was screaming insults. Which meant that someone was about to be shot.

Boris didn't move from his spot near the hole in the wall. "Vanya is trying to cross the street," he said. "Thirty rubles says he doesn't make it."

"Stop it, Boris," Alexi said wearily. "I'm tired of your jokes."

"No, seriously," Boris continued, his voice a deep rumble that matched his size. "I'll give you two-to-one odds. Vanya wasn't well this morning; he was throwing up again. I think his antiradiation pills have stopped working, or else he got another bad batch. He's so doubled over with cramps that he can barely walk. Thirty rubles says a Union bullet finds him before he's gone two steps."

"Boris, please."

"Forty rubles, then. At three-to-one odds."

"I just want to find my—"

"Fifty rubles. Four to one. My final offer."

Alexi's fingers encountered something that was wedged between two pieces of concrete. A piece of smooth glass, framed in wire. His glasses! He tugged gently, but they were stuck. He started to wiggle a chunk of concrete, praying it wouldn't crack the lens.

"Sixty rubles?" Boris asked hopefully.

An explosion just outside the building sent Alexi and Boris sprawling. Chunks of pavement rained in on them, thudding down through the hole where the ceiling had been. One bounced off Alexi's helmet. With a loud hissing noise his respirator activated, blowing a cloud of stale dust into his nose. Sneezing violently, he pushed himself to his hands and knees. Damn. Where was that crevice his glasses had been in?

It was getting darker. The blur that was Boris was getting harder to see as the patch of light coming in through the hole dimmed. A bright orange glow, coming from somewhere in the street below, lit the hole for a moment, then began to fade.

Private Maltovich! Bring up that chem-sprayer on the double! Move it, or I'll shoot!

The voice came over Alexi's helmet speaker, loud and clear. The blow on his helmet must have knocked it back on-line. That would be Vanya, getting yelled at by the *leitenant* again. Vanya's voice sounded exhausted as he radioed back to the squad's much-despised commanding officer.

Da, Leitenant. I'm moving.

Poor Vanya. But at least he could see where he was going.

"Boris, if I take your bet, will you help me find my—"

The blur that was Boris moved suddenly. Leaning out the hole, he emptied the entire magazine of his AK-51 in a deafening roar. Smoke from the aging weapon—an antique, even in Alexi's great-grandfather's day—drifted back to where Alexi crouched.

"The bet's off, Alexi," Boris said. "Vanya's across the street now."

"We never had a bet," Alexi reminded him.

Boris shouted down through the hole. "Hey, Vanya. Give them a squirt for me!"

Alexi heard a dull pop, followed by the sound of spraying liquid. Something splattered against the outside wall of the ruined building, then moved up the space between the buildings like storm-blown raindrops. A harsh chemical smell wafted in from the street outside. Alexi heard a wet, bubbling sound as the deadly chemicals reacted violently with whatever it was Vanya was hosing down.

Alexi located his glasses once more by feel, and carefully pried at the chunk of concrete that had trapped them. The speaker in his helmet blared in his ear, making him wince. The respirator still blew cold air in his face.

Move forward, damn you! You've got to get closer, you incompetent, spineless—

"Ten rubles says Vanya 'accidentally' sprays the *leitenant*," Boris muttered.

"It wouldn't matter if he did," Alexi said. "Soldatenkof's armor would save him. I hear they paint the officers' jackets with a toxin-repellent coating."

"That's just a lie they tell to keep the Chem Grunts from trying," Boris shot back.

"Vanya won't even try," Alexi said. "He knows what the consequences would be if he succeeded." As he spoke, he felt the chunk of concrete that had pinned his glasses finally come free. He lifted it up and used it to give the right side of his helmet a good thump. Mercifully, the *leitenant*'s voice dissolved back into static.

Alexi lifted his glasses up to his face and squinted at the lenses. A blurry reflection of himself stared back: a scrawny fellow with watery blue eyes and baby-fine blond hair that hung limp on his sweaty forehead. Alexi offered a brief prayer of thanks that the glasses were undamaged, save for a scratch in one lens. Straightening the bent wires, he slipped them over his ears.

Outside, the patter of automatic-weapons fire had fallen silent. Alexi heard a faint whirring noise and the creaking of metal joints. He wiped a smudge of dust from the lens of his glasses and looked across the shattered room at Boris.

The large bear of a man, clad in tattered sand-on-green combats and a dull black helmet embossed with a red star, glanced back at Alexi. The heavy three-day growth of beard that framed his face, disappearing down his neck and blending into his hairy chest and shoulders, was gray with dust. Compared to the others in the squad he looked almost healthy, except for the dark circles under his eyes. He wrenched the empty magazine of his AK-51 free, and slapped a fresh one—his last—into place.

"Better take those glasses off again, Alexi," he said in a mournful voice. "You're not going to like what you see. Five thousand rubles says we don't make it out of here alive."

Then he laughed, leaned out the hole again, and fired the AK-51 in a series of short bursts at something in the street. Alexi heard the sound of bullets pinging off metal. Then Boris jerked back inside the wall.

The answering response was swift: a dull whoosh, and an explosion that punched a smoking hole in the wall a few meters away from Boris. Broken concrete fountained into the room, and Alexi threw up an arm to shield his face. The force of the blast knocked him to the ground.

He spat dust from his mouth. "What is it?" he gasped.

"Another assault suit!" Boris shouted. "And this one's got more than just a machine gun." He was still in a crouching position; he had braced himself by flinging a meaty hand against the wall when the rocket hit. But the explosion had torn open his shirt, exposing his chest. Tattooed on one of his pectoral muscles, just visible under his thick chest hair, was the bright orange warning symbol for radioactivity: a deadly three-petaled flower. In a fit of masochistic pride, all 460 of the radiation-poisoned soldiers in the so-called Battalion of Death had gone out and gotten them a few months ago. Except Alexi. He shouldn't have been part of the battalion in the first place. But just try telling the bureaucracy back in Moscow that . . .

Alexi crept forward on hands and knees. Outside, heavy footsteps crunched through the rubble as an assault-suited Union soldier advanced. Boris risked a brief look out the hole and described what they were up against.

"This suit is rocket-equipped. It looks as if the launcher is gyro-mounted on the shoulder—"

Cradling his AK-51, Alexi took a peek through the hole, too . . .

And found himself face-to-face with an incoming rocket. His eyes had only a second to register the sleek needle of death before it exploded with a hot flash of light and noise. He had a dim awareness of being thrown backward through the air. When he landed, something was horribly wrong. What were his legs doing lying next to Boris? And what was that long red thing that had flown from his gut like a streamer as he was hurled through the air?

Boris's body was a blackened husk. White teeth clenched in pain in a face that had most of its flesh burned away. His voice was a dull croak.

"Make that . . . ten thousand . . . rubles," he gasped.

Alexi's mind began to slip from his body as his blood and guts puddled beneath him. He lay faceup, staring at the night sky through the hole in the ceiling. Dimly, he noticed a bright streak of light across the heavens. His dulled mind fought to identify it. Was it another rocket, like the one that had . . .

killed . . .

him?

2

"Boris, wait." Alexi laid a hand on the shoulder of the man ahead of him. They were creeping through the ruins of Vladivostok, assault rifles in hand. Boris had just climbed a pile of rubble and was wrenching open what used to be a second-story door on the ruined building.

"What's wrong, Alexi?" he rumbled. "This will make a fine vantage point." Keeping low, he stepped inside and quickly scanned what remained of the building's interior, cursing as his foot slipped on a piece of loose rubble. Then he motioned Alexi to follow.

Alexi was nervous, sweating. His glasses slid down his nose, and he pushed them back with a grubby finger. He could see that the footing was unstable. It would be just his luck if he tripped and sprained an ankle, or lost his weapon, or his . . .

The thought almost reminded him of something. He paused, trying to remember what he'd been about to say. Bullets spanged off the corner of the wall he was hunkered down behind, and Alexi involuntarily ducked.

"I don't know, Boris," Alexi answered. "I just have a bad feeling about it."

Which was pretty much how Alexi felt about everything, these days. Bad. He was tired of fighting a useless war, tired of watching the soldiers in his squad die, only to be replaced by more missile fodder. Earlier that day, he'd received word for the third time that it was impossible to amend the medical classification code that had assigned him to an infantry battalion, instead of to the space-recon regiment he'd signed up for when he joined the military, three long years ago. They actually expected him to be consoled by the fact they'd made him a corporal and given him an armored vest. But it didn't matter what rank he was. He was trapped here on Earth, and there was no way out.

Except to die. He'd just have to wait, and the bullet with his name on it would find him.

Or the rocket.

Now where had that thought come from?

"I'm going to circle around to the left, down to street level," he told Boris. "The heavy-assault suits will have to advance up this street to rescue the one that's been knocked down. I don't really think we stand much of a chance, but I'm going to try to find a good place to shoot from."

The big man grunted. "Bet you thirty rubles you don't even make it across the street," he said.

Alexi felt his face go pale. "What?"

Boris chuckled. "Just kidding," he said. Then his voice grew less brusque. "Listen, if you're going to cross, wait a moment before you move out. Let me get into position. I'll cover you from up here."

Alexi turned away from the doorway and skidded down the pile of rubble to the street, nearly losing his balance as a nearby explosion rattled the ground. Pushing his glasses back up his nose, he peered out from the base of the ruined building, then jerked back behind the corner when a hail of heavy machine-gun fire chipped cement from the wall a meter above his head. The street was a shooting gallery; his brief glimpse around the corner had told him why. The

Union heavy-assault suit that had been downed was lying in a crater at the center of the road, a few meters to the right. Its mechanical legs were crippled and it was unable to walk, or even to stand. But the machine gun mounted on its shoulder was sweeping the road with bullets, making it a formidable obstacle. The Union soldier inside it was safe in his steel shell. Bullets and frag grenades wouldn't hurt him one bit.

The heavy-assault suit stood out in vivid color against the gray of the concrete on which it lay. So arrogant were the troops that rode in these hulking behemoths that they didn't even bother with camouflage paint. Like the pilots of the first of the World Wars, they painted their suits in brilliant colors. This one was a checkerboard of orange and black, with a word written on its chest in English that Alexi couldn't read.

To Alexi's left, farther down the street, a figure in Neo-Sov fatigues popped up from cover like a gopher from a hole. It was the new conscript, Irina. She stood just long enough to hurl a stick with a bulbous orange head. The grenade sailed past Alexi, bounced once on the pavement, and rolled into the crater in the street that the assault suit was occupying.

Alexi ducked and shielded his eyes. A second later there was a muffled *whumff*, and a lurid orange glow came from around the corner. Alexi heard a frantic whirring as the disabled legs of the suit fought to lift it upright, then silence. So much for that Union soldier—and for that piece of cover. The crater in the road would be poisonously radioactive for the next few hours, until the glowing cloud of highly unstable isotopes that filled it reached the end of their incredibly short half-lives. In the meantime, it was a good thing there wasn't a wind blowing. Alexi's respirator wasn't working, and he didn't relish the thought of breathing in highly radioactive dust. Especially when he was the only member of the squad who didn't receive an issue of antiradiation pills.

As the gloom of dusk deepened, the glow in the crater

seemed to get brighter. Static crackled in Alexi's helmet speaker: the *leitenant*'s angry voice.

Private Maltovich! Bring . . . sprayer . . . or I'll . . .

A moment later, Vanya lurched out of the doorway of a ruined building across the street and began moving in Alexi's direction. His narrow face with its high, balding forehead was a sickly shade of green, and there were dark circles under his eyes. One hand holding his helmet respirator over his mouth, he staggered under the weight of the twin tanks of the chem-sprayer on his back. His tall black gumboots flapped against his skinny calves as he ran.

Alexi heard the roar of a machine gun and saw bullets chipping the concrete at Vanya's feet. The Chem Grunt tripped and fell—and that saved him. For the moment, at least, a pile of rubble stopped the bullets. But whoever had fired those bullets was on the move; the cover wouldn't last long. Somewhere down the street to Alexi's right, another Union soldier in an assault suit was advancing.

Christ. Just Alexi's luck that his squad should wind up in an area of the city that had not one but *two* of the monstrosities. The assault suits were thinly spread across the city—the enemy was trying to take Vladivostok with just a handful of them. But despite their small numbers, they were easily a match for the two battalions of Rad Troopers the Neo-Sovs had poured into the battle so far.

Alexi gripped his AK-51, trying to psyche himself into leaning around the corner and firing back at the heavy-assault suit. There was always a chance that a bullet would strike a vulnerable spot on the steel suit—although if there were any weak points, Intelligence hadn't gotten around to letting the average grunt know about them. But despite the fact that he'd made up his mind to just get it over with and die today, Alexi couldn't bring himself to do anything so foolhardy. It was as if his body were refusing to obey orders out of an involuntary sense of self-preservation.

Above and to Alexi's right, Boris leaned out of a hole in

the building he'd gone into and sprayed the street with rifle bullets. As the machine gun from the advancing Union assault suit swung up, seeking this new target, Vanya rose from cover and struggled the last few meters across the street.

"Hey, Vanya!" Boris shouted down from above. "Give them a squirt for me!"

Vanya sagged against the wall next to Alexi. He looked bad. The front of his fatigues were stained with wet splotches—the remains of the freeze-dried eggs that had been their only meal all day. Even though he'd been starving, Alexi hadn't been able to chew the rubbery, gray mottled mass that smelled more like the plastic in which it had been vacuum-sealed than it did like food. No wonder Vanya had gotten sick.

Vanya, a musician in the Moscow Folk Orchestra before the war, had long, delicate fingers that had once danced across the mandolin. Now they were spotted with overlapping scars from chemical burns. He struggled to unlimber the hoses of the chem-sprayer, then turned a valve at the base of each of the corroded nozzles that were paired at the end of the hoses.

"Let's give him a Russian serenade, Alexi," he said with a pale grin. "You on assault rifle and me providing accompaniment on chem-sprayer."

Alexi couldn't help but grin back. "*Da.* Count me in."

Vanya picked up on Alexi's unintended pun. "In four-four time then," he said. "And one, and two, and three, and . . ."

Alexi poked the barrel of his assault rifle around the corner and opened fire. At the same time Vanya stepped out into the street, aimed, and pulled the dual triggers. Toxic chemicals spewed out of the hoses, the streams mingling in midair with a sizzling hiss. The first few splatters of the black, tarry substance hit the side of the building that Boris had sheltered in. Flaking paint sizzled and began to slide down the wall. Then Vanya got the pressurized, bucking hoses under control and sent a stream of the foul-smelling chemical spewing up the street. It arced high into the air, landing with a gentle splatter. The streams fell just short of the heavy-assault suit, which was painted bright green, with what looked like a yellow thunderhead on its chest and an inscription.

Angry screaming staticked in Alexi's helmet speaker. Vanya released the trigger of the sprayer and the stream of chemicals sagged back until only a dribble fell from the twin nozzles. He lurched back to where Alexi stood, making it behind the corner of the building just as a fresh burst of machine-gun bullets raked the street.

Vanya glanced back over his shoulder, and Alexi turned to see what he was staring at. *Leitenant* Soldatenkof—well in the rear of the squad, as usual—had the barrel of his Viper pistol pointed at the pair of them. Alexi could hear only fragments of his screamed insults over the radio in his helmet. And those words that did come through the speaker were almost incoherent. But the tone of the *leitenant's* voice told him everything he needed to know.

You incompetent . . . worthless piece of . . . make an example of . . .

A thin line of neon red—the laser-light sighting system of the weapon—stretched from the sight on the barrel of the Viper to a spot on the wall next to Alexi and Vanya. The *leitenant's* angry eyes glared at them from behind his pistol. Only twenty-two years old, the *leitenant* was a product of one of the Neo-Soviet's elite Suvorov military training academies. But the soldiers in the two squads under his command used to joke that Soldatenkof was instead the product of one of Russia's foremost madhouses. Prone to violent rages and commanding out of the barrel of a gun, Soldatenkof was a short man who stood only as high as most of his soldiers' shoulders. He had deep-set eyes and a protruding forehead with a blue vein that throbbed when he was angry. Day and night, he wore a helmet and a full suit of field armor, emblazoned with the red hammer and sickle of the reforged Soviet state. A solid yellow stripe on each shoulder marked him as a *leitenant*—or as a coward, if you listened to the jokers in the squad.

The *leitenant*'s armor was one of the things that prevented his squad from killing him. The other preventative measure was the army's standing order that any squad that lost its officer in questionable circumstances would be summarily executed. It didn't seem to matter that it was nearly impossible to prove that enemy fire had taken out an officer. Once an officer died or disappeared, the squad was under a death sentence. The standing order was designed to encourage soldiers to sacrifice themselves so that their officers might live. In fact, the only thing the policy encouraged was desertion.

Daring another brief look around the corner, Alexi saw the bright green assault suit advancing. The hulking metal monstrosity lurched down the street, feet crumbling concrete to dust and power-assisted joints whirring. The thing was twice the height of a man, bristling with weapons and wrapped in layers of reinforced steel. One arm was mounted with a heavy machine gun, and a rocket launcher was nested on the other shoulder. Somewhere inside all that mechanized steel and bristling weaponry was a Union soldier, but the mirrored surface of the faceplate had turned Alexi's enemy into a faceless, terrifying metal monster. The single gold stripe on the shoulder of the armored suit was the only clue as to the identity of the soldier inside it. Whoever he or she was, the soldier's rank was *leitenant*. Alexi wondered if the Union officer was as big a bastard as Soldatenkof was.

As the noise of the suit's approach grew louder, the nozzles in Vanya's hands began to shake, spattering dribbles of chemical goo onto his feet. The rubber in his asbestos-impregnated boots began to smolder. He turned as if to run, and Alexi jumped back out of the way. Resigned to death though he was, Alexi didn't relish the thought of having his flesh melted by chemicals.

The movement saved him. Alexi couldn't hear the bark of the *leitenant*'s handgun—it was lost in the roar of Boris's AK-51 and the zinging twangs of bullets bouncing off the assault-suited Union soldier. But it had to have been *Leitenant* Soldatenkof who fired. The red light of the Viper's sighting laser had slid across Vanya's turning shoulder a fraction of a second before a bullet struck the chem tank, dinging a dent into it. Vanya's eyes widened in fear as one of the tank's seams sprang a leak. Frantically, he began loosening the straps that held the tanks to his back.

Soldatenkof's second shot was even less accurate. It tore through the twinned hoses of the chem-sprayer, severing them both. Without the pressure of the nozzles to hold them back, chemicals surged up and out of the tank, mixing in a bubbling black foam as they emerged from the frayed hose ends.

Alexi yelped and danced back from the rapidly growing puddle of toxic goo on the ground. At the same moment something bright flashed just above him: a rocket. His ears registered the explosion and then began to ring. Concrete rained down on him, knocking him to the ground.

Above Alexi, a second rocket slammed into the ruined building and exploded with a *whoosh* that sent flame and dust through the hole that Boris had fired from. Alexi looked up and saw smoke and dust curling through the opening. There was no way Boris could have survived that blast.

Dazed, on hands and knees, he glanced up at the sky and saw the moon rising above the jagged skyline of Vladivostok. Since the Change, it was the only part of the heavens that had remained the same. The constellations had all been rearranged, the other planets in the solar system had been left behind, and the sun had disappeared from sight. In its place was the angry red eye of the Maw.

The scientists were still at a loss to explain exactly

where the Maw had come from or why the Change had occurred. But thanks to the space-exploration teams, they were starting to get some answers. They knew that the Maw was the heart of a galaxy-sized space anomaly they had named the Maelstrom. It dominated this anomaly like the eye of a hurricane. Except that while the eye of a hurricane is an empty void, the center of the Maelstrom was a superdense implosion of matter and energy, capable of consuming entire worlds.

The moon—the only familiar object left in the sky after the other planets had disappeared—was a stepping-stone into space, a point of departure for exploring the mysteries of the reconstituted heavens. Alexi looked enviously at the twinkles of light that marked the moon bases. But for the clerical foul-up that assigned him to the rad squad, even though he wasn't radiation-poisoned, he would have been there now.

Then he sighed. With his luck, even if he had made it into space, he'd probably have been posted to the part of the moon where the fighting was going on. Funny, to think that World War III was raging just as fiercely across its cratered face.

A streak of light flashed between the moon and the Maw, and continued down through the night sky, toward the western horizon. A falling star?

No use wishing upon it. Alexi was stuck here on Earth.

As the ringing in his ears subsided, Alexi realized that someone was screaming beside him: Vanya. Clawing his way out of the rubble, Alexi pawed at the broken concrete to expose Vanya's face. He immediately regretted his action. The gurgling screams stopped as Vanya's head imploded with a sucking noise. The chemicals had corroded his skull until it was no stronger than wet tissue. Now the puddle of brains and flesh that remained were bubbling. The smell that rose from the mess was a violent combination of seared flesh and sharp chemical.

Leitenant Soldatenkof was still screaming. Glitches of it came through Alexi's staticky headphones.

Pick up . . . sprayer and . . . that armor suit to . . .

Alexi suddenly realized that the *leitenant* wanted him to continue the attack—using a piece of equipment that Soldatenkof's own foolish action had destroyed, costing Vanya his life. It was the final straw.

"You pompous idiot," Alexi spat back. He had no idea whether the microphone in his helmet was working. He hoped it was. He'd already made up his mind to die today, so he might as well tell the *leitenant* exactly what he thought of him. He gestured at the ruined chem-sprayer and Vanya's bubbling corpse. "If you hadn't shot at Vanya, it wouldn't have—"

This time, the *leitenant*'s aim was better. Alexi blinked as a line of red light caught his eye, and then a bullet from the Viper smacked into his forehead. He sagged to his knees as blood trickled down his . . .

cheek, onto his . . .

chest, onto the . . .

ground . . .

which rushed up together with the blackness to claim him.

3

Alexi skidded to a halt as he reached the bottom of the pile of rubble. Despite the fact that he was sweating from his scramble over the debris that choked the streets of Vladivostok, a chill ran down his spine under his armored vest. No. This way was no good. Staying there would be too dangerous. He wasn't sure why, but . . .

He peeked around the corner of the building and saw a downed heavy-assault suit, lying in a crater in the road. The machine gun mounted on it swung this way and that, seeking a target. Alexi ducked back.

He glanced to his left, and saw *Leitenant* Soldatenkof glaring from behind cover at someone across the street. Somehow the sight of the pistol in the *leitenant*'s hand was even more unnerving than the bullets that chewed their way down the rubble-strewn street, coming from the direction of the heavy-assault suit. Alexi had done nothing wrong—he was always careful never to raise the *leitenant*'s wrath—but somehow he *knew* that if he stayed here, Soldatenkof would shoot him. He could even picture where the bullet would hit: right between the eyes.

He shuddered.

Alexi scrambled back the way he had come, then changed direction and clambered over a burbling sewer pipe and down into a basement. It was all that was left of a three-story building that had been reduced to a skeleton of twisted metal girders. Overhead, chunks of window glass dangled from what remained of aluminum window frames, tinkling against each other each time an explosion rattled the ground. A twisted metal fire escape leaned at a crazy angle against an outside wall. A piece of something—a human leg—lay on one of the girders, as if placed there by an unseen hand. The thigh was a mess of chewed flesh, ripped open by the explosion that had tossed the limb there. But the boot was spit-polished, a glossy black that belonged on the parade square.

Alexi shook his head in wonder at the oddities of battle. He felt dizzy, disoriented. And it wasn't just the foul-smelling fumes that wafted up from the puddles of raw sewage that his boots were splashing through. He had a pre-monition that something or someone was coming his way . . .

Static crackled in his helmet speaker. The *leitenant* was yelling at someone again. During a lull in the officer's insults and threats, Alexi heard Boris bet that he could shatter the assault suit's faceplate with a tightly grouped burst—that he would be the one to kill the soldier inside it. The *leitenant* yelled at him to keep the communications frequency clear, then ignored his own advice and added a full minute's worth of insults.

Alexi suddenly stiffened as a figure appeared up above in his peripheral vision, ducking between the girders. Heart pounding, he pointed his assault rifle up at it, pulling the trigger even as he turned. The spray of bullets chewed a diagonal line up the basement's concrete wall. Just as it reached the top, the soldier there slipped on a loose piece of rubble, falling to one knee. The bullets passed harmlessly overhead.

Alexi gasped, and checked his fire. He'd nearly shot Irina, the squad's newest member.

"*Prastitye pazhalsta*," Alexi called out, hoping the apology was enough. "I . . . didn't realize who it was."

Irina turned, and Alexi saw that she carried a stick with a bulbous orange head in her hand. A second rad grenade hung from the webbing at her belt. A third . . .

Alexi paled. The third grenade teetered on the lip of the basement wall. Then it fell down into the basement, landing with a splash on the sewage-covered floor. Alexi backed away from it in horror, expecting at any moment to see the walls lit up with the bright orange glow of more than two thousand rads. He had a vivid picture of himself reduced to a mere shadow on the wall by the flash of the explosion. . . .

"Don't worry," Irina called down. "It wasn't primed." She made no move to recover the sewage-covered grenade. Instead she grinned and hefted the rad grenade she still held. "Which way is the machine gun? I'm going to take Boris up on his bet."

Alexi jerked a thumb over his shoulder, indicating the way he'd come.

"*Spahseebe*," Irina cheerfully replied, and ran off in that direction.

Alexi shook his head. Irina had been assigned to the rad squad to replace Tamara. That had been just ten days ago, shortly before the squad was ordered to Vladivostok. Not only was Irina visibly healthier than all of the others in the squad, she was an annoyingly patriotic presence in a six-person squad filled with sarcastic cynics and brooding fatalists. She was proud to be a member of the Battalion of Death, even more so after Alexi told her the history of the unit's nickname.

Back in the first of the three World Wars, early in the twentieth century, the original Battalion of Death had been made up entirely of women—an unusual thing, for that period of history. They had sworn to fight unto death, as an example to the "cowardly" men who were deserting in droves after the Russian Revolution. Irina saw it as her patriotic duty to set a similar example. She actually followed *Leitenant* Soldatenkof's orders without need of the goad of a laser sight. As a reward, she got to carry the deadly rad grenades.

Until recently, Irina had been a ranger in the Lapland Nature Reserve, up near the Finnish border. It had been her job to protect what was left of its wildlife from poachers. Whenever she got the chance, she'd preach to whoever would listen about the need to do whatever it took to protect this last scrap of wilderness. And the facts backed her up. The Neo-Soviet Union was a nation that had been poisoned by toxic waste and radiation from a chain of nuclear-power-plant accidents that stretched all the way back to the infamous Chernobyl disaster, back in the twentieth century. As early as the 1990s, scientists had calculated that fifteen percent of the country was "ecologically unsafe." Today, just over a century later, that figure stood at seventy-five percent. Why they bothered fighting to keep it was beyond Alexi. If the Union wanted his country, they could have it, in his opinion.

But Irina didn't share these doubts. She hunted Union soldiers with the same amount of zeal that she'd put into hunting poachers. The irony was that the grenades she wielded came from the munitions factories in Monchegorsk that she'd raged against. Factories like the one that had irradiated a vast swath of the nature reserve she worked in, causing her to seek medical assistance, which resulted in her conscription. And yet she didn't seem to have the same bitterness that Alexi did.

It was enough for Alexi that he was fighting in Vladivostok. Just over a century ago, the port had been a transit point for prisoners and dissidents bound for the Gulag camps of northern Siberia. Shipped east by the Trans-Siberian Railroad in cattle cars, they were loaded into the holds of ships and taken north to the gold mines of Kolyma, the Auschwitz of the original Soviet state. Twenty million died, and their crushed bones were used to build the roads that connected the camps to the mines.

One of Alexi's ancestors—his great-to-the-power-of-four-grandfather—had been sent to the Gulag in winter aboard a ship on which the political prisoners revolted. The sailors turned the hose on them, and when the ship eventually docked, three thousand corpses were entombed in a block of ice in the hold.

Alexi was also descended from even earlier exiles to Siberia. On Alexi's mother's side, his ancestors had been sent to the "land of chains and ice" centuries before the first Soviet Union came to be. But like the political prisoners of a later century, their crimes had been mere excuses to send them east. One of Alexi's ancestors had been exiled for participating in an illegal prizefighting match, another for fortune-telling. The fortune-teller was rumored to have foretold the death of Peter the Great in 1725 a little too accurately, and was banished as a political conspirator by his successors.

Alexi shook his head. Strange, that he should be defending a land that had treated his forebears—and himself—so poorly.

An explosion rattled the ground, and something splashed into the murky water behind Alexi. He whirled around, certain that someone was watching him—but saw only darkness in the corner of the ruined basement. A ring of ripples spread outward from a spot on the sewage-covered floor where something had landed—probably a fragment of debris thrown up by the explosion.

Alexi tensed. Had something moved?

Alexi squinted, convinced his mind must be playing tricks on him. That corner of the basement seemed darker, somehow. As if a shadow had settled over it. But there was nothing there... .

He was getting jumpy. He'd nearly opened fire on a shadow. He needed to sit down, to rest. So what if he sat this battle out? He hadn't asked to join this squad, he didn't really care about Vladivostok—and one man wouldn't make a difference, anyhow.

A chair sat at the center of the basement. Alexi pulled it over to one wall and sat with his back against the cement. Trying to tune out the sounds of the explosions and bursts of rifle and machine-gun fire, and ignoring the static in his helmet speaker, he stared up at the darkening sky. It seemed appropriate, somehow, to be looking up at it from a basement filled with sewage. The sludge around his feet had just thawed; the temperature had finally risen above freezing to a balmy ten degrees Celsius just two days ago. A typical July day in Vladivostok, now that the chill of nuclear autumn had gripped the Earth.

Five years had passed since the Change, and Alexi still hadn't gotten used to the way the heavens looked. The familiar constellations had disappeared, as if wiped away by a careless sweep of God's broom. In their place were jumbled points of light that astronomers were still struggling to classify into planets, asteroids, and stars. Shifting wisps of what looked like electrified mist drifted across the sky, causing the points of light to twinkle. These tendrils looked something like the aurora borealis, except that they were a ghostly white instead of electric blue.

As to where the sun had gone, not even the scientists could say. It had vanished on the day of the Change—yet not completely. Dawn, day, dusk, and night followed each other as they always had, as if the sun had merely become invisible. The sky turned its familiar blue during the day and became inky black at night.

Dominating the sky was the Maw, an angry eye of boiling blue-white light twice as large as the sun and spotted with dark gouts of red. It rose in the east and sank in the west each day, appearing halfway through the day and only sinking below the horizon late at night, a reminder that the Earth was still rotating once every twenty-four hours.

After the Change, the scientists had tried to reassure a panicked public that the Earth was in no immediate danger of being sucked into the fiery depths of the Maw—that although it appeared to be closer than the sun had been, it was in fact several light-years away. But their reassurances had been lost in the chaos and upheaval that followed the Change. To appear so large in the sky, the Maw had to be huge beyond imagining. Distant though it might be, to a public unaccustomed to thinking in terms of light-years, its mere size was threat enough.

From somewhere nearby came the sound of a rocket exploding. The noise caused Alexi's thoughts to drift back down to earth. He wondered if anyone had died in the blast—and where the rocket had been launched from. He glanced around the walls of the basement and decided he was safe enough where he was.

The war had been raging for five years, ever since the Change. Alexi would have thought that, in the wake of the chaos and upheaval that followed the Change, the Neo-Soviets and the Union of North America would have set aside their differences. But instead Alexi's nation had launched a nuclear attack just minutes after the Earth was transported into the Maelstrom. Perhaps the Neo-Soviet leadership had anticipated the Union would fall as easily as China had. But the Union had fought back, and now World War III was raging both on Earth and on the recently colonized moon.

When he had signed up for military service, Alexi had set his heart on the stars and the mystery of space. He thought that by joining the military, rather than waiting for the Neo-Soviet bureaucracy finally to grind its way around to conscripting him, he could choose the arm of service he wanted. He'd honestly believed that his education—and the fact that he had served the state well as a schoolteacher, instilling a proper appreciation of the history of the original

Soviet Union—would merit him a ticket into the space arm of the military. He yearned to probe the mysteries of how and why the Earth became trapped in the Maelstrom. At the very least, he hoped to get off this poisoned planet.

Instead he was assigned to a military unit that would never leave the Neo-Soviet Union, let alone Earth. His education and teaching experience had merited him only a minor rank within one of the infamous rad squads—radiation-poisoned conscripts who were used as missile fodder in situations where trained soldiers could not be spared. He'd been condemned by his eyesight. But at least he didn't have to take antiradiation pills, like the rest of the squad.

Alexi heard a second explosion—also a rocket, by the sound of it. After so much time in battle, he could tell the sounds apart, just as Vanya could identify musical notes that were right next to each other on the scale. Alexi wondered whose death the explosion heralded.

Something overhead caught Alexi's eye then. A shooting star? No—more than that. The streak of light in the sky was increasing, growing.

Alexi stood. The chair splashed over sideways into the muck.

The Maw blazed brightly in the sky, a disturbing glare of white-blue light. Between it and the moon, a bright star blazed in the sky. A feathery streak of reddish yellow light trailed behind it. A meteor, then, burning up during its entry into the Earth's atmosphere. Or perhaps a piece of space debris—one of the satellites that had gone silent in the seconds after the Change, its orbit degraded until it fell back to Earth.

Over the nearer sounds of battle, a faint whistling reached Alexi's ears. Whatever was falling from the heavens, it was big.

Slinging his AK-51 over his shoulder, Alexi climbed out of the basement and began ascending the fire escape. Metal scraped against metal as the staircase slipped to a steeper angle, then held. Alexi ignored it, climbing ever higher and seeking a better view. At last, when he was level with what had been the third story, he could see over Vladivostok's hills.

The meteorite streaked toward the horizon. Far to the northwest, Alexi saw a flare of light as it struck the Earth. It had landed somewhere in northern Siberia, up near the Arctic Circle.

Longitude 100 degrees east . . .

Where had *that* thought come from?

Staring at the horizon like a man trying to remember the location of an important object he had misplaced, Alexi neither saw nor heard the assault suit that clanked toward the base of the twisted girders. Gyros softly whirred as a machine gun trained on the spot where Alexi—obviously an enemy sniper or spotter—stood with a rifle slung across his back.

It was only when the machine gun opened up with a roar and bullets began spanging off the metal girders beside him that Alexi jerked into furious motion. Scrambling to unlimber his AK-51, he tried to bring its barrel down to point at the bright green metal monstrosity below. But his rifle strap caught on a protruding bit of metal.

He was trying to tug his weapon free when the bullets finally found him, punching into his chest like a swarm of exploding bees. His boots slipped on his own blood . . .

and he fell, hallucinating that he was finally floating up into space, toward the streak of light . . .

down toward the heavy-assault suit, whose machine gun chewed his torso into two pieces before it hit the ground.

4

Alexi stared at the rad grenade he'd picked out of the sewage. It was a Neo-Soviet weapon; the Union forces, not wanting to risk irradiating their own soldiers, didn't use anything so crude. Irina must have dropped it; she was the only one the *leitenant* trusted with rad grenades.

Normally, Alexi wouldn't have picked it up. The Neo-Soviet munitions factories were noted for their abysmal quality control; the grenade was almost certainly leaking radiation. But Alexi smiled as he hefted it in his hand. A rad grenade was the one weapon that was guaranteed to penetrate *Leitenant* Soldatenkof's armor. . . .

Alexi laughed grimly. If he did muster up the guts to throw a grenade at the *leitenant,* his satisfaction would be short-lived. He'd only be ensuring his own death by firing squad. And although he'd started off the day with the decision just to let himself be killed and end it all, now Alexi wasn't so sure that was what he wanted.

Alexi suddenly felt a strange compulsion to look up. He did—and saw a streak of reddish yellow light between the moon and the Maw. A shooting star.

The sight sent a shiver down his spine, driving from his mind the fantasies of killing the *leitenant*. Instead he felt strangely drawn to the meteor. He wanted to get closer to it, to climb the fire escape that had somehow survived the destruction of the building and get a better look at the falling star. But when he clambered up out of the ruined basement and placed a hand on one of the ladder's rungs, he shivered with a chill that came from somewhere other than the cold metal under his hand. Alexi was not ordinarily a superstitious man, but it felt as though someone were walking over his grave. He pulled out the gold cross that hung around his neck and kissed it for luck, then tucked it back inside his armored vest.

In one of the incredible periods of silence that sometimes settle over a battlefield, Alexi heard the sound of heavy, thudding footsteps, perhaps a block or two away. It was completely irrational, but he was suddenly certain that the grim reaper herself was walking toward him.

Herself?

Alexi suddenly remembered the rad grenade that he still held in his hand. It would take out the assault suit.

What the hell. If he was going to die today, he might as well die a hero.

Alexi ran toward the sound. As he drew nearer, the noise clarified into the individual sounds of gyro stabilizers and the faint creak of moving metal parts. It was the unmistakable signature of the heavy-assault suit—a turtle shell of rocket-studded steel that turned an ordinary soldier into a walking tank. The Neo-Soviets had focused their weapons development on mutants and chemicals, and were still racing to come out with their own version of the heavy-assault suit. The Union had beaten them in the race and were now proving the worth of this new weapon in Vladivostok.

Over his helmet speaker, Alexi heard the *leitenant* screaming at Vanya.

"Vanya!" he shouted into his microphone. "Don't run! It's Alexi—I'm coming to help you."

Why had he said that? Alexi didn't know. It had been pure impulse, illogical. But he had a vivid picture in his mind of Vanya turning and running, and the *leitenant* shooting him in the . . .

The image was gone. Now the *leitenant* started directing his curses at Alexi instead, ordering him to maintain radio silence so that his orders could be heard.

Alexi rounded the back of the building that Boris was hunkered down in just as a rocket tore open the corner of one of its walls in a loud explosion. He couldn't say why, but he knew that the assault-suited enemy's next shot wouldn't miss. If he didn't move quickly, Boris was a dead man.

"Boris!" he yelled into his microphone, praying that it was working. His headphones were cutting in and out in bursts of static; for all he knew, his microphone was glitching, too. "Draw the assault suit's attention, Boris. A second or two is all I need!"

Alexi emerged onto the street behind the heavy-assault suit, which was painted a bright green. As Boris leaned out a hole in the building above, electric engines whirred and the Union soldier brought the rocket launcher on its shoulder to bear. At this range, it couldn't miss.

Boris's voice crackled in his headphones: "Five thousand rubles says I don't make it out of here alive, Alexi."

Alexi laughed. Bullets might bounce off the assault suit; metal fragments might fail to pierce its steel hide—but the deadly gamma radiation of a rad grenade would penetrate its armor plating like a laser burning through tissue.

With the fierce energy of a madman—or a hero, which was perhaps the same thing, really—Alexi gave the end of the rad grenade he'd picked up in the basement a vicious twist, priming it. Then he hurled it at the armor-suited figure. It clanked against the monster's metal back and fell to the street at its feet as Boris ducked back inside the building. Alexi, well out of the tightly focused blast radius of the grenade, simply stood and watched.

The grenade did not go off.

Conscious of the new threat, the heavy-assault suit turned. It stood a meter or two away from the lip of the crater where the crippled assault suit still lay. The glow of a rad grenade—one that *hadn't* been a dud—filled the crater, backlighting the scene in a dull orange glow. The machine gun on the green assault suit rotated toward Alexi . . .

"Irina!" he screamed. "Your other grenade—throw it!"

The grenade was already in the air; Alexi simply hadn't seen it. Or maybe he had seen it out of the corner of his eye—which was his explanation, later, of how he somehow *knew* that Irina was hiding behind that particular jumble of broken concrete, and that she still had a grenade to throw, even when he hadn't been anywhere near her.

Irina's grenade went off.

A cloud of luridly glowing orange blossomed around the assault-suited soldier. The explosion triggered the grenade that was lying at its feet, and the glow brightened. To Alexi, it was as beautiful as a sunrise—something he hadn't seen in five long years.

The assault suit teetered as the soldier inside it attempted to hurl it into motion. It pirouetted on one foot—then crashed over onto its side in the street. A hatch in the back of the thing opened, and the Union soldier inside wriggled out. The soldier wore a silvery, form-fitting body suit that covered her from neck to toe, hiding none of her graceful curves and lean, toned body. Her face had Asian features: almond eyes and a snub nose. It was a delicate, beautiful face, with intelligent eyes: a face that belonged on a soldier's tattered snapshot of a sweetheart back home. But instead of a photo-perfect smile, her face held a look of terror. Her mouth was wrenched open in a silent scream, her body bent nearly double as spasms gripped her. Radiation burns were already blossoming like poisonous roses on her cheeks as she lay writhing on the broken concrete.

The *leitenant*'s voice sputtered out of the speaker in Alexi's helmet.

That was a good . . . Irina . . . see that . . . commendation for . . . act of heroism.

It didn't surprise Alexi that Irina would get all of the credit for their joint kill. What did surprise him was the depth of his emotion that the Union soldier's death had triggered in him. He lifted his glasses to brush away a tear that had welled in his eye. What the hell was this? He hadn't cried in three long years—not for any of the comrades killed in battle. He'd seen them blown apart, stitched with bullets, burned, crushed . . . He hadn't even cried when his own sister was reported missing in action after the disaster that was the Battle of Petrograd. Yet when he drew breath as he stared at this woman—this enemy soldier—it stuttered in his throat. His chest ached and he trembled, as if he'd just lost a dear *tovarish*.

And the greatest absurdity of all was that he felt an urge to go to the woman, to hold her in his arms.

Just like the time . . .

The time . . .

Alexi shook his head fiercely, to clear the not-yet thought. Slinging his AK-51 over his shoulder, he lifted his wrist and pushed a button on the side of his watch. Its face lit up with a green glow. The time was 9:31 P.M.

Alexi did not realize it then, but it was the last time he could ever be absolutely certain what time it really was.

5

Alexi stumbled through the streets, his arms around his comrades' shoulders. His shoulder was wet—oh yes, it was the bottle in Vanya's left hand sloshing vodka onto him as they lurched along.

Vanya was on Alexi's right, a battered-looking mandolin slung over one shoulder. Nevsky, the Mongolian conscript, was on his left, gnawing on a thick ring of garlic sausage. The three of them weaved along the road, past the gray concrete buildings and barred windows of the shops. Automobiles were parked at either side of the street, but none looked as if they had been anywhere in some time. Many had flat tires or broken windows. The petrol shortage was severe enough that only military vehicles were allotted fuel. Jeeps and two-ton trucks rumbled through the silent streets, soot-belching engines trumpeting their gluttony.

It felt good to be drunk, to unwind. To be completely irresponsible. Be as numb in body as he was in spirit. But where was he?

Drunk as he was, it took Alexi a moment to realize that he remembered nothing that had come before this moment.

He had been fighting street to street in Vladivostok and then . . .

Somewhere between that battle and now, he'd filled his stomach with food, changed into a freshly laundered uniform, and had a bath—or so he assumed, since his hunger cramps were gone and his clothes and skin smelled of soap.

And vodka. Which was probably why he couldn't remember anything.

With the abandon of the thoroughly drunk, Alexi decided that he didn't care. All that mattered was this moment.

The vodka should have made Alexi completely relaxed and happy, but every now and then he had the distinct impression that someone was watching him. He glanced around, and figured out why. A queue of locals were waiting in front of the GUM—the state department store. Several held plastic ration cards. By their hungry eyes and mutters, Alexi guessed that they were waiting for a food shipment to come in. Their eyes followed the three soldiers, their expressions stony.

Alexi could understand why. These people were hungry, while the soldiers were well fed. Or at least, well supplied with what passed for food, Alexi thought ruefully, thinking about the food paste and dehydrated chips of what looked like sawdust that were a soldier's standard rations. But the civilians' stares made him nervous. Were they hungry enough to mug the three drunken soldiers for the sausage Nevsky was carrying?

Alexi wished he had his AK-51 with him, antiquated though that weapon might be. Command, however, forbade the carrying of weapons behind the lines. They were probably afraid that, if the people did riot, the soldiers would support them. Just as they had during the first of the World Wars in 1917, when troops ordered to fire on demonstrators in Petrograd had handed the civilians their rifles instead.

One of the women spat into the street as they passed.

Vanya waved the vodka bottle at her. "*Dohbridyen!*" he

shouted. "We have every right to celebrate. This is our first leave in two years!" His voice wasn't slurred; he'd obviously not had as much to drink as Alexi.

The woman glared at him and turned away. On the other side of Alexi, Nevsky belched loudly. The smell of sausage wafted from his lips.

"Show some respect," he bellowed. "You're looking at a hero of the Neo-Soviet state."

Alexi was surprised when Nevsky clapped him on the back. "This man saved our country from an alien invasion," Nevsky continued. "If it weren't for him, terrible monsters from outer space would be marching through Novosibirsk right now, cutting every last one of you to pieces with their—"

What in Christ was Nevsky raving about? Aliens from space? That was a good one.

"Nevsky, hush." Vanya nodded meaningfully at an officer who had just turned the corner and was walking toward them down the street. Nevsky's lip curled, but he took the hint. Straightening up, he even managed a deliberately sloppy salute as the officer drew nearer. The fellow, dressed in the crisp uniform of the Intelligence Corps and carrying a clipboard computer tucked under one arm, took a second look at them. He crossed the street to approach the trio.

Vanya cursed. "Now you've done it," he whispered fiercely to Nevsky. "So much for our leave."

Vanya handed his mandolin and the vodka bottle to Alexi, then stepped forward to greet the officer with a proper salute. Alexi clutched the mandolin and bottle to his chest, trying not to spill the vodka. His stomach was starting to feel queasy, but whether it was from the drink or the look in the officer's eye, he couldn't say. The world tilted a little bit, then came back into proper horizontal alignment as Nevsky grabbed the back of his collar, propping him up.

The officer stopped and looked them over. Then he consulted his clipboard computer. "I'm looking for a Corporal

Alexi Minsk of the Sixty-sixth Rad Squad. Have you seen him?"

Alexi blinked at the officer, suddenly hopeful. Had his reassignment to the military's space arm at last come through? No—wait a minute. Command wouldn't send an Intelligence officer to give him the news. It would be a lowly clerk. Not a reassignment, then.

Alexi's mind slowly fought its way through the fuzz of vodka, seeking another, more rational explanation. After a long moment's thought, he concluded that an officer searching for him just couldn't be a good thing. When an officer came looking for you, it either meant disciplinary action, or extra duties, or a death in the family—not that Alexi had any living relatives. Alexi's glasses were on, but he was having trouble focusing, thanks to the vodka. He started to speak, but his words came out slurred.

"Shir, I—"

"I know Corporal Minsk," Nevsky said.

Alexi's heart sank. He wanted to flail a hand at Nevsky to shut up, but between the vodka bottle and Vanya's mandolin, his hands were full.

Nevsky continued in a rush. "Minsk is a tall fellow with a black mustache and a fierce expression—a real man's man. He's down at the bathhouse." He flailed an arm in a gesture that took in the whole road.

The officer winced slightly and backed away from Nevsky's breath. His look of disgust deepened as Nevsky deliberately began scratching at one of the radiation sores on his forehead.

The officer turned to Alexi. His eyes took in the rank stripes on his sleeves. "What's your name, Corporal?"

Alexi glanced down at his chest, wondering why the officer hadn't just read his name tag. Oh—the mandolin was hiding it. He looked up, and caught Vanya's slight head shake and Nevsky's wink.

He said the first name that popped into his mind. "Corporal Raheek, sir."

The officer frowned slightly, as if puzzled by the unusual surname. Then he snapped the clipboard computer back under his arm.

"If you see Corporal Minsk, send him down to the *stavka*," he said. "We have a few more questions we'd like to ask him."

"Yesshir," Alexi slurred. He couldn't salute, so he nodded instead. The slight motion left him feeling dizzy.

When the officer left, Vanya took his mandolin back from Alexi. "Quick thinking, Corporal Raheek," he said with a wink. "But why'd you choose such an odd name?"

"Hmph," Nevsky added between bites of sausage. "It sounds Indian. Knowing Alexi, it's the name of some obscure historic figure from the previous century. Am I right, Alexi?"

Alexi blinked in puzzlement. Where had the name come from? He had no idea.

"It makes no difference—it worked." Vanya tugged Alexi's sleeve. "Let's go before the officer figures out who you really are."

They moved on past the queue of people outside the GUM store, and around the corner. But even though the officer was gone—Alexi nearly tripped, looking back over his shoulder to make sure—Alexi still had the distinct impression that eyes were following him.

Nevsky appropriated the bottle and drank a hefty swig of vodka, washing down a bite of sausage. "Nicely done, Alexi," he said. He patted the breast pocket of his combats and winked. "I wouldn't have wanted him to confiscate my medical supplies. Greedy bastard officers always take the best for themselves."

He pulled a bottle of red-and-blue capsules from his pocket and spilled a few of them into his cupped palm, showing them to Alexi. "These are the latest antirad pills from the Union," he whispered. He tipped them back into the container and sealed the lid. "And unlike ours, they work, hey, Vanya?"

The musician grinned and rubbed his stomach. "I feel better than I have in weeks—good enough to perform, even." He looked around. "Come on—we're almost there."

Right, Alexi thought drunkenly. Almost there. Wherever there was.

His companions each took one of Alexi's arms and steered him down the road. As he staggered along between the two, Alexi's mind cleared enough for him to wonder where he was. On leave in Novosibirsk, if he'd heard correctly. And that was good news.

The vodka was a warm glow in his stomach. He grinned. Life was good. Food, drink, clean clothes—and friends to hold you up. What more could a soldier ask for?

They were approaching a large building crowned by a gigantic silver dome. A sign that hung from the portico proclaimed it to be temporarily closed—although judging from the weather-beaten look of the sign the closure wasn't all that temporary.

Alexi and Nevsky were jerked to a halt as Vanya stopped suddenly. Vanya gestured at the building with a sweeping motion. "The Novosibirsk Opera and Ballet Theater," he announced. "Largest theater in Siberia." He swallowed, and when Alexi glanced sideways, he saw that Vanya's eyes were glistening.

"Such a beautiful building," Vanya said wistfully. "And such beautiful music that used to fill it. What a shame. It makes me wonder what we are fighting for. A people without bread should at least have music."

"Or vodka," Nevsky said, tipping the empty bottle to his lips and watching as the very last drop slid into his mouth.

The front of the building was decorated with large sculptures from the 1900s. In the heroic, larger-than-life style of the latter half of that century, they depicted a peasant, soldier, worker—and a man and woman pointing proudly into the future. If only the couple had known what the next two centuries would bring, Alexi thought, they would have dropped their arms in shame long ago.

In front was a statue of a balding man with mustache and goatee. Nevsky stared up at it as they passed.

"Hey!" he said, rubbing a hand across his almost-bald head. "Looks like they had rad poisoning back in the 1900s, too." He flung the empty vodka bottle, which shattered on the statue's chest. "Have a drink, you poor bastard, whoever you are!"

The feeling of someone watching him was suddenly back. Alexi looked around warily, but the only eyes he could see looking at him were those in the statue's frowning face. Had the vodka induced paranoia? Given the importance of the historic figure the statue represented, it was no wonder. He shook his head at Nevsky. "Don't you recognize him?"

Nevsky shook his head. "*Nyet.*"

"That'sh Lenin. Father of our country."

"Never heard of him."

A series of bangs came from one side of the building, and then the sound of breaking glass. Alexi tensed as his mind flashed back to the battle of Vladivostok. After three solid days of fighting, his body still reacted instinctively to sudden noises—especially here in the quiet of Novosibirsk.

"I found a way in," Vanya cried out from around the corner. "Hurry, before someone spots us."

Alexi and Nevsky walked around the side of the building, toward the noise. Vanya had pulled the boards off a window and broken the glass. He reached in and turned the latch, opening it. Then he lifted his mandolin carefully inside and clambered in after it.

Alexi followed, boosted inside by Nevsky. He found himself in an ornate theater lobby with plush red rugs and pillared walls. Vanya led them into the darkened theater itself, and they descended toward the stage between the dusty rows of seats. Standing near the stage, Alexi surveyed the theater. It was like a huge cavern, its hundreds of seats like empty eyes.

Vanya pushed something into Alexi's hand—a flashlight—and clambered up onto the stage. "Turn it on," he instructed. "And sit down, both of you."

Alexi did as he was told. The lone beam of the flashlight illuminated Vanya with a soft yellow glow. Behind Vanya, the curtain rustled softly as his back brushed it. Alexi folded a front-row seat down and sat heavily on it, his booted feet splayed out in front of him. Nevsky did the same.

Vanya's long fingers plucked at the strings of his mandolin as he tuned it. His lips turned down in a sour grimace as one of the strings snapped. "It's not a very good instrument," he said to Nevsky. "Hardly worth the water-purification tablets you traded for it."

Nevsky shrugged and continued to munch on his sausage. "Doesn't matter," he assured Vanya. "That woman looked as though she could use them. Did you see her poor kids? Dysentery. The young one wouldn't have lasted much longer, if I hadn't given them to her." He tore another chunk off the sausage. His chewing noises were overloud in the hushed cavern of the empty theater.

Vanya sighed and tugged the broken string free. He coiled it neatly and stuffed it in the pocket of his pants. Then he bowed slightly to his audience of two, placed his long, delicate fingers on the strings, and took a deep breath. Suddenly his fingers flew across the strings. Nevsky stopped chewing and Alexi sat up, enraptured. The flashlight beam swung up into Vanya's face, but the musician only closed his eyes. He ignored it—just as he must have been ignoring the pain of his chemical-burned fingers. Despite the vodka he'd drunk, he played beautifully. Eyes closed, swaying in time with the music he played, Vanya was transported to another place and time—and the music carried Alexi right along with him. The mandolin cried and trilled, its lone sound filling the acoustically perfect theater. Its strings spoke of longing, of passion, of dreams unfulfilled . . .

With a final, lilting chord, the tune came to an end.

For a heartbeat or two, Alexi and Nevsky sat in silence. Then Nevsky clapped his hands together and leapt to his feet. "Bravo!" he shouted, his voice echoing through the empty theater. "Encore!"

Vanya's lips twitched in a smile. "Even with the missing string?" he asked. He winced. "It doesn't sound so good . . ."

"It'sh beautiful," Alexi shouted. "Another!"

Vanya gave a slight bow. Then he sighed. "One makes do, in times like these," he said.

He launched into a quicker piece. Alexi found his boot tapping as Vanya's fingers skipped lightly through the lively strains of a Slavic folk tune. Nevsky, unable to contain his exuberance, heaved himself up onto the stage. As Vanya's fingers flew across the strings, Nevsky's boots rapped out the rhythm of the *trepak*—the stamping dance.

Alexi clapped his free hand on the arm of his seat, laughing. The flashlight beam wavered across the stage and back again. "Where'd you learn that, Nevsky?" he shouted. "I thought you were Mongolian."

"My grandfather was a Slav," Nevsky called back, hands raised and boots stomping up dust on the stage. "Watch. He also taught me this!"

Nevsky launched himself into a low, double-footed kick that landed him sprawling on his back. Vanya ignored him and continued to pluck out the folk tune, his rapid fingers blurring on the mandolin strings.

Alexi laughed and staggered to his feet. He balanced the flashlight on the arm of his seat and clambered up onto the stage. As Nevsky rose to his feet, brushing the dust from his combats, Alexi pretended to applaud him.

The Mongol bowed deeply, nearly losing his balance again. As Vanya ended one song and began another, he waved at Alexi with a flourish.

"Your turn," he said. "Go on—I know you know the words to this song. Entertain the audience. Maybe the critics will print a good review in the *Red Star.*"

Alexi turned to face the empty theater, blinking in the beam of the flashlight. The piece Vanya was playing now was a classic love song from the late twentieth century—a rock ballad by Boris Grebenshikov. It was meant to be played on electrically amplified guitar, but Vanya was doing a passable rendition on mandolin. Alexi had heard the song only one time before—in a museum that played the underground *magizdat* cassette on an old-fashioned magnetic tape player. But he still remembered the words. Most of them, anyway. Closing his eyes to help himself remember, he began to sing. He heard Nevsky jump down from the stage and the creak of his seat as he settled into it.

When Alexi reached the part describing the lover, he stumbled over the name. For some reason, the English name Juliana came out instead. Alexi shook his head, unable to re-call the next verse. Beside him, Vanya merely shrugged and continued to play.

"What's wrong, Alexi?" Nevsky called from the front row. He had picked up the flashlight and was holding it. "A sudden case of stage fright?"

Alexi squinted at him over the flashlight glare, and Nevsky obligingly moved the beam to one side. "I don't know," Alexi said. "I guess I'm too drunk to re—"

His eyes widened. The flashlight had briefly illuminated something three rows behind Nevsky—a seated figure who stared up at the stage with eyes that were twin pools of darkness. A tall, thin bald man—or a radiation-poisoned woman whose hair had fallen out. The person sat perfectly still, attention riveted on Alexi. Something long and slender and silver lay across the figure's bony knees—something that made Alexi's throat tighten in fear.

Nevsky finally sensed the person behind him, or perhaps just noticed Alexi's fixed stare. Twisting around in his seat, he swung the flashlight around to illuminate the rest of the theater. But as suddenly as he had appeared, the thin man was gone.

But not completely. Alexi could still feel those eyes upon him. He backed slowly across the darkened stage, coming to a startled halt as the curtain brushed his back.

Silence fell as Vanya came to the end of his song. He lowered the mandolin and stared at Alexi, echoing Nevsky's question.

"What's wrong?" He squinted out at the darkened theater. "Did that officer find us?"

Something behind the curtain—a hand—tapped Alexi on the shoulder. Yelping in surprise he ran—right off the stage. He landed on the floor in a sprawled heap, knocking the air from his lungs. But his drunkenness saved him. Loose-limbed, he suffered no cracked ribs or broken bones. Just two badly scuffed palms.

The eyes were still watching him. He could feel it. Alexi scrambled to his feet.

"That was nice, Vanya," he said, jogging up the darkened aisle, tripping over steps with hands splayed in front of him like a blind man. He'd been weaving on his feet a few short minutes ago, but now he suddenly felt sober. "Keep playing. It's just—I suddenly feel sick. I need to get some air."

He heard Nevsky's laugh from the front row. "Save a bucket for me, Alexi," he joked. "My stomach isn't feeling so good, either."

When Alexi reached the lobby he broke into a run. He clambered out through the open window and walked rapidly across the front of the opera house, ducking slightly as he passed the heroic statues. Only when he was back on the street did the feeling that someone was watching him finally fade.

He crossed *ploshchad* Lenina, dodging out of the way as a truck filled with MVD soldiers rumbled past. They were young—no more than teenagers—sitting on benches in the back of the tarp-covered truck with new-looking Kalashnikov rifles. Their faces were fresh, their cheeks plump and hair still thick. One of them actually noticed Alexi's corporal stripes and saluted him as they passed by. Recruits then, rather than radiation-sickened conscripts. Young enough that they didn't know any better. Young enough that they should have still been in school.

Alexi grunted. Probably not a single one of them knew who Lenin was, either.

He trudged down Krasny *prospekt*, past the entrance to the metro station. The subway didn't run anymore; the underground had been turned into a bomb shelter, back in the days of the China-Soviet War. Next to it was a museum, closed like the opera house. Alexi almost considered breaking in for a look—the museum was supposed to have an excellent display on the building of the Trans-Siberian Railroad, responsible for the founding of Novosibirsk in 1893. But something held him back. He had a sudden irrational notion that museums were places inhabited by the dead—restless spirits who had left behind their clothing, tools, and art just a few short moments ago. Alexi didn't want to be stared at by their haunting photographic images. One pair of eyes watching him was enough. And they *were* watching him, even now . . .

He looked around. He'd reached *ulitsa* M. Gorkogo. A jeep was just turning into the triangular intersection. Alexi suddenly recognized the officer occupying its passenger seat—the Intelligence officer who had been looking for him earlier. The last thing Alexi wanted to do was be confronted by him.

He ran to the closest building: the blue-and-gold-domed

Vosnesenky Sobor, Cathedral of the Ascension. Thankfully, the front entrance wasn't locked. Alexi pulled open one of the heavy wooden doors and slipped inside.

It had been years since Alexi had been inside a *sobor.* He'd done his share of praying on the battlefield—what soldier didn't?—and still wore around his neck the Orthodox cross that his mother had once worn—the one set with four diamonds and a chunk of black stone. But he didn't consider himself a religious man. It wasn't faith that had kept him alive during the three long and grueling years he'd been in the army. It was sheer dumb luck. Why, in Vladivostok alone, Alexi might have been killed a dozen different ways. Yet somehow, while the rest of the Battalion of Death was being slaughtered all around them, he and his squad had survived.

Unlike the museum and the opera house, the *sobor* was still open for business. The sweet smell of incense hung in the air, and thick white candles flickered in glass-bottle containers. The only other person in the building besides Alexi was an elderly woman polishing a brass rail at one side of the room—a concession for worshipers who were ill with radiation or toxin poisoning, or who had been crippled in the war. Unlike places of worship in Western Europe, Russian churches had no benches to sit on. Worshipers stood to sing and pray.

The woman, whose wrinkled face was shrouded by a head scarf, glanced pointedly at Alexi. Realizing that he was still wearing his beret, he scooped it from his head. Holding it in his hands, he stood and debated whether to stay inside the *sobor.* It was warm, but the smell of incense was cloying. The warmth of the candles was lulling the alcohol back into Alexi's brain, and he felt himself swaying on his feet. But the Intelligence officer was probably still looking for him . . .

He crossed to the iconostasis that divided the main body of the *sobor* from the sanctuary at its eastern end. Made from tiered rows of heavily gilded icons, the wall had a door at its center. Only the priests were allowed to pass through this Holy Door into the altar area behind it.

Alexi stood in front of the iconostasis, letting his eye range over the rows of icons. The "canvas" of each icon was a slab of dark wood, thickly painted with muted oils that had cracked with age, and highlighted with gilt. The bottom row of icons showed local saints; not being from Novosibirsk, Alexi didn't recognize any of them. The icons above them showed Old Testament prophets and patriarchs, and winged archangels. At the top was an icon of Christ on his throne, with the Virgin and John the Baptist flanking him on either side. The solemn, bearded figure of Christ Pantokrator looked gravely down at Alexi. Once again, he got the sense that someone was watching him.

He glanced back over his shoulder, and saw the elderly woman. She was leaning on the handle of her broom, staring at him. No—staring at his hands. Her ancient face was crinkled in a frown.

What was wrong? Alexi might stink of vodka, but he had bared his head and was acting in a respectful manner. He glanced down at the beret he held, and saw that there was blood dripping from his scuffed hands. It trickled down his palms, dripping onto the yellowed tiles.

With a disapproving shake of her head, the cleaning woman disappeared through a side door. Probably to get a mop. Alexi scuffed a boot across the drops of blood on the tiles, but only succeeded in smearing the blood and making the stain worse.

He was just about to turn and leave when he heard a creaking noise. He glanced up—and saw that the Holy Door had opened a crack. Thinking that one of the black-robed priests was going to emerge and admonish him, Alexi opened his mouth to apologize. But the figure that stepped through the door wasn't even human.

Nearly three meters tall and thin as a famine victim, the

figure had a human shape. But try as he might, Alexi couldn't bring it into focus. The person's outline wavered and shimmered like a heat wave; the more Alexi tried to focus on it, the less distinct it became. Those strangely articulated limbs—were they folded wings?

The only thing Alexi could see clearly was the metal staff that the figure held in one hand. Alexi's heart hammered a warning in his chest as he stared at the wickedly sharp blade that tipped the end of that shaft. Was this a shepherd—or the grim reaper?

Knuckles whitening as he gripped his beret, Alexi took a step backward. But then the figure spoke—in perfect Russian. The voice was overlaid with a hissing sound, like the white noise of pattering rain.

"Do not be afraid," it said. "We must talk."

"Who . . . what are you?" Alexi asked. A thought suddenly struck him: during the fighting in Vladivostok, on several occasions he'd felt a sudden urge to do—or not do—something, to go in a certain direction—or not. The feeling had been similar to déjà vu. And each time he had that feeling, it had caused him to pause and reconsider his actions—to do things that Alexi knew had either saved his life or spared him from becoming wounded. Had someone—or something—been watching over him and whispering in his ear?

"Are you my guardian angel?" he asked at last.

The figure cocked a blurred head to one side. After a moment's thought, it answered. "I am a holy person, yes. I have been seeking you."

"But I'm just a soldier," Alexi protested, taking another step back. "What do you want with me?"

"I have come to warn you—to warn all humankind," the angel said. "And to help you to save humankind, if I can."

Alexi listened, awestruck. The silence stretched, and his

head spun—though whether from the vodka or from the sudden realization that came into his mind, he couldn't say.

"Me?" he asked at last.

"You," the angel answered. "My arrival on your planet was . . . not welcomed. I was knocked from the sky. I searched for a human of power, with whom to communicate. Someone in whom the flame burned brightly. A holy person, like myself."

"Uh . . ." Alexi swallowed and glanced around the *sobor*. It was still empty. "I think you want to speak to the priest, then."

The angel ignored his protest. "The ancient souls whispered to me from the darkness. You are the one. You lead, and I follow. Together we will reach the end of time. And stop it."

Now Alexi knew he was drunk. None of this was making any sense. Guardian angel or not, the figure in front of him was speaking gibberish. Alexi wondered if Nevsky had added a hallucinogen to the vodka, to spice it up a little.

Slowly he began backing away from the shimmering angel. If he was hallucinating, it could be anyone standing in front of him: the elderly cleaning woman, or the priest—or even worse, the Intelligence officer or Soldatenkof himself. Christ only knew what sort of gibberish Alexi was spouting off. If he didn't watch out, they'd lock him up in a madhouse. Or just declare him unfit for duty and shoot him.

"I'm drunk," he said, articulating the words as clearly as he could. "I need to lie down and sleep it off. Perhaps we can continue this conversation another time?"

Despite the fact that the figure was a mere blur, Alexi had the distinct impression that it was unhappy with his answer.

"Some other time?" it echoed. "That now is already here."

Visions of being sent to a penal battalion for being drunk and disorderly inside a *sobor* shuddered through

Alexi's mind. He had to get out of there. His heart was pounding and it was getting difficult to breathe. And the room was starting to spin. Turning his back on the hallucination, he bolted for the door.

6

Alexi awoke with a start. Where was he? Inside something dark. He reached out from under the blankets that covered him and touched the wall beside him with one hand. Cold metal, filmed with a glisten of ice. He drew his hand away and shivered.

He sat up. He'd been lying on a bench made of nylon webbing in a place that smelled of dried mud, diesel fumes, and cracked vinyl. Inside a vehicle of some kind. But without his glasses, his surroundings were a blur. His helmet was also gone; his head was bare, and his ears were numb with cold.

Alexi patted his chest, looking for his glasses. He found them where he always kept them when he slept: buttoned safely inside the breast pocket of his combats, under the heavy jacket he was wearing.

He looked forward through an open doorway and saw the reflective sheen of an instrument panel. By the fading glow of its light he could make out the familiar contours of a helicraft cockpit. The engine was silent, and there was no motion—it was on the ground, then. Alexi was in the back, lying on one of the benches that folded up against the walls of the cargo bay when not in use. The rear door, which could flop down like a metal gangplank to disgorge soldiers, was closed.

Snow was falling softly outside the helicraft. It had already coated much of the cockpit windows, patches of white that blocked any view of the outside. Something had awakened him—a faint scraping noise. Maybe branches blowing against the outside of the helicraft?

Branches meant a forest, and that meant . . .

Alexi gripped the edge of the bench on which he sat, his heart beating. How had he come to be there? Had the transport helicraft crashed, knocking him out and causing amnesia? Where were the others in his squad? The last thing he remembered clearly was the fighting in Vladivostok. He had been . . . Torn to pieces by a rocket? No, that wasn't it. Been shot by . . . No. That wasn't it either. Then his mind seized on the one thing he knew with certainty. The Union soldier, the one in the heavy-assault suit. He'd attacked it with a grenade, and . . .

His head ached from trying to remember what had occurred between then and now. He had some hazy memories of being drunk, and on leave. But that might have been just a dream . . .

He chafed his hands together, shivering in the cold. His breath fogged in front of his face. Where was he?

He heard breathing. It came from a blanket-wrapped figure that lay on the bench on the opposite side of the cargo bay. Alexi glanced down and saw the familiar contours of an AK-51 at his feet. Slowly, he reached for it. The heavy jacket he was wearing creaked, and the figure stirred slightly. Alexi paused, not really understanding why his heart was beating so furiously. He was inside a Neo-Soviet helicraft. The figure on the bench across from him had to be a friendly soldier. But silent alarms were ringing in Alexi's mind, putting him on the alert.

AK-51 in hand, he crept across the cargo hold toward

the sleeping figure. He located the face by the fog of breath coming from the open mouth, then prodded the chest below it with the barrel of his weapon.

The soldier sat up.

"What is it, Alexi? Is Raheek back?" A woman's voice.

"Irina?" Alexi asked, tentatively.

Then he realized that the woman's Russian had been heavily accented. In that same moment, he remembered where he'd heard accents like that before: in the shouted, half-intelligible surrenders of Union soldiers.

Alexi raised the AK-51 to his shoulder and sighted down the barrel at the enemy. Despite the cold, nervous sweat trickled under his arms.

"Don't move!" His shout sounded hollow in the cargo bay. "Don't move or I'll shoot!"

In the dim light, Alexi could only just make out the enemy soldier's features. She looked Korean, with wide cheeks and a short flat nose. Her short black hair was covered by a Russian *ushanka*—a fur cap with earflaps. Despite the cold, she wore only a lightweight shirt and combat pants, both of them too big for her, over a silver bodysuit of some kind. Her feet were covered with tight-fitting, soft rubber boots that looked like something a diver would wear.

Alexi suddenly realized where he'd seen her before. This was the Union soldier that he and Irina had killed—the one inside the bright green heavy-assault suit. Was she really alive? Or had her ghost come back to haunt him? And if it had, what was it doing wearing a Neo-Soviet uniform?

"What are you doing, Alexi?" The woman's voice was sleepy and slightly irritable; she stared up at him without fear, despite the fact that an assault rifle was pointed at her chest.

Alexi shivered, and the barrel of his AK-51 trembled. His hands were aching with the cold where he gripped its metal stock; he wasn't certain if his numbed fingers would be able to pull the trigger.

"How do you know my name?" he asked. "And how is it you are alive? I thought—"

"I'm alive because I brought the helicraft to a safe landing after the rotors iced up," the woman answered. "And thanks to me, so are you. If I hadn't found a bare spot among the trees, we'd have crashed."

"You were flying the helicraft?" Alexi asked in amazement. A blizzard of possibilities whirled through his mind. Had the Union soldier captured him? Had his squad captured her? Had she somehow overpowered and disposed of everyone else? None of the scenarios made any sense.

The woman stared back at him with a suddenly wary expression. "We made a truce," she said slowly. "That we would cease hostilities until we found out whether Raheek is telling the truth—if it really was a meteorite. If you were thinking of going on alone, you should have shot me when I was still sleeping."

"Meteorite?" Alexi's mind fought for a handhold on a reality that was as slippery as ice. He'd been in combat in Vladivostok, and had looked up to the heavens at the swirling mass of the Maw, and had seen . . .

"You mean the shooting star I saw?"

"Don't be so coy. You were the one who figured out where it must have fallen. It was lucky that you taught history before the war, *Leitenant*."

Leitenant? Alexi glanced at his shoulder, and saw a solid yellow band on the shoulder board of the jacket that he wore: an officer's stripe. Suddenly he realized why the jacket was so heavy. He was wearing a flak jacket. He sniffed, smelling it for the first time. The jacket stank of boiled meat, and was uncomfortably tight on Alexi, narrow though his shoulders were. He glanced at the chest. The name that had been printed onto the jacket's pectoral plate had been gouged away. Only traces of the block letters remained: S - - DA - - - - - F.

Yet another mystery settled like a snowflake onto

Alexi's already overburdened mind. How had he come to be wearing *Leitenant* Soldatenkof's armored jacket? Panic seized him. If the *leitenant* wasn't wearing his jacket, he was probably dead. And that meant a court-martial and firing squad for Alexi.

He focused on the immediate problem. The enemy.

"You are my prisoner," he told the Union soldier. He steadied the aim of his weapon. "I want some answers. Now. Where are—"

"I knew I couldn't trust you, Sov," the Union soldier spat. "But you'd be stupid to shoot me. Pull that trigger, and you'll be stuck here in the Siberian wilderness in a downed helicraft with a radio that doesn't work. Then it will be just you and the alien, with not another human being for hundreds of kilometers."

"Alien?" The mystery was deepening, the questions piling up like accumulating snow. Alexi had no idea what the enemy soldier was talking about. "What are you—"

The rear hatch opened with a loud squeal of metal and the cracking of breaking ice. As it thudded to the ground, cold gray light spilled into the cargo bay. Alexi's combat training took over. He turned and crouched in the same motion, keeping the barrel of his AK-51 trained on the known threat: the Union soldier. But what he saw in the open cargo door, backlit by the watery light of an overcast sky, caused him to forget all about the enemy soldier he had just been confronting. Astonished, he let his assault rifle droop at the same time that his jaw involuntarily sagged open.

The figure that stood in the doorway was only vaguely human-shaped. Freakishly tall and thin, it had gangly legs and strangely jointed arms that folded back upon themselves twice, causing the arm to bend at a Z-shaped angle. One of its overlong hands gripped a metal staff tipped with a blade that crackled with sparks of electricity. The creature was entirely naked, without any visible genitalia. Its skin was a vivid blue. Its head was smooth and bald, an overlong forehead giving it an egg shape. It stared at Alexi with eyes that were twin pits of shadow. Falling snow settled on its shoulders, melting and running down its bare skin in tiny rivulets. The creature seemed oblivious to the cold.

Without understanding how, Alexi knew with a cold certainty that this was the alien that the Union soldier had spoken of. The Neo-Soviets were fond of mutants; radhounds, "pukker" dogs, and other bioengineered beasts were already in use on the battlefield, and there were rumors that the scientists were also genetically altering humans in an attempt to create a race of superwarriors. Yet Alexi somehow *knew* that this creature was not something cooked up in a Neo-Soviet military research lab. It was something entirely new—something entirely alien.

Something entirely terrifying.

The creature's free hand—the one that wasn't holding the staff—snaked forward in a strange, double-jointed motion. At the same moment, the fears in Alexi's mind avalanched into motion. Whipping his AK-51 around, he pulled viciously on the trigger. The cargo bay filled with a roar as the assault rifle bucked in his hands, spewing out a deadly stream of lead. Alexi screamed over the jackhammer roar of his weapon, giving vent to his terror as he fought to correct his aim against the recoil. . . .

And suddenly the alien creature wasn't where it had been.

Some corner of Alexi's mind shouted a warning at him. In his peripheral vision he caught a glimpse of the helicraft's cockpit. Something was obscuring its snow-shrouded windows and instrument panel: a patch of impenetrable blackness, a darkness that Alexi could feel, as well as see. Colder even than the wind that blew in through the rear door, the darkness swelled back into the cargo bay, bulging out toward where Alexi crouched. In that same instant, his mind registered the Union soldier, hurling herself off the bench in a tackle.

In the split second that it took him to decide between the two targets, his ammunition ran out. The AK-51 fell silent. The Union soldier crashed into him, knocking Alexi back against the side of the cargo bay. The back of his head smacked into the ice-filmed metal, and bright points of light danced in front of his eyes. Suddenly dizzy, unable to hold his weapon, he felt himself borne to the floor and flipped facedown as the enemy soldier pinned him in an arm lock. The textured surface of the cargo bay's metal floor bit a pattern into his cheek.

Alexi stared in horror at the blackness that was bulging out of the cockpit. Then the darkness hesitated. After a moment, the black void shrank back into the cockpit, then disappeared with a soft *pop*, like a the sound of a blowtorch being shut off. The alien creature stepped out of the spot where the blackness had been and leaned over Alexi as the Union soldier held him down.

"You are being foolish," it said in perfect Russian, using the form of the pronoun usually reserved for children. Its voice was overlaid with a soft hissing that reminded Alexi of the static crackle of the speakers in his missing helmet.

"We don't need him," the Union soldier said. "He can't be trusted—he was going to shoot me, and he just tried to shoot you." She tugged on the arm that was bent behind his back, sending a jolt of pain up it. Her knee was on the back of his neck, forcing him to lie still.

"I do need this one." The alien turned its head slightly, so that its shadowed eyes stared down at the other human. The creature was so tall that its bald blue head nearly touched the ceiling of the cargo bay. Bone-thin and naked though it was, the creature had an aura of power and authority about it. "Set it free."

The pressure on Alexi's arm slackened, then ceased. The knee disappeared from the back of his neck. The Union soldier stood, then took a step back from him.

Alexi sat up, shaking his head to clear it. "What—"

"The impact site is not far," the alien said. "A walk of less than one-twentieth of your planet's period of rotation. There is sufficient light now for the journey. We will leave."

Alexi's head was clear now, but he still felt dizzy, as if the deck of the helicraft were shifting beneath him. Except that it wasn't the helicraft that was unsteady—it was his entire universe that had come unhinged.

"I don't understand." He fought to banish the tremble from his voice. "Who . . . where are . . ."

The alien's arm zigzagged out with impossible speed, like a striking snake. Alexi gasped as bone-thin fingers wrapped around his chin and cheeks, forcing his head back. He eyed the alien's staff, with its razor-sharp blade. Sparks danced across the metal.

The alien's shadowy, blue-black eyes stared into Alexi's. "Something is wrong with his mind," it said. "He is no use to me in this condition."

Alexi heard a sharp whir. The alien's staff spun in a blur, coming to rest with its point just under Alexi's right ear. The blade crackled with menace. Alexi's nostrils filled with an ozone smell. He struggled to back away from the weapon, but the alien's fingers had a death grip on his face.

Alexi's mind finally caved in as he realized what was going on. He was going to die—the alien was going to cut his throat.

A spark tickled Alexi's ear.

Either that, or electrocute him.

The staff suddenly blazed with the brilliance of a lighted sparkler, the sparks crackling against Alexi's temple and ear. Just as the alien began to draw the blade across his throat, Alexi's consciousness slipped away.

7

The roar of the helicraft's engines and the stink of diesel fumes rushed at Alexi in a wave. He blinked. Where . . . ?

He sat on one of the benches in the helicraft's cargo bay, jammed in between Boris on his right and Nevsky on his left. Across from him on the opposite bench were the other members of his squad. Irina was busy running a cleaning tool through the barrel of her AK-51 and Vanya was applying antiseptic cream from the helicraft's first-aid kit to chemical burns on his hands. His sprayer was tucked under the bench below him, its chemical-crusted nozzles emitting an acrid stench. Piotr leaned back against the wall, eyes closed. The cargo bay was lit with only running lights to save the soldiers' night vision; dim red bulbs on the floor illuminated the soldiers from below with a macabre glow, throwing their faces into shadow.

A thought entered Alexi's mind as he glanced at the bear of a man beside him: Boris should be dead. He glanced around. So should Vanya. And so should . . .

For a moment, his imagination and paranoia ran hand in hand. The others in the squad *were* dead. *He* was dead. The helicraft was carrying them up to heaven. . . .

No. That was a crazy thought. He'd saved them all from death by taking out the heavy-assault suit. Only one of them was even wounded: Irina. A bandage around her left calf was dark with dried blood.

Alexi looked around, focusing on the normal—the everyday. Up in the cockpit, the pilot and copilot were strapped into their seats, staring out the windows as they flew the helicraft. *Leitenant* Soldatenkof stood between them, shouting into the microphone of the helicraft's radio. His back was to the cargo bay, and yet still the members of the squad kept glancing at their officer, in the same way that soldiers glance at an unexploded round, wondering when it is going to go off.

Alexi peered out the tiny window in the wall behind him and saw the city of Vladivostok sliding past below as the helicraft flew away from it. Explosions blossomed with bright flares of light in the streets of the former port, and its ruined buildings reached up with skeletal fingers to the sky. On the horizon, the Maw was just setting in the west, a swirling blood-specked implosion that dwarfed any destruction that mere humans could wreak. Alexi pressed the button on his watch.

The time was 2:16 A.M. Where had the last four and a half hours gone?

Boris glanced out the window, grinned, then shouted at Alexi over the roar of the engine and the chuff of the helicraft's rotors. "I'm glad we're out of there, even if you did cost me two hundred rubles, Alexi. I hear the Union heavy-assault suits have already slaughtered the equivalent of an entire battalion. Our troops are catching hell. Thanks for getting us out of it, *tovarish*."

The other soldiers were listening. They stared at Alexi with something he'd never seen in their eyes before: admiration. There was also an undercurrent of something else—embarrassment.

"Uh . . . You're welcome."

Irina nudged a tarp-covered object on the floor with the toe of her boot. "That was nice shooting, Alexi," she shouted. "Lucky for us you're half-blind."

The other squad members broke into relieved laughter. Their faces were strained with the weariness that comes after a battle. But it wasn't just that. The thing on the floor was what was making them uncomfortable. Several were deliberately not looking at it.

Alexi felt like a man who had just walked in on comrades sharing a private joke. Not the butt of it—just unable to understand the punch line.

He stared at the floor. Lying among the clutter of equipment, covered by a stained tarp, was a shape that looked like a body. Was it the Union officer Alexi had killed? No—it was too tall, too thin. The person under the tarp would have stood nearly two and a half meters tall.

Alexi felt a chill of fear. He wasn't frightened of the body—not in the same way that the other soldiers were. Instead he was frightened that he would see a familiar face under that tarp. The thought was irrational; Alexi had already glanced around the cargo bay and seen that all of the members of his squad were alive. And even if one of them was missing—if it was a squad member lying under that tarp—Alexi didn't really care. He'd never gotten close to anyone in the squad. There was no point. If a bullet didn't get them, radiation poisoning would. In a very real sense, he was living among dead men and women.

The tension was getting to him. Who was it, under the tarp?

The helicraft tilted then, as the pilot sent it into a turn. A hand slid out from under the tarp. Cold and stiff, it had turned a deep shade of blue, like the lips of someone having a heart attack. Except that this blue was deeper, richer—a natural skin tone.

Raheek!

The word exploded in Alexi's mind like a grenade, filling him with anxiety. Before he realized consciously what he was doing, he bent and flipped back the tarp.

In the instant when he saw the body, two emotions washed over him: shock at seeing such an alien creature—and relief. This was someone else.

It wasn't . . .

The name that had been in his mind a second ago was gone.

The body was tall, and lean—as thin as a starving man but with an overlaying of stringy, tough-looking muscle. The forehead was twice the height of a human's and the arms were strangely jointed, with two elbows instead of one. A loincloth of what looked like fur covered the groin, and the flat chest of the creature was studded with four nipples—and numerous bullet holes. The alien's hair was pure white, except where purplish blood had clotted in it. As the helicraft turned the other way and the angle of the floor tilted, the head flopped to one side, revealing a gaping bullet wound in the back of the skull.

The entire body of the creature was covered with intricate white lines that reminded Alexi of the henna patterns that the women of India decorated themselves with. Wondering whether they were tattoos or part of the alien's natural skin coloration, he touched the body, running a finger along one of the lines. The skin was cold and waxy. . . .

"What are you doing?" Nevsky smacked his hand away. "Don't touch it!"

Irina leapt from her seat to flip the tarp back over the creature's face. The former ranger wasn't scared of much—but she was frightened of this alien.

"Are you mad, Alexi?" she shouted, her eyes wide. "What were you thinking? We have to keep it covered. We don't know if its tattoos are still active."

Alexi was at a loss to explain his actions. For that matter, he was at a loss to explain how he had come to be on a troop-transport helicopter, instead of fighting house to house through the streets of Vladivostok. Was he going mad? He glanced nervously at Vanya's chem-sprayer. He had an uneasy feeling that he'd been exposed to its chemicals. Had they caused temporary amnesia?

"I never thought we'd see one face-to-face," Nevsky said. His wide, moon-shaped face held a mixture of wonder and fear. He scratched at his head, and a patch of dark hair came away. His scalp was mottled with small blisters—like many of the others in the rad squad, Nevsky's body wasn't responding well to the antiradiation pills. Nevsky tossed the chunk of hair under the seat, not looking at it. As the squad's unofficial medic and purveyor of black-market medicines, Nevsky knew better than any of them what hair loss meant. He'd been a nurse before the war, and had watched hundreds of patients die of radiation poisoning.

Alexi nodded at the tarp that covered the body on the floor. "What is it?" he asked.

"Remember the attack on the deep-space exploration ship, *Novyy Proezd 30*?" Nevsky gave a hard look at the corpse on the floor. "This blue bastard is one of the aliens that did it. It took an entire company of spaceborne *spetsnaz* to clear just six of these creatures from the *NP-30*."

"And now they've made it as far as Earth," Boris rumbled from Alexi's other side. "I'm doubly glad we're out of Vladivostok now. God only knows what those creatures were doing there. Fifty rubles says Command didn't even know the aliens were on Earth."

"Now that's a sucker's bet," Nevsky shouted back across Alexi. "Most of the time Command doesn't know where its *own* soldiers are, let alone soldiers from another planet."

The burst of laughter that filled the helicraft suddenly cut short. Everyone in the squad stiffened as *Leitenant* Soldatenkof stomped back into the cargo bay. Vanya tried to hide the tube of antiseptic cream up his sleeve, but it fell onto the floor near Soldatenkof's boot. The officer wasn't interested in black-market contraband, however. Instead he stopped where Alexi sat, then leaned over him to brace one hand on the wall. Even though they were airborne and out of combat, the officer still wore his armored jacket and pants. Alexi winced at the smell of sweat that leaked out of the open front of the flak jacket.

"Minsk!" Soldatenkof bellowed.

Alexi, who had been pointedly avoiding the *leitenant*'s eye by studying the crusted sewage on his boots, was forced to look up when he heard his surname.

"Sir?"

"Forward, soldier. Into the cockpit. On the double!"

Alexi slid a glance at Boris. The larger man shrugged slightly.

Soldatenkof cuffed Alexi. "Let's go, slug! Intelligence wants to talk to you. MOVE!"

Alexi stood as quickly as he could. When the *leitenant* got that tone in his voice, somebody usually died. It was a wonder the officer hadn't drawn his Viper already. Alexi jogged forward, lurching as the floor of the helicraft tilted this way and that. Praying that he hadn't done something to irritate the *leitenant* during the four and a half hours that were missing from his memory, Alexi searched for reasons why Intelligence would want to speak to him.

Soldatenkof shoved Alexi into the cockpit with a hand at his back, then picked up the radio microphone and shouted into it. A voice crackled back from the radio in the helicraft's instrument panel as the *leitenant* pushed the microphone into Alexi's hand.

Corporal Minsk, the leitenant tells me that you were the one who took down the alien. We need a full report. Leave nothing out. Tell us exactly how you were able to overcome it. Over.

Alexi stared at the microphone, dumbfounded. How was he to make a report on something he didn't remember? He wet suddenly dry lips, trying to think what to say.

The *leitenant* jabbed Alexi's arm with a forefinger. "Idiot. They're waiting for you to speak. Push the button on the side of the microphone, you moron."

Alexi bit back his retort. He was tired of the *leitenant* treating him like a slow-witted child. Alexi knew a thing or two about how to get children to listen to you—and neither insulting nor belittling them was the way to do it.

He pressed the button. He'd thought of a way to stall for time. "Hello, Intelligence. Corporal Minsk here. Should we be discussing this over an open radio?"

The transmission is encrypted, Corporal. Make your report.

"Tell them how you were able to kill the creature," the *leitenant* hissed angrily in Alexi's ear.

Alexi pressed the button and spoke into the mike. "Uh—" He thought about the alien on the floor, and the gaping wound in the back of its skull. "I shot it?" he guessed.

Pain flared in the back of his own head as the *leitenant* smacked him with an open palm.

"Details!" he shouted at Alexi. "They want a detailed report!"

The microphone was slippery in Alexi's sweaty hands. "Uh, *Leitenant*," he said hesitantly, finger hovering over the mike button. "Just how *did* I kill it?"

Soldatenkof grabbed Alexi by his armored vest and shook him. The vein in his forehead was throbbing. Spit sprayed into Alexi's face as he shouted.

"Tell them"—*shake*—"why"—*shake*—"you weren't"—*shake*—"affected!" Soldatenkof screamed.

The microphone flew from Alexi's hand as the *Leitenant*'s final push slammed him into the pilot's seat. His glasses fell onto the floor and slid as the helicraft lurched to one side. Cursing, the pilot shoved Alexi off his seat, and shouted something back at Soldatenkof. Alexi dropped to his hands and knees as the helicraft came level again, and lunged after his glasses as they slid back across the tilting floor. The radio crackled behind him.

Say again, Corporal. We did not receive your last transmission. Over.

Alexi picked up his glasses. As he hooked the wire frames over his ears, he saw the bright red spot of the Viper's laser sight on the floor in front of him. In that moment, a sense of déjà vu washed over Alexi. Was the *Leitenant* going to kill him—again?

"Put that weapon away, *Leitenant*!" the pilot shouted.

The beam of laser light was trembling as Soldatenkof fought to control his rage. For some inexplicable reason, he hadn't shot Alexi yet, much as he wanted to.

Alexi looked up. In the rear of the helicraft, the eyes of every squad member were trained on the drama that was unfolding in the cockpit. Boris had picked up his AK-51 and was glaring; Nevsky, sitting beside him, used the flat of his hand to push it gently to one side.

"Put the pistol away now, *Leitenant*," the pilot shouted at Soldatenkof. "You're aboard my helicraft, and I'm in command here. There will be no shooting on board. That's a direct order!"

The laser light winked out.

All of this had happened in a matter of heartbeats. During the entire exchange, Alexi was only half-listening. Instead his eye was caught by something in the very back of the helicraft, beyond the benches where the squad sat: a patch of shadow that was darker than it should have been. At first, Alexi thought it was a smudge of oil or dirt on the lens of his glasses, or a discoloration of the helicraft's rear cargo door. But it wasn't any of those things. The blackness had a shifting quality about it—a kind of solid formlessness that Alexi's mind couldn't quite shape into a proper outline. . . .

Alexi jerked back in surprise. Was that a blue face looking out from the center of the patch of black?

In a blink, the face was gone.

The *leitenant* hauled Alexi to his feet. The microphone swayed at the end of its cord. Soldatenkof grabbed the mike and spoke into it.

"Intelligence, please stand by." His eyes blazed fury at Alexi as he spoke. "A full report is coming momentarily. Over."

"Ah . . . *Leitenant* Soldatenkof," Alexi began. He glanced back at the patch of blackness that nobody else in the squad seemed to have noticed. "There's something I think you should know . . ."

8

—*in hell is Alexi?*

Piotr's voice, crackling in his headphones. Where . . . ?

Alexi seemed to be asking himself that question a lot today.

He jerked back in terror as he saw what was crouched next to him: a tiger as big as a horse. Twin fangs lanced up like sabers from its snarling mouth, and eyes sparkled in the moonlight as it prepared to spring.

Recoiling in horror, Alexi fired a burst from his AK-51 at it. The bullets punched into the tiger's hide, tearing away bits of fur. Clods of stuffing rained out the other side of the creature, filling the air with a musty smell.

Stuffing?

Alexi held his fire. He reached out and gave the tiger a poke with his finger. Then he looked around.

He stood in a building filled with broken glass cabinets and stuffed animals. Snakes, bears, birds—and the saber-toothed tiger that he'd just shot. And all of them with glittering glass eyes that stared hungrily at him out of the darkness. He walked slowly from one to the other, looking at the exhibits in the moonlight that filtered through the shattered skylight in the ceiling. A museum, then. That's where he was. His mind flashed back to the times before the war, when he'd taken classes of schoolchildren to look at similar displays. What was he doing there now, assault rifle in hand, armored vest on his chest, boots crunching the shattered glass underfoot?

The answer was quick in coming. Alexi thumped a hand against his helmet to clear the static from its speakers.

Boris's voice: *We've got . . . pinned down . . . harbor. Where's . . . with those grenades?*

Soldatenkof: *Get moving, you useless . . . take it out or I'll . . .*

Piotr: *Does anyone else . . . grenades?*

Over the static in his helmet, Alexi heard the stutter of automatic weapons and explosions, coming from the streets outside the museum. He kept walking, looking at the beautifully painted backdrops that showed each animal's natural habitat. A lot of work had gone into creating the displays, and now they were pockmarked by bullets. What point was there in fighting a war, if your land and culture were being destroyed?

Nevsky: *Where the hell . . . Alexi? I thought . . . bringing up the . . .*

"I'm here," Alexi said into the microphone in his helmet. Something bumped against his thighs as he walked. He glanced down at his belt and saw a web bag filled with fragmentation grenades. Where had they come from?

"Uh . . . Are we still in Vladivostok?" he asked.

Soldatenkof: *Get your pathetic . . . into position immediately, Minsk! And quit joking around. There's a heavy-assault suit . . . the docks . . . where the S-56 is beached.*

Boris: *Twenty rubles says Alexi doesn't . . .*

Ah. The S-56, one of the famous "red banner" submarines. A relic of the Great Patriotic War—the second of the World Wars. It had been hauled onto shore like a beached whale—back when there was still an ocean lapping at the docks of Vladivostok—and turned into a museum ship. So they *were* still in the city.

Alexi looked at his watch. It was 10:44 P.M. Where had the last hour gone? The last thing he remembered was taking out the heavy-assault suit with a rad grenade. How did he get here?

He turned a corner, looking for a way outside. This room was filled with a display of artworks from the Futurists, members of a movement that had flourished at the beginning of the twentieth century. Many of the paintings were torn or burnt, but the few that remained showed utterly abstract geometrical shapes: circles, squares, rectangles, and triangles. The art wasn't to Alexi's taste—yet one of the pieces caught his eye: a painting that was dominated by a large black triangle, poised on one of its points.

Alexi stopped to read the inscription beneath it. The painting was by Kazimir Malevich, an artist who claimed that Futurism had freed art from having to depict the material world. He claimed his paintings were doorways to a "higher reality."

Alexi shook his head. Ridiculous. And yet the painting fascinated him. The triangle in it beckoned silently, as if luring the viewer into an unknown, sharp-edged future. The thought sent a chill up Alexi's spine.

Tearing his eyes away, Alexi walked into another wing of the museum. Here a more practical display caught his eye: a relic of a war fought over 150 years ago. Amid a display of artifacts from the Great Patriotic War was a motorcycle and sidecar that had been lovingly restored. A mannequin dressed in a uniform from the previous century slouched in the sidecar, just behind the machine gun that was mounted there. Alexi toyed with the idea of adding his own AK-51 to the display. He might as well; it was as much of an antique.

Then he saw the dead soldier. She lay on the other side of the motorcycle. Her sand-on-green fatigues and the red star on her helmet identified her as Neo-Soviet. The orange radiation sign tattooed on her exposed chest told Alexi she was from the Battalion of Death. Although her chest and guts had been torn open by what looked like a sword slash, her face was untouched. It was a shame that someone so pretty had to die. . . .

Alexi pushed the thought aside. She was a soldier, nothing more. A member of the rad squad. In a few months—a year or two, at most—she would have been dead from radiation poisoning, anyway.

Piotr's voice screamed over the speaker in Alexi's ear.

. . . told you I saw . . . in the hole on the left . . . naked soldier with blue skin? I've never seen anything like . . .

Blue skin? That reminded Alexi of something. His mind reached for the thought, but he could no more grasp it than he could a cloud of smoke. There was a face attached to the thought: a bald head, deep-set eyes . . . But like a face from a dream, only its outline remained, without any features colored in. Except the color blue.

Which reminded Alexi of something from his history classes.

"Someone's running around in woad?" he asked, chuckling. "So we're fighting ancient Celts, are we?"

Corporal Minsk! Soldatenkof screamed. *I ordered you to bring back grenades, you dolt. What's keeping . . . court-martial for you, you spineless . . .*

Which was the *leitenant*'s way of saying that he'd shoot Alexi if he didn't get himself back to the squad's position. Fast.

Alexi's boot thumped against something that gave off a hollow metal thud: a petrol can. He kicked it again, and it sloshed. Its metal side was marked with a red star—the dead soldier must have been carrying it. Had she honestly been thinking that the ancient motorcycle would still run?

Alexi peered into the sidecar. It was filled with loot—but not the sort an ordinary soldier would steal. It wasn't antique jewelry, or gilded religious icons, or any of the other valuables the museum had to offer.

It was filled with books.

Alexi smiled. It would take him months to read through all of those.

What the hell. Maybe he didn't want to die today, after all.

Scooping up the can, he unscrewed the cap and poured the gurgling contents into the motorcycle's gas tank. The sharp smell of petrol filled the air. Slinging his assault rifle over his shoulder, he tossed the bag of grenades in on top of the books that already covered the mannequin's lap. He almost hauled the mannequin out, but on a whim decided to leave it in place. He might as well have some company on this ride. He sat on the motorcycle's creaking leather seat and tried the kick start.

The engine coughed.

He tried again.

The engine sputtered once. A fart of exhaust and dust wafted up from its tailpipe.

He jumped on the kick start again. And again. And again.

The engine roared to life.

Amazing!

Grinning fiercely, Alexi snapped a salute at the dead woman on the floor—a fellow comrade who must have shared his love of literature. Then he opened up the throttle and shifted. The motorcycle lurched forward, steering sloppily on underinflated tires. Hoping the brittle rubber wouldn't break, he steered the bike around the broken glass on the floor, and out through the shattered front doors of the museum.

The motorcycle's headlamp was no longer working, but the moon and the Maw provided enough light for Alexi to find his way. He rode the bike down *ulitsa* Svetlanskaya, a street that was relatively free of rubble. He roared past the huge monument in the Square of the Fighters for Soviet Power in the Far East and steered for the waterfront.

"Alexi here," he shouted over the sputtering roar of the bike, hoping the microphone in his helmet was working. "Hang on! I'm coming. And I'm bringing you a treat."

Wind whistling in through the open faceplate of his helmet—the visor was still stuck in the up position—Alexi turned right onto *ulitsa* 1 Maya. Something red flickered in his peripheral vision as he started the turn, and a bullet spanged off the sidecar. Then a burst of bullets stitched across the mannequin's chest, spraying chips of plastic everywhere.

He revved the bike and finished taking the corner with the wheel of the sidecar in the air. The mannequin bounced out onto the road as the sidecar thumped back down onto the pavement.

"Thanks for taking a bullet for me, *tovarish*," Alexi shouted back at it.

The beached sub was just down the hill. Artillery fire from the recent fighting had torn gaping holes in the sub's sides at several points; every now and then gunfire would erupt from one of them. Then the rad squad, who were hunkered down behind debris on the beach, would pop up to return fire with a hail of bullets that bounced off the rusting metal walls of the sub. Without grenades, the squad wasn't going to be able to oust the enemy from the improvised bunker.

Alexi roared past ruined buildings—the abandoned headquarters of the previous Soviet state's Pacific Fleet. They'd been turned into a civilian office complex after the Change altered the eastern shoreline, leaving Vladivostok a landlocked city; scattered files drifted across the darkened streets. Alexi waited for his own side to start shooting again, then gunned the bike and roared to the spot where *Leitenant* Soldatenkof, Boris, and Irina had taken shelter behind a block of concrete that used to be part of the docks.

"Hey!" Alexi shouted. "I brought the grenades."

He killed the engine and leapt off the bike. Tossing the bag of grenades out onto the ground, he picked up a book— a copy of *War and Peace*—and held it above his head.

"And books!"

A rifle cracked. A bullet struck the book, knocking it from Alexi's hand. Gulping, he ducked down below the concrete. When he picked up the book, there was a ragged round hole where the word *peace* had been.

"About time you got here," Boris muttered. "I was offering ten-to-one odds that you'd finally deserted."

Leitenant Soldatenkof slapped the book out of Alexi's hands and picked up the bag of grenades. Then his face purpled.

"Minsk, you idiot," he shouted. "What good are these? I told you to bring back rad grenades! You're not only a sluggard—you're stupid! And for that, you get the honor of making the attack on the sub. With *frag* grenades."

Alexi glanced at the beached submarine. Stutters of red flared from a hole in its side. The enemy inside it had to be an assault-suited Union soldier, but for some reason he had gone to ground, taking cover inside the sub. Maybe the assault suit was disabled and the Union soldier had shed it— which would mean that a frag grenade would work, after all . . .

Bullets spanged off the concrete near Alexi's head. He suddenly wished he had deserted, after all. There was cover here and there on the beach—mangled chunks of machinery, bits of broken concrete—but the spaces between them were long indeed. And Alexi had never been much of a sprinter.

"*Leitenant*, I . . ." He looked at the newest addition to the squad, who squatted beside Boris. "Irina's better at throwing—"

"Irina's wounded."

Alexi took a second look at Irina and saw that Soldatenkof was not lying. A bandage around her left calf was just starting to soak through with blood. Knowing Irina, she'd probably insisted upon staying with the squad, despite the wound. She was tougher than any of the others in the squad.

"But—" The rest of the protest died on Alexi's lips as the red laser sight of the Viper settled on his chest. At point-blank range, his armored vest wouldn't stop the slug.

The *leitenant*'s voice was harsh and unyielding: "You make the attack. Now move!"

Alexi wet his lips and clutched the bag of grenades. He glanced at Boris, but the big man only shrugged. Alexi heard Boris say, "five hundred rubles" over his helmet speakers and knew his chances weren't good. Then Boris glanced in his direction. "Ready?" he asked.

Alexi nodded.

"Go!" Boris shouted. He and Irina leaned out from cover to rake the sub with rifle fire. Heart pounding, Alexi sprinted from behind the block of concrete and ran for a rusted-out forklift that was tipped over on its side. Vanya was hunkered down behind it. Bullets chewed up the ground at Alexi's feet as he ran, and something thudded—hard—into the bag of grenades he carried against his chest. He prayed they wouldn't explode. He leaped behind the forklift next to Vanya, who was bent down over his chem sprayer, jamming a splinter of metal into the nozzle.

"What's wrong with the sprayer?" Alexi panted.

"The nozzles are plugged," Vanya answered. Then he grinned at Alexi. "It's just like cleaning a trumpet. Except the spittle is toxic."

"Will it be cleared anytime soon?" Alexi asked. If the chem-sprayer were working, Vanya could fill the submarine with toxic chemicals at a distance. Alexi wouldn't have to . . .

Vanya shook his head. "No, Alexi," he said. "You'll have to play this one solo."

Alexi's helmet crackled to life with Soldatenkof's exasperated yelling. *Get moving, Minsk! We . . . time to . . . assault suit moving toward . . .*

Boris cut him off. *Six hundred rubles says . . .*

Alexi took a deep breath. The next piece of cover—a jumble of broken concrete that a dead Neo-Soviet soldier was draped over—was within throwing distance of the largest of the holes in the sub's hull. But the run to it would leave Alexi completely exposed. He made sure his AK-51 was slung out of the way on his back, then patted the web bag of grenades. They'd already stopped one bullet for him.

Then he ran.

This time, he could hear the bullets hissing past his ears, cutting the air around him. Sweat running down his sides, he pounded across the open ground. Only a meter or two to go . . .

His foot caught on something: a loop of cable buried in the broken concrete. Alexi crashed to the ground, knocking the wind out of himself. The bag flew from his hands, scattering the grenades. Panting, dazed, Alexi lay there for a moment. Then a bullet chipped a piece of concrete directly in front of his face. Acting purely on instinct, he pulled himself into a crouch and dived for the pile of rubble, landing on it in a painful belly flop next to the dead soldier.

Without the grenades, which now lay in perfect view of the hole in the sub.

Alexi could hear the enemy moving inside the submarine. The soldier was firing his weapon nonstop, crashing about in there.

He looked back over his shoulder. He couldn't see any of the other members of his squad; they were all hidden behind cover, waiting until the grenades were thrown. Any moment now, the *leitenant* would see the spilled grenades, and would realize that Alexi had failed. And then Alexi's back would make a perfect target for the *leitenant* to vent his rage upon. . . .

Now Alexi could hear screaming inside the sub. Had the enemy been wounded?

He gasped as a soldier ran past his position. A Union soldier, in the tight-fitting silvery bodysuit they wore inside their heavy-assault suits. Running *away* from the sub. Then something very odd happened. A ball of light—almost like ball lightning, except that it had swirling shapes inside it that were suggestive of howling, screaming faces—streaked across the open ground. It slammed into the Union soldier's back. The stricken soldier threw back his head and began to scream.

Neo-Soviet rifle fire cut him down. Then an acrid smell filled the air as Vanya's chem-sprayer soaked him from head to foot. The Union soldier fell, still screaming in terror until the air bled from his lungs.

Then it was quiet, aside from the crackle of gunfire and muffled explosions coming from the fighting elsewhere in the former port city. It sounded like the battle was moving deeper into Vladivostok.

Irina leaned out from behind her cover and fired a burst from her assault rifle at the submarine, then disappeared behind the cement block again.

The submarine was silent. No one fired back at her.

What was happening? Alexi stared at the dead Union soldier, whose body was rapidly being consumed by the chemicals from Vanya's sprayer. Why had the fool shucked his armored suit and run out into the open where he would be shot? What could possibly have frightened him so badly? And what had that ball of screaming light been?

Alexi glanced back to the cement block that the *Leitenant* was sheltered behind. Despite the armor that covered him from head to foot, Soldatenkof hadn't yet had the courage to show his face. But with the lull in the shooting, he'd be looking in Alexi's direction any moment. . . .

Alexi ground his teeth in frustration. He was caught between a rock—a pile of broken concrete, actually—and a hard place. Then he sighed. Now was as good a time to die as any. If he stayed put, the tension alone would kill him.

In a shambling crouch, he broke cover and ran for the grenades. Scooping one up, he charged at the sub. He twisted the primer on the bottom of the grenade, bowled it underhand through the gaping hole in the sub's rusted hull, and slammed up against the side of the submarine, under one of its fins, sheltering himself. The grenade exploded. Fire and smoke fountained out past Alexi, littering the beach with twisted metal fragments. The rush of air from the explosion carried with it the smell of burnt flesh and hot metal.

More silence. Nothing stirred within the sub.

The members of the rad squad broke cover and ran forward, assault rifles at the ready. Leading from behind, as usual, was *Leitenant* Soldatenkof, who shouted orders at them over his helmet radio from the shelter of the concrete block. Static crackled in Alexi's helmet speaker; he couldn't make out what the officer was saying over the ringing left in his ears by the exploding frag grenade. He lifted the strap of his AK-51 over his head and began lifting the weapon to his chest.

A figure stepped from the submarine. Alexi caught only a glimpse of it: incredibly tall, strangely jointed arms, blue skin covered with intricate white lines, one hand holding what looked like a scythe-tipped metal pole. Then it shoved him back with one hand in a motion as fluid as it was swift. In that same eyeblink-quick movement, the creature plucked the assault rifle from Alexi's hand before he could pull the trigger, and tossed it to one side.

Alexi found himself sprawled on his back, his glasses hanging from one ear as the AK-51 clattered to the ground somewhere to his right.

He looked up, trying to focus on the impossibly tall, incredibly swift blue creature. But the human-shaped creature was nothing but a blur. And that blur was . . . shifting. The white lines on its blue body squirmed like writhing snakes, pulsating in a strobelike effect.

A thought entered Alexi's head: his squad was about to die. Each and every one of them would stand like ripe wheat waiting to be cut down by the blue creature with his deadly scythe. . . .

The creature was ignoring Alexi—for now. Why wasn't anyone shooting at it? Were the others in the squad holding their fire because Alexi was too close to the thing? Why didn't Vanya spray it? Why didn't someone shoot?

Reaching a trembling hand to his face, Alexi hooked his glasses back over his ears. He scrambled sideways across the concrete like a crab, away from the creature, searching for his rifle. There! Only a meter away. He picked up his AK-51 . . .

And looked up at the other members of his squad. They were standing still, weapons held loosely at their sides. Even *Leitenant* Soldatenkof had risen from cover and was staring at the creature with his mouth hanging open, slack-jawed as a half-wit.

Alexi heard the creature moving behind him. He started to turn his head . . .

A warning voice whispered in Alexi's mind: Don't look!

And then he almost remembered . . .

His glasses were off . . . a rocket . . . No, a blade at his throat . . .

Without really understanding why, Alexi took off his glasses. The creature passed him by, striding toward the nearest Neo-Soviet soldier—Vanya. The musician-turned-soldier was a motionless blur; the nozzles of the chem-sprayer in his hand hissing as they sprayed a blurry arc of black gunk onto the ground a short distance ahead of him. Vanya stared at the blue-skinned creature as if hypnotized.

The blur that was the creature raised something long

and slender that glittered in the moonlight: its scythe-bladed staff. The staff started to swing . . .

Alexi squeezed the trigger. His AK-51 bucked in his hands. He had only the vaguest of targets to aim at: the taller of the two human-shaped blurs. He ran the risk of hitting Vanya or one of the other squad members—or even the *Leitenant*. But if he didn't shoot, they'd die anyway.

Alexi wasn't able to see the back of the creature's head tear open as a round from the AK-51 caught it. Not clearly. But he could see the results. The staff flew from the creature's hands, and then the creature itself folded up like a Chinese fan, the life suddenly gone from it.

In that same instant, the other members of Alexi's squad came to life. At least three of them—Alexi wasn't sure who, since they were still blurs—fired a burst from their own weapons at the thing as it lay twitching on the ground. As Alexi put his glasses back on, Vanya was just about to reduce the creature to a bubbling mess when the *leitenant* ran over to him and smacked the twin nozzles of the chemsprayer away.

"Idiot!" Soldatenkof cried. "Don't destroy it! Intelligence will want the body intact, you imbecile." He looked around. "Someone get a tarp so we can move it," he shouted.

"What is it?" Vanya asked the *leitenant* as Alexi approached. "Some sort of mutant?"

Boris and Piotr ran toward the beached submarine and clambered inside. Their voices crackled back over Alexi's helmet speakers.

Just an empty assault suit in here. All clear!

And Neo-Soviet dead. Ugh . . . body parts every-where . . . slaughterhouse in here . . . thirty rubles says . . .

Curious, Alexi knelt beside the blue-skinned creature. Purplish blood was puddling on the cement underneath it. The white lines on its body were still now. Its face . . .

It wasn't . . .

A name hovered at the edge of Alexi's consciousness,

then vanished. He glanced back at the submarine and saw Boris emerge from a hole in its side.

"Whatever that blue thing was, I'm glad it's dead," he shouted. "Nice shooting, Alexi. Thanks. I don't know what that creature did, but it felt as though I was hypnotized. I couldn't—"

"That's enough chatter," the *leitenant* snapped, cutting Boris off. "No one is to speak of this—person—further, until given permission by me to do so. Especially over your helmet radios. Understood?"

Boris and Piotr jogged back to where the rest of the squad had gathered. As they stared at the creature on the ground, the *leitenant* glared at each of the squad members in turn until they nodded.

Alexi stood, and looked around for the blue-skinned creature's weapon. He had seen where it had landed, but now he couldn't find the strange metal staff. He couldn't be certain, but had that area of the beach suddenly turned a darker color—a shade of black that was somehow more dense than it should be?

"The creature," Alexi murmured, speaking his thoughts aloud. "How can we be sure there was just one of—"

Suddenly the *leitenant*'s face was centimeters from his own. "Minsk! You half-witted dreamer," he screamed. "No talking about it! That's a direct order."

"But . . ." When Alexi looked back, the patch of darkness was gone. Something important had just happened—something he understood only at a subconscious level.

He had no idea what it was.

Instead of arguing with the *leitenant*, he turned away to fetch a tarp.

9

The hissing noise was the first thing Alexi noticed. That—and the darkness.

He wasn't in the helicraft anymore.

He froze.

"Alexi, what's wrong? Did you hear something?"

That was Piotr's voice.

Alexi's hands no longer held the microphone. Instead they gripped his AK-51. He stood in a concrete-walled hallway, in utter darkness except for the beam of light that came from the halogen bulb in his helmet. The hissing was coming from somewhere up ahead, up past the point where the corridor had partially collapsed.

Piotr stood beside him, holding a frag grenade in one hand and his Uzi in the other. His breath fogged in the chill air, forming tiny ice crystals on the fur of his *ushanka* cap. He wore a padded greatcoat over his combat fatigues. So did Alexi; his armored vest was gone.

The last thing Alexi remembered, he'd been on board a helicraft as it flew away from the battle in Vladivostok. The *leitenant* had been about to shoot him because he couldn't remember how he'd killed the blue-skinned alien. He'd been trying to point out something to the *leitenant*, something in the helicraft that none of the other squad members had noticed. . . .

Except that he *did* remember how he killed the alien: by taking off his glasses so he wouldn't be affected by the hypnotic tattoos, and shooting it. And he *had* made the report to Intelligence.

And the patch of darkness in the back of the helicraft . . .

Only a shadow.

Yes, the memory was clearer now. The *leitenant* had called Alexi forward to the helicraft cockpit to speak on the radio. As he'd handed Alexi the microphone, Alexi thought he saw something moving in the back of the cargo bay, but it had been nothing more than the shadow of one of the squad members, a product of the cargo bay's flickering interior lighting. He'd begun making the report to Intelligence . . .

And found himself here.

Wherever here was.

Piotr shifted nervously from one foot to the other. He'd been an actor in Moscow before being conscripted into the rad squad—back before the radiation blisters marred an otherwise perfect face. His chiseled features and long dark hair gave him the appearance of a noble *boyar*, and his actor's training enabled him to hide his emotions well; he was one of the few members of the squad who could keep the contempt out of his expression when he looked at *Leitenant* Soldatenkof. But his face was an open book. Piotr was scared. His dark eyes were wide in his pockmarked face.

"What do you hear, Alexi?" he asked. "Something up ahead? Or are they radioing us? Can we return to the surface?"

Radio. Yes. That might give him some clues. But the speaker was producing its usual static hiss.

Alexi thumped the heel of his hand against his helmet. But the static didn't clear up.

Should he tell Piotr about his blackouts? Alexi didn't think it was a good idea—not after what had happened to Tamara. When she'd gone crazy and started talking to her grenades as if they were babies, the other squad members had at first turned a blind eye. Then she'd primed one, and held it to her breast. Boris had wrenched it from her and tossed it away only a second or two before it exploded. A short time later, Tamara and Piotr had been sent ahead to scout out a downed Union bomber plane. Shots were fired, and only Piotr had returned. He'd claimed that the plane's automated weapons systems had killed Tamara, but Alexi doubted it. If the plane's weapons were still functional, it would have required a miracle for Piotr to escape without a scratch. Nothing was ever said about the incident—not even by the lieutenant. Alexi had just gone along with the silence, adding his unspoken vote in favor of Piotr's actions.

Alexi didn't want Piotr thinking that he had gone mad, too.

"Where are we, Piotr?" Alexi asked. He decided to stretch the truth a little, in case he'd been providing Piotr with position reports up until now. "I've ah . . . lost track. My helmet radio has just gone dead."

"We must be too far underground to pick up a signal," Piotr answered. He glanced up, but the bulb in his helmet had nearly burned out and emitted too feeble a glow to illuminate even the ceiling overhead. "Too much concrete above us. We should climb back up to where they can hear us."

Alexi turned his head, swinging the beam of the helmet's built-in flashlight around. Underground, then. In a bunker, perhaps?

The light picked out a pattern on the floor. Half-hidden by grime were stripes that ran along the middle of the corridor—a broad band of yellow and one of red. They reminded

Alexi of the stripes used in hospital corridors, to direct people to the various wards. The yellow stripe turned a corner to the left; the red one disappeared just ahead, under the pile of broken concrete that had fallen from the ceiling. Pieces of wire and a broken light panel dangled just above the chest-high debris. Faint sparks crackled from their frayed ends. The hissing noise came from just behind the collapse.

Piotr gestured at the spot where Alexi's helmet light illuminated the red stripe. "We don't have to follow it all the way to the end. We'd never get past that collapse, anyhow. Do you see the sparks? There must be some sort of emergency generator—those wires are live. We could just say the lab was clear and go back."

"Lab?" Alexi asked. "What's inside it? Maybe we should take a look."

"*Nyet.*" The once-handsome man's eyes grew still more fearful. "Let it be."

Alexi's mind whirled. "Let what be?" he asked.

Piotr laughed. "That's the spirit, Alexi," he said with a broad wink. "We saw nothing. The tank was crushed—just like the others. Our recon is done."

Alexi glanced at the spot where the ceiling had collapsed. Was the hissing noise getting louder?

"Should we be turning our backs on it?" he asked.

Piotr turned on his actor's charm. Smiling, affable, he clapped Alexi on the back. "Come on, *tovarish*," he said. "Let's just tiptoe away. I've never known you to do anything you don't have to. Or have you suddenly turned hero on us, now that you've been recommended for a decoration?"

"I have?" Alexi asked. Then he quickly added: "Oh—for killing the alien, *da?*"

Piotr grunted. "Don't get *too* boastful about it, or they'll promote you. And then you'll turn into a bastard, like every other officer. And then I'd have to shoot you."

Alexi looked sharply at Piotr. The words had been spoken entirely without expression—Alexi couldn't be certain it was just a joke. He took one last look in the direction of the hissing noise, then nodded. The light from his helmet bobbed across the floor.

"Which way?" he asked.

Piotr gestured with his Uzi. "We followed a green one in. And then the red. But I think the yellow is a faster way back to the surface."

They turned down the side corridor and began trudging back along the yellow line. As they walked, their footsteps echoing off the concrete walls, Alexi couldn't shake the feeling that there was something just behind them—something menacing and evil. Was that faint sound the scrape of metal on concrete—or had Alexi's helmet speaker started crackling again? Alexi had the strange feeling that he knew what the thing making the noise was—but every time he tried to picture it in his mind, the image vanished. He kept glancing back over his shoulder, splashing the corridor behind them with light, until Piotr stubbed his toe on a piece of hospital equipment that looked as if it had been chewed up by a frag grenade. Cursing, he made Alexi take the lead.

"You want us to break our necks, Alexi?" he asked in an exasperated voice. "*Nyet?* Then keep that light pointed for—"

A noise erupted out of the darkness—a cross between the roar of a strangled lion and a sound like metal being sawed with a dull blade at high speed. Echoing down the corridor, it approached like the roar of a subway train through a tunnel. Fear washing through his gut like ice water, Alexi turned to see what was bearing down on them. . . .

Piotr went down.

The rad soldier screamed as he was pulled to the ground. A flare of red erupted from the barrel of his Uzi as his fingers convulsively pulled the trigger. Bullets crashed into the ceiling, showering chips of cement on Alexi's shoulders. One or two spanged off the metal of a light fixture overhead, and glass exploded from it. Piotr's other hand flailed, and the grenade he had been holding rolled away.

Backpedaling rapidly, Alexi pointed the light of his helmet down at Piotr. An animal about the size and shape of a chimpanzee, but with exaggerated muscles and metallic spikes radiating out of its spine, was sitting on Piotr's chest. It had a short, thick tail and bare skin that gleamed like burnished copper. One of its lumpy knees pinned Piotr's arm to the floor.

Alexi brought up his AK-51, aimed . . . but Piotr was in the way. He didn't want to shoot him by mistake.

As Piotr screamed and fought to twist his Uzi around to shoot the thing, the creature opened oversize jaws that looked like a spring-loaded leg-hold trap. Its mouth was filled with rows of bright metal teeth. Slamming its head down, it sank these teeth into Piotr's neck. Alexi heard a wet crunch, and Piotr's scream choked off abruptly. The Uzi fell silent and clattered onto the ground.

Alexi took a cautious step back from the creature, struggling to fight down his panic. Another step. As the creature fed, pulling an artery from Piotr's mangled neck and slurping the hot blood from it, Alexi aimed his AK-51 at its head. Then he fired.

The assault rifle bucked as bullets roared out of it. The barrel began to steam in the cold corridor. Bullets slammed into the creature, some striking sparks as they ricocheted off the steely spikes on its back.

What *was* this thing?

In the middle of the hail of bullets, the creature looked up. Its heavy brow was crinkled, as if it was frowning at Alexi for interrupting its meal. The assault rifle was taking its toll; bullets had torn deep creases into the creature's metallic hide and thick liquid was oozing from them. The creature rocked back on its haunches and threw up a heavily muscled arm as if to fend off a blow. Then it began to hack, like a cat coughing up a hairball.

Alexi's magazine ran out of bullets. Wrenching it out of the assault rifle, still backing away from the blood-fouled creature, Alexi tore open his greatcoat and yanked another magazine from the pocket of his fatigues. The creature continued to make strangled, coughing noises as it sat on Piotr's chest, the steely claws on its feet embedded in his flesh like knives in soft cheese. Was it going to roar again?

The answer came just as Alexi snapped the magazine into his AK-51. Opening its mouth impossibly wide, the creature coughed up a stinking wad of phlegm twice the size of a fist. It splatted onto Alexi's chest, just on the spot where he'd wrenched open his greatcoat a second before. Instantly, he felt a burning sensation, as if his chest were on fire. An acrid smell rose from the shirt of his combat fatigues as the fabric melted against his skin. The acidic stench brought back a flash of memory—of the arts and crafts classes in the high school where he'd taught. Then he realized what that smell reminded him of: hydrofluoric acid, used for etching glass.

Screaming, he threw his assault rifle down. By the time he'd wrenched off his greatcoat, the acid had eaten deep into his chest. His skin was a bubbling, steaming mass of red blood and gooey phlegm. The pain was overwhelming. He couldn't breathe. Something inside his chest cavity collapsed as air rushed from it—a lung?

As the first trembles of shock overtook him, Alexi sagged to his knees. He'd been killed by . . . spit? He'd had a feeling that he might die today, but he never expected it to be like this.

A stray thought entered his mind: If he'd died when he was supposed to, back in Vladivostok, it would have been much cleaner and quicker. . . .

Alexi's fought to lift his head as he held himself up, hands splayed on the cold concrete floor. The light from his helmet illuminated the creature from below, throwing its jutting brows, heavy shoulders, and apelike arms into shadowed relief. Still eyeing him, the creature growled—a rumble that was a cross between a cat's purr and the rattle of two metal gears clashing together.

Alexi fell face forward onto the bubbling cavity that had once been his chest. The creature gave a small belch, glanced down at Piotr with satisfaction, and went back to its grisly meal.

As Alexi's consciousness slipped from his shock-numbed body, his mind groped for a word to describe the horrific creature. At last he found one: growler.

Where had he heard . . . ?

10

oris laughed out loud.

"Growlers?" he asked in a mocking tone, leaving a lazy trail of blue smoke in the air as he gestured with a hand that held a foul-smelling cigarette. "Is that the best name Command could come up with? It sounds like something out of a children's cartoon! Ten rubles says the officer who thought that one up was the same fellow who came up with the name 'glowworm' as a code for rad grenades."

Alexi's head jerked back as laughter rippled across the rest of the squad. He stiffened in his chair. Had he nodded off? He clutched at his chest, wondering why it didn't hurt any more. He was amazed to find that the shirt of his combat fatigues was intact. His chest was whole, the flesh solid under his probing fingers. He was breathing. . . .

He sucked air into his lungs in a ragged gasp. Beside him, Boris turned and gave him a strange look. "Is my cigarette bothering you, Alexi?"

The smoke was pungent. To make their tobacco last, the soldiers cut it with something that, when it burned, smelled like vegetables left too long in a pot on the stove. Alexi waved the smoke away from his face, and Boris shifted the cigarette to his far hand.

It must have been the smoke, irritating his lungs as he slept.

It must have been a dream . . .

But now the dream was gone, all memory of it vanished.

Alexi glanced around. He was sitting on a folding metal chair behind the other squad members, in a room with walls painted a dull military green. The other five members of the squad were all here, watching as the *leitenant* slapped a pointer across the flat of his hand in annoyance. His Viper pistol lay on the table beside him, next to a worn leather briefcase. Even though the squad members were unarmed, Soldatenkof wasn't taking any chances.

Pinned to the wall beside the *leitenant* was an enlarged color photograph of an apelike creature with more teeth than face and metallic-looking horns growing out of its back. It lay on its side inside what looked like a glass-fronted coffin; the picture had been taken through the glass from above the lid, then rotated so the creature was in a vertical position. The silhouette of a human figure beside it showed the thing to be twice the height of a human. Stamped across the top of the photograph, in red, were the words TOP SECRET.

Alexi stared at the creature—a thing from his worst nightmare. His stomach clenched as if he'd eaten something bad.

Boris was whispering something—a joke that had the other squad members chuckling—but Alexi's mind was elsewhere. He tried to remember his dream. He and Piotr had been in a dark, close space, somewhere underground . . .

Soldatenkof's pointer cracked across the tabletop. "Pay attention, you dolts," he snapped. "What I tell you could save your worthless lives."

The laughter died away.

Irina, sitting just in front of Boris, turned and hissed angrily at him. "I want to hear what the *leitenant* has to say, even if you don't. He's talking about an incredible moment in Neo-Soviet history. Just imagine it: an alien race. And our nation was the first one to make contact."

Piotr—who for some reason Alexi was startled to see alive and well—leaned over to elbow Irina. "We were the first ones to take them captive, you mean," he whispered at her. "And just look where it got us. But that's what comes of poaching—eh, Irina?"

As the *leitenant* droned on at the front of the room, Alexi swiveled in his seat to look behind him. Through a grubby window high in the wall he could see snow falling. It was light outside. The combats he was wearing were worn, but clean. He could smell the detergent that had been used to launder them—and the lingering scent of vodka on one shoulder. The squad had been away from the fighting for some time, then.

The last thing he remembered was staring out through the window of the helicraft cockpit at the Maw as it sank below the horizon in a darkened sky. . . .

He must have been exhausted, after the battle at Vladivostok. By the time the helicraft whisked them away, they'd been in the thick of battle for three solid days, playing a game of cat and mouse with the heavy-assault suits—with the rad squads faring about as well as a mouse in a cat's jaws. It was no wonder the past few hours were a blank. Alexi remembered the times in basic training—when he'd literally slept on his feet—when he'd dozed off even as he was marching.

The thought cheered him up. He wasn't going crazy, after all. But he wished he'd been paying attention during the *leitenant*'s briefing. There was something about the creature in that photograph, something that was causing Alexi to experience a feeling like heartburn, deep in his chest. . . .

"The growler in this illustration is much larger than the creatures you're likely to encounter," the *leitenant* continued. "The growler that was spotted in yesterday's flyover is considerably smaller, about the size of a large dog. Intelligence believes it came from one of four cryotanks that were assumed destroyed after a Union smart bomb leveled the building they had been housed in. But obviously at least one of the cryotanks must have come through the bombing intact, if a growler was spotted on the surface. Intelligence has concluded that the lower levels of the building survived the bombing."

Soldatenkof gave his squad a brief, falsely reassuring smile. "None of the cryotanks in that building was large; all held growler pups. Even if all four have survived and have escaped the cryotanks, they'll be sluggish and disoriented after being on ice for so long. According to Intelligence reports, they're small and won't pose much of a threat."

Boris leaned over to whisper in Alexi's ear. "And we all know how accurate Intelligence reports are, don't we?" he muttered. "Fifty rubles says they turn out to be as big as a house."

Alexi didn't want to take that bet. Given the unreliability of what they'd been told about Vladivostok—that the Union troops attacking it were inexperienced and only lightly armored, certainly without heavy-assault suits— Boris was probably right.

Alexi leaned closer. "Uh, Boris."

The bear of a man looked at him eagerly. "Yes, Alexi? I didn't think you *had* fifty rubles." He held out a meaty palm in anticipation.

Alexi ignored it. "I ah . . . fell asleep earlier. What's the *leitenant* talking about?"

"We're being sent to kill those creatures," the big man rumbled. He nodded in the direction of the photograph at the front of the room, then took a deep drag on his cigarette and expelled a foul-smelling blue cloud of smoke. Nicotine had stained his fingers a deep yellow. His lungs were probably equally filthy, but to a man slowly dying of radiation poisoning, the threat of cancer was a small one. The fingernails were missing from Boris's hands—a reminder of the poisons that were all that was keeping him alive: the chemicals in the military-issue, antiradiation pills.

"What are growlers?" Alexi asked. "Something our scientists cooked up?"

Boris gave Alexi a strange look. "You really were asleep, weren't you?" he whispered back. "Funny, you looked as though you were listening."

"I'm tired," Alexi said. "Vladivostok left me weary to the bone."

Boris's frown deepened. "Even after two days of leave?"

Alexi recoiled. Two days? He'd lost two entire *days*? Even worse, they were two days of leave. What had he done—drunk so much vodka he'd blacked out?

At the front of the room, the *leitenant* was busy relating what little the military seemed to know about the so-called growlers. It basically boiled down to what any fool could guess from the photograph—that their claws and teeth were lethal weapons, as long and sharp as bayonets.

Whispering quickly, Boris recapped what the *leitenant* had said earlier. "The growlers are aliens. A space-recon team found them inside an artificial asteroid, apparently in hibernation, just after the Change. First contact with an alien race. Very exciting—and very hush-hush. The *Novyy Proezd 30* was sent to fetch them. They put the comatose growlers in cryotanks that duplicated the cold and airless conditions inside the asteroid, and brought them back to Earth for the scientists at Tomsk to play with. On the way back to Earth, the *NP-30* was attacked by another alien race: those blue-skinned bastards like the one you shot."

Alexi blinked in confusion. "But what—"

Boris winked. "Two thousand rubles says the blue boys didn't much like the growlers. Or that they wanted them for themselves."

At the front of the room the *leitenant* was droning instructions, listing off the equipment the squad would be carrying. They would be issued winter greatcoats, extra grenades, an experimental new chemical for Vanya's sprayer . . .

"How many were brought back to Earth?" Alexi asked.

"The *leitenant* says there were only a dozen of them—including the four pups that were put on ice in the research lab, one of which was spotted in yesterday's flyover," Boris whispered back. He took one last drag on his cigarette, then lifted his foot and ground the stub out on the sole of his boot. "But you know how that goes—I wouldn't even offer odds on there really being twice or even ten times as many. Nobody would take the bet."

Alexi eyed the photo at the front of the room nervously. The *leitenant* had taken a map out of the briefcase that lay on the table beside him, and was posting it on the wall. The map was titled TOMSK 13. It showed a series of identical buildings, one of them circled in red.

Alexi knew nothing about Tomsk 13, aside from the fact that it was a military research facility. Top secret, secure, guarded by an elite Ministry of the Interior unit.

Tomsk itself—the city of half a million souls that lay a few kilometers to the south—had been suffering the ill effects of the military research facilities for more than a century. Back in 1993, an explosion in the nuclear-weapons plant Tomsk 7 had thrown radioactivity over a 120-kilometer-square area. The next year a tuberculosis epidemic—possibly cooked up in a government weapons lab—swept the area. Now it seemed that dangerous aliens had been added to the mix.

Reaching into the briefcase a second time, Soldatenkof pulled out a black-and-white photo that showed Tomsk 13 from the air. All of the buildings in the facility had been reduced to rubble. Three of them—including the red-circled one—had vanished entirely; large craters on the aerial photograph marked the spots where they had once stood.

Boris was counting under his breath. "Ha!" he exclaimed.

A little too loudly.

A thin spot of red light appeared on Boris's wide chest. For a moment, Alexi was reminded of the laser pointers he'd used when teaching his history classes. Then metal scuffed on the floor as the squad members sitting in front of Boris hurriedly pushed their chairs away, out of the line of fire.

"Do you have a comment, Private?" the *leitenant* asked.

"As a matter of fact, I do." Boris smiled like a student who had thought of something his teacher had overlooked.

"There are ten buildings on that map," he said. "If each one held four cryotanks, that's forty growlers. I'd like to know why Intelligence is so certain we won't encounter another thirty-six of them."

The purple vein throbbed in the *leitenant*'s temple. Alexi held his breath, waiting for the finger on the Viper's trigger to tighten.

"They're gone," the *leitenant* spat.

Boris took a deep breath as he looked at the laser that was lined up on his chest.

"How do we know that?" he asked. "Sir."

A sadistic look crept into Soldatenkof's eyes. The laser sight winked off, and Soldatenkof holstered his weapon. He was enjoying himself now; there would be no "disciplinary killings" today.

"We know there are no other growlers left in Tomsk 13," he said, "because those that did escape from their cryotanks after the Union bombed the site chewed their way through the entire company of MVD troops that guarded the facility."

Boris's eyes widened. Off to Alexi's right, someone gave a low whistle. The Ministry of the Interior troops were elite soldiers with modern weapons—the best the Neo-Soviets had to offer.

"Three months have passed since the Union's surprise bombing raid on Tomsk 13," Soldatenkof continued. "Not a single growler has been seen in the area since then. But Intelligence has received scattered reports of them from across Siberia—as far away as Alaska. They're spreading out across the north. They aren't coming back."

Soldatenkof picked up his pointer and tapped the red-circled building on the map. "Command has ordered us to go in and deal with the last of the growlers to awaken—the pup that's roaming around Tomsk 13."

Alexi couldn't help himself. Burning with curiosity, he broke the soldier's number one survival rule of not drawing an officer's attention to oneself.

"Why us?" he asked.

Beside him, Boris rumbled: "Good question, Alexi. Funny, isn't it, that we've suddenly got top secret clearance."

"Why you?" Soldatenkof echoed.

Alexi didn't think it was possible, but the *leitenant*'s expression became even more sadistic. "Because after the MVD failed to contain the growlers, Command ordered Tomsk 13 neutroned. Unfortunately, the blast didn't take out the growlers that were down in the lowest levels of the complex; the concrete must have shielded them. The blast released fast-decay isotopes; there's only residual radiation left. Not enough to bother soldiers who are already on anti-rad pills—"

"And already sick as dogs," Boris muttered.

"—but enough to incapacitate our regular troops," Soldatenkof concluded. "Command doesn't want to waste them on a mop-up mission."

"So it's in with the missile fodder," Boris grumbled. "Us."

"But I'm not . . ." Alexi paused when he saw every soldier in the rad squad looking at him. Their faces held a mixture of envy and pity. They all knew he didn't belong with them—that he wouldn't even be here if a clerical error hadn't lumped bad eyesight in the same category as radiation poisoning.

"Don't worry, Minsk," the *leitenant* said with a smile. "You'll be issued antiradiation pills. Just like the rest of the squad."

11

Alexi stared at the stripes that ran the length of the concrete corridor. Just ahead of where the light from his helmet illuminated the floor, part of the ceiling had collapsed. Sparks crackled from the frayed ends of wire that hung down from a broken light panel. Just beyond the collapse, something hissed faintly. The sound reminded Alexi of a serpent about to strike.

He knew what he'd see next: Piotr, standing beside him, wide-eyed and frightened, holding a frag grenade in one hand and an Uzi in the other. And he could predict, almost word for word, what Piotr was about to say.

"Let it be, Alexi," the former actor said. He smiled and gave a falsely hearty wink. "We found nothing. The cryotank was crushed under that collapse, *da*? Our recon is done. Let's get out of here."

Piotr glanced down the corridor that led away to the left. He gestured with his Uzi at a yellow line on the floor. "I think the yellow is a faster way back to the surface."

A wave of déjà vu gripped Alexi. He was frozen in his tracks, unable to move. Whatever was beyond the collapsed ceiling, they couldn't turn their backs on it. The yellow line somehow seemed prophetic. It was the coward's way out. And cowards died.

Just as Soldatenkof would when . . .

The thought evaporated. Alexi forced himself to swallow. His mouth was suddenly very dry. He spat on the floor—and when the beam of his helmet light caught the puddle of spit, he shuddered.

Gripping his AK-51, he walked toward the ceiling collapse, every nerve on alert.

"Alexi!" Piotr called. "Where are you going?"

"Stay here, Piotr," Alexi said. "Or follow me. Whichever you choose. But I have to see what lies ahead."

Piotr muttered the Neo-Soviet soldier's favorite curse—a suggestion that Alexi have intercourse with his own mother—but followed him a moment later.

Carefully avoiding the broken electrical wires, Alexi climbed over the pile of rubble. It was a tight squeeze; the debris under his boots shifted, and he smacked his helmet against the fallen light fixture. Static crackled in his ear. He could hear Soldatenkof berating the squad for having found nothing yet. The *leitenant's* voice was slightly slurred, as if he'd been drinking.

Alexi slid down the other side of the blockage and found himself in a large room. He shined his light around it—and stiffened at what he saw. Piotr clambered in behind him, and Alexi heard a sharp intake of breath.

"Oh Christ," Piotr whispered. "There must be a hundred of them."

The room was a laboratory of some sort, filled with what at first glance looked like aquariums. The glass sides of dozens of small tanks reflected Alexi's helmet light back at him. Several of the tanks were broken—probably by the partial collapse of the ceiling. But about half were intact. The insides of these tanks were frosted over, as if covered by a thin layer of ice. But that icy coating was melting, leaving clear patches. Through them, Alexi could see tiny apelike creatures, about the size of cats, squirming inside the tanks. Each was curled in a fetal position, with muscular arms wrapped around its torso and spines down its back. Even as Alexi and Piotr watched, one shifted inside its tank, scraping its spines across the glass. Both humans took an involuntary step back.

Alexi glanced at Piotr. "Growlers?" he whispered.

The other soldier nodded, eyes wide. "The scientists must have been breeding them."

Their voices were almost lost in the hissing noise that filled the room. The air held strange smells: ozone, medical disinfectant—and a sharp acidic odor that made Alexi shudder. He suddenly found it difficult to breathe.

Alexi cleared his throat, then spoke into his helmet microphone. "*Leitenant* Soldatenkof, do you copy? This is Corporal Minsk. We have located several dozen—"

The roar of Piotr's Uzi filled the room, making Alexi's ears ring.

"What's wrong?" Alexi shouted.

Then he saw it. Scuttling across the floor toward them was a tiny growler with a horn jutting out of its forehead. Its multicolored skin was as pretty as a parrot's—a wild mottling of red, yellow, and turquoise—but its mouth held a vicious collection of fangs. Despite the bullets that gouged its flesh, it ran straight for Piotr's leg and sank long, wickedly sharp fangs into his calf.

Screaming, Piotr pointed his Uzi straight at the thing and blasted it with a hail of lead, oblivious to the bullets that were also pulping his own foot. Alexi brought his own weapon to bear—and only under the combined firepower of assault rifle and submachine gun did the thing finally release its hold. It scuttled away under a bank of cryotanks, leaving a smear of steaming ichor on the floor.

Piotr sank to his one good knee, groaning. He dropped the Uzi and grenade on the floor and clutched his ruined leg just below the knee. His pockmarked face was white with shock.

Just then, Alexi heard a cracking noise. He spun toward the tanks, illuminating them with his helmet flash. A row of spines was jutting through the glass of one of the tanks, cracking it open like an egg. Even as he watched, the crack grew and spread.

"Christ," Alexi muttered. "I've got to get out of here." He started backing out of the room, AK-51 leveled at the tanks.

"Alexi!" Piotr begged. "Don't leave me."

Alexi hesitated. The other soldier was still clutching his leg, unable to move. His trouser leg was soaked with blood; a large puddle was spreading on the floor around his boot. Already he was trembling with shock. The only way he'd make it out of here was if Alexi carried him—all the way to the surface. And with something—something larger and even more menacing than the dozens of little growlers in this room—following him every step of the way.

Piotr's eyes pleaded with him. But Alexi reminded himself that this was the soldier who had shot Tamara. And that Piotr was a dead man, anyway. If the growlers didn't get him, radiation poisoning eventually would. The thought steeled Alexi's resolve.

"Don't worry," he lied. "I'll get help. Just hang on until I get back."

He turned and ran. As he scrambled up and over the pile of debris that had collapsed into the corridor, he glanced, once, over his shoulder. He shuddered at what he saw.

Four of the glass-walled cryotanks cracked open at once, spilling infant growlers onto the floor. Landing on their apelike feet, they immediately bounded for Piotr. Three of them sank slavering teeth into the wounded soldier, chewing gaping holes in his sides. The fourth clamped its jaws onto Piotr's face, cutting off his scream. His hands fumbled until they found the frag grenade, which he primed with a last desperate twist. Then the grenade exploded, showering bits of human and growler across the room. A fragment of bloody steel zinged off Alexi's helmet, knocking the speaker in it out of commission.

Heart pounding, Alexi ran down the corridor as fast as his feet would carry him. Piotr had said the yellow stripe led to the surface. All Alexi had to do was follow it . . .

But even as he ran, he knew there was no way out of this dungeonlike corridor. Not for him. Not this time—or any other time.

Alexi screamed as the *thing* he had been expecting bounded toward him out of the darkness: a growler about the size and shape of a chimpanzee, but with exaggerated muscles and metallic spikes radiating out of its spine. The creature skidded to a stop, distended its fang-filled jaws, and began to cough.

Weeping with fear, Alexi leveled his AK-51 at it and squeezed the trigger until the weapon was hot in his hands. The bullets bounced harmlessly off the growler's hide.

Then it coughed a wad of acidic phlegm onto Alexi's chest.

Collapsed on the floor, dying as a puddle of spit ate into his chest, Alexi was filled with a single thought that kept repeating itself.

Not again. Oh Christ, not again . . .

12

Y ou," the *leitenant* said to Piotr.

"And you!"

The barrel of the *leitenant*'s Viper jabbed into Alexi's chest. Startled, he took a step back and looked around.

He saw shattered gray walls, a dull red Neo-Soviet star emblazoned over a gaping doorway, pavement choked with rubble, and a large crater in the ground to the left. Snow drifted down from an overcast sky. Alexi looked up and saw the glaring eye of the Maw, rising behind the clouds in the east, a dull clot of fire in a leaden gray sky.

Was he back in Vladivostok? No, the air was too quiet, too still, the landscape too flat and bleak. Somewhere else then.

The last thing Alexi remembered was the briefing. Had he suffered another blackout? Then it came to him. This must be Tomsk 13.

Thoughts tumbled wildly through his mind as he fought to find his mental balance. All the while, Soldatenkof kept screaming at him.

". . . hear me, Minsk? That was an order, you mindless

drudge! Or do you still think you're too good for this squad?"

Alexi's self-preservation instincts cut in. "Yes sir!" he shouted. "I mean, no sir!"

The rest of the squad laughed.

They stood next to a helicraft whose engines were still gently chuffing as the rotors wound down. Snow whirled across the ground as if invisible dervishes were dancing. The rear hatch leading to the helicraft's cargo bay stood open; Alexi heard a washboard-scraping noise and saw Vanya hauling spare tanks for his chem-sprayer down the drawbridge-style door. The other squad members stood around in greatcoats and gloves, holding their weapons and breathing steam into the cold air.

Alexi tried desperately to remember what Soldatenkof had just told him. His mind came up blank. He glanced down at the *leitenant*, and the visor of his helmet, which had been stuck open for days, slammed shut, causing another ripple of laughter. Cursing the army's useless equipment, Alexi forced open the visor—and suddenly had an idea.

"*Pazhalsta, Leitenant*," he said hesitantly. "Could you, ah . . . repeat that order?" He thumped a hand against the side of his helmet. "The speaker in my helmet is acting up again. It's all static. I couldn't hear you."

The vein throbbed in Soldatenkof's forehead. He had to unclench his jaw before he could speak. "I said that you and Piotr are to get your worthless carcasses down there." He pointed at a hole in the bottom of the crater. "You're to do a recon of the basement-level corridors. Look for intact rooms—for laboratories. Contact me by radio immediately if you find any cryotanks."

Alexi stared at the hole in the ground, and the darkness that it led to. A shudder of déjà vu washed through his body. The *leitenant* was asking him to step into a hell filled with growling demons. Alexi somehow knew that if he went down there, he'd never come out alive.

"But *Leitenant* . . ." he protested.

Soldatenkof was suddenly in his face. "Minsk," he hissed, "if you refuse a direct order, you'll be disciplined." His hand was on his Viper.

"I'm not refusing to go . . ." Alexi stammered, knowing full well that he was. He glanced at Piotr for support. The pockmarked soldier was pointedly ignoring him, tying the chin straps of his *ushanka*. "It's just . . ."

Inspiration struck. If Piotr was wearing a fur cap, that meant he didn't have a radio.

"It's my helmet," Alexi said. "Its radio isn't working properly, and Piotr isn't even wearing a helmet. We won't be able to radio you if we find anything."

Alexi held his breath. It was unheard of for Soldatenkof to back down once he'd issued an order, no matter how ludicrous it might be. He'd rather shoot his entire squad and carry out the order himself than allow a lowly private to contradict him. But there was a chance that the *leitenant* might think that locating the cryotanks was important enough to . . .

"Nevsky!" Soldatenkof shouted. His eyes never left Alexi's.

"*Da.*" Nevsky's answer was resigned. He stared accusingly at Alexi from under a brow that was mottled with radiation blisters that were as red as the star on his helmet. One hand scratched the bare spot where an eyebrow had been.

"You're on the recon with Piotr," Soldatenkof said. "Move out."

Grumbling, the two soldiers began clambering down into the crater. Alexi sighed his relief.

"As for you, Minsk," the *leitenant* continued with a malicious grin. "You'll stay up top here—where the residual radiation is strongest. Pair up with Irina."

Alexi gulped.

"Now let's find that growler!" the *leitenant* shouted. "Boris and Vanya, head north. Irina and Alexi, south. Move out, and prove yourselves worth your rad pills, for once. A bottle of vodka to the team that bags the pup!"

Chuckling to himself, the *leitenant* watched as the squad trudged away in twos, then climbed into the back of the waiting helicraft. Alexi saw him reach for something under the seat, then tip a bottle to his lips.

"Coward," Alexi muttered to himself—keeping his voice low enough that his helmet mike wouldn't pick it up. Then he trudged after Irina across the snow-dusted rubble of the research facility.

After they'd rounded one of the bombed-out buildings, Irina turned and put a hand on Alexi's chest. Her other hand covered the microphone in her helmet.

"I know you're lying," she hissed. "Your helmet was serviced while we were on leave." Her brown eyes stared up into Alexi's. She was a tiny, wiry woman, no taller than Soldatenkof. But her eyes were as fierce as a mink's.

She jerked her head to the left. "We can cover more ground if we split up. You continue south, and I'll scout to the east. Radio me if you see anything."

Alexi wasn't about to argue. Maybe if he was on his own, he could find a place to hunker down and take shelter from the radiation that was probably beaming from every above-ground surface. He glanced at the snow that swirled around his boots, and wondered if it carried a deadly dose of gamma radiation. The snowflakes were melting on his cheeks, trickling down onto his lips . . .

"Da," he told Irina. "I'll keep in radio contact."

He trudged away, AK-51 in one cold hand. If he just kept walking south, he would eventually reach the Trans-Siberian Railroad. He could hop a boxcar west to Moscow and lose himself in the huddled masses of that decaying city. . . .

Then he laughed at himself. Who was he kidding? If the ground was as hot as the *leitenant* had hinted, Alexi would die of radiation poisoning long before he made the capital.

In his imagination he could already feel the gamma radiation beaming in through his greatcoat, soaking into his skin, making it itch. Without the army's antirad pills, he was a dead man.

As he trudged along, Alexi's stomach grumbled. Patting his greatcoat, he found a food paste tube inside one of its pockets. He slung his AK-51 over his shoulder and unscrewed the lid. He squeezed a wad of brown goo from the bottle and touched the tip of his tongue to it.

He spat to get the taste out of his mouth. The stuff was moldy. Wiping flakes of snow from his glasses, Alexi read the label: sausage. He grunted. More like oatmeal and glue, with a little rancid fat thrown in to help it congeal. But that was nothing new. All through history, soldiers had been forced to make do with substandard rations.

Alexi screwed the lid back into place and put the tube back in his pocket. Then he started walking again, choosing his direction at random. He wasn't really hoping to find the growler. He was just hoping to stay warm. And alive.

Alexi's boot clunked against something on the ground. Looking down, he shuddered as he saw a helmet that was perforated with jagged holes. The ragged ends poked toward the inside of the helmet. Alexi pictured one of the growlers chewing on the head of a soldier, punching those holes through heavy-gauge steel. He wondered who had worn the helmet, and what her final thoughts had been as she died. Had the MVD soldier realized that the battle was already lost—that her own military was about to drop a neutron bomb on her? Was her ghost laughing now that the growlers were spreading out across the tundra of Siberia, infesting the wasted Earth like an opportunistic disease?

The radio in Alexi's helmet sputtered static. *Tovarish Alexi! . . . hear me?*

So his helmet radio hadn't been fixed, after all. The static glitch was still there. But the visor had been oiled—it flopped down again, and instantly fogged up with breath. Cursing the army technicians, Alexi wrenched it open again.

"Alexi to Irina," he answered. "Your transmission is breaking up, but I can—"

Irina's voice continued to crackle in Alexi's ear . . . *moving toward you.*

Alexi tensed, remembering their mission. The growler they had been sent to kill could be anywhere. He glanced around at the multitude of hiding places offered by the collapsed walls and piles of blasted rubble. He suddenly wished that Irina hadn't chosen to go off on her own.

"What was that, Irina? *Pazhalsta*—please—can you say again?"

A burst of automatic-weapons fire split the stillness of the snowy air. This time, Irina's voice was less calm. Her breathing sounded heavy, as if she were running.

. . . is approaching your . . .

Alexi saw it then: a low, dark shape sprinting toward him down the gap between two of the bombed buildings. Snapping the butt of his AK-51 to his shoulder, he pointed his weapon at the moving figure, trying to get it in his sights. It was small, the size of a dog—and fast.

Alexi fired a burst—and missed.

Impossible to hit as it swerved with superhuman grace, the creature zigzagged from cover to cover. Cold sweat sprang from the pores under Alexi's arms as he tried to train his weapon on the moving figure, knowing that this minute might be his last. The radio in his helmet blared a static-obscured warning.

Alexi had only a second to aim his assault rifle as the creature burst into the open and hurtled toward him. Then he saw what it was. Too late—a stream of bullets erupted from the AK-51 with a deafening roar.

The dog Alexi had just shot yelped with pain as a bullet struck it, and flopped over onto the pavement.

Adrenaline still pumping through him, his assault rifle

warm in his hands, Alexi ran to where the dog lay whining. It was a hound—a purebred, by the look of it. A once-beautiful animal, like the wolfhounds Alexi's grandfather used to keep. Alexi remembered them romping with him and his sister along the turquoise waters of Lake Baikal. He'd known it was impossible for a boy to outrun such sleek animals but had foolishly bet his sister that he could do it, even so. And when the dog won, racing to the finish line drawn in the sand in response to his sister's whistles, Alexi had reluctantly surrendered his favorite toy dinosaur to her. He didn't tell his sister that he'd planned on giving the toy to her anyway, on her birthday. It would have spoiled her fun at "winning" the bet.

Those were the heady days of childhood. Before the Change, before the war. These days, even a skinny dog like this one would be lucky to avoid being butchered for the cooking pot. Alexi wondered what it was doing in Tomsk 13.

Setting his weapon aside, he reached out to stroke the hound's grimy fur. As his fingers ran along its neck, Alexi felt the sharp points of shoulder bones under the dog's wasted flesh. The dog shuddered under his hand—a death throe?

Three years of fighting had numbed Alexi. But a lump welled in his throat as he compared the memories of his grandfather's dogs to the wasted animal that lay in front of him. Curse the war, for making Alexi take the life of such a beautiful creature as this dog. Humans could choose to fight and die, but animals were caught in the middle of it. Hungry, scared, abandoned, and without masters to tend to them, they were the true innocents.

The snow was falling more thickly now; in a short time it would provide a shroud for the dog.

A noise intruded on Alexi's thoughts: the drone of an aircraft, far overhead. Alexi craned his head back, but couldn't see anything beyond the cloud cover.

Suddenly the dog lurched to its feet. It was a tough one, this hound. The half-starved animal had fallen over more from shock than anything else. But Alexi's joy was short-lived. Staring at the bullet hole in the animal's flank, watching it seep blood, he knew the animal would eventually die without medical care. And with medicines so short that Nevsky was forced to buy them on the black market for the squad, there weren't any antibiotics to be given to a mere dog.

Whining, the hound licked Alexi's hand. He scratched it behind the ear, and reached into his pocket for the tube of sausage paste. The dog would be hungry enough to appreciate it. . . .

Booted feet thudded around the corner. Irina skidded to a stop in the snow. Alexi heard the rustle of her greatcoat as she raised her weapon.

He threw up a hand. "*Nyet!* Don't shoot!"

Irina held her fire.

"*Tovarish!*" she panted, lowering her weapon and looking at the hound. "I thought it was a growler."

The dog whined. Alexi squeezed some of the sausage out of the tube, and the whines became hungry slurps.

"What are you doing?" Irina asked.

Alexi could not see her eyes in the shadow of her helmet, but the censure in her voice was clear.

"Feeding a dog. Are you going to criticize me for wasting rations—*tovarish*?"

"It could be a rad-hound." Irina whispered, as if her words alone would set off a bomb.

Alexi jerked his hand back from the dog. The animal whined, looking up at the paste tube. Saliva dribbled from its mouth. Well trained, it waited for him to lower the food, even though it was starving.

A rad-hound? The thought had never occurred to Alexi. But it was possible, especially here in what remained of Tomsk 13. Neo-Soviet officials were often accompanied by personal guard dogs—mutants that were trained to protect their masters at any cost. These "rad-hounds" would hurl themselves at a target and then trigger an explosive charge that had been implanted inside their abdomens. Once triggered, it sent shards of steel flying in all directions, like a mobile land mine.

This dog looked normal enough. It certainly didn't have the grossly augmented musculature of a rad-hound. But that didn't mean its body cavities hadn't been tampered with. Especially since it was running loose in the ruins of a military research facility.

"Stand aside," Irina said. "It's best to shoot it."

The dog looked up at Alexi with equal parts of hunger and obedience. Its eyes never left the tube.

"*Nyet,*" Alexi decided. "Leave it be. If it was to have exploded, it would have done so when I approached. It's just a normal dog."

Alexi's voice was firmer than his resolve. But he was tired of this pointless war. He wanted to let something live, for once. Still, it paid to be cautious. He raised the tube of sausage paste above his head, then tossed it away, into the ruins. The dog limped after it and disappeared from sight.

Irina snorted, then turned on her heel. As she walked away, Alexi could hear her muttering into her helmet, no doubt complaining to the *leitenant* about Alexi's incompetence.

Something overhead caught Alexi's eye. He looked up—and saw a large white circle fluttering down from the sky. Suspended below it was a dull silver object that was difficult to see against the falling snow and gray sky. Just as Alexi realized what he was looking at, the parachutist aimed a weapon at him. The machine gun belched fire from above and bullets churned the snow at Alexi's feet into slush. One of the slugs smashed through the open visor of Alexi's helmet, perforating the clear plastic and slamming it shut.

The parachutist landed just behind him. The dull silver

bodysuit the soldier wore was unmarked, save for a patch on each shoulder and rank designators on the sleeves. But Alexi didn't need to see the combination of stars, maple leaves, and eagles that made up the Union shoulder patch to know that this was the enemy.

Neither did Irina. In one smooth motion she wheeled around to face the parachutist. In that same instant, the Union soldier whipped his compact machine gun to his shoulder. Alexi realized that he was standing between the two—in a space that was about to be filled with flying lead.

He dived for cover.

The visor of Alexi's helmet was crazed—a mass of cracks crisscrossed the clear plastic. He couldn't see the ground as he hit. But as the two weapons roared behind him, he realized his mistake. As he skidded on his belly in the snow, a ragged chunk of glass from a blown-out window frame caught his right arm. It tore open his greatcoat and gouged into his flesh just above the elbow. In seconds, the sleeve of his greatcoat was soaked. Alexi's arm throbbed as hot blood pumped out of it. He groaned, realizing what had happened. An artery . . .

Dazed, he sat up, clutching at the pain with his left hand. Through the bullet hole in his crack-obscured visor, he could see that both Irina and the Union parachutist were down, their bodies sprawled heaps in the snow. Red puddled around them, staining the snow.

Farther away, Alexi could hear gunfights erupting. Somewhere to the north, the helicraft's engines were revving. He looked up and saw another Union parachutist. Dizzy now from loss of blood, he hallucinated that the parachute was a gigantic white snowflake, drifting down from the sky to cover him gently like a soft, cold blanket. . . .

Alexi shook his head violently. Something rattled next to his ear. At the same time that his thoughts cleared, so did the radio in his helmet.

Got him! Boris shouted jubilantly. Then, *Uh-oh. Here comes another.*

Fall back to the helicraft! Soldatenkof screamed. *You've got two minutes, and then we're taking off. Move it!*

Alexi didn't feel like moving anywhere. He closed his eyes and clenched his teeth, fighting back the pain. If he didn't get to the helicraft, Soldatenkof would leave him. . . .

But what about Piotr and Nevsky? They're too far below to make it.

That was Vanya's voice. Panting, as if he was running. Alexi waited for Boris to lay odds on whether the chem grunt would make it to the helicraft, but the bearish man's voice was missing from the radio traffic. Then he heard Vanya scream into his radio. The panting stopped.

A rocket exploded, throwing a flash of red into the sky from behind a building to the north. That had to be the helicraft's ordnance.

Alexi tried to get his feet under him. The slight motion sent more blood pumping through his fingers. No good. He'd bleed to death before he took a single step.

"*Pazhalsta,*" he groaned into his mike. "It's Alexi. I'm wounded. Won't someone help—"

Soldatenkof's terrified voice shrieked out of Alexi's helmet speaker. *What in the name of the Savior is that?* he screamed. *Get this helicraft into the air before that thing—*

The rest was lost in what sounded like a lion's roar—so loud that it rattled the broken window glass beside Alexi in its frame. Fighting to remain conscious, Alexi imagined that the saber-toothed tiger from the museum had come to life. Except that a lion would have to be as big as a mountain to make that noise, and would have to have vocal cords made of strung steel.

Someone was still shooting. And the helicraft rotors were whirring. But the radio in Alexi's helmet gave out only a faint static. The voices of the squad had fallen silent, replaced by a ghostly hiss.

A cold feeling in Alexi's gut told him that the rest of his squad—to the last soldier—was dead. He was the only one to have survived.

Alexi tried once more to stand, then collapsed again. Flakes of snow puffed into the air as he landed on his back on the cold cement. He let go of his throbbing arm and pulled off his helmet with his uninjured hand. Snowflakes drifted down onto his bare cheeks as he pulled out the cross he wore around his neck and began to pray. He was getting colder, starting to hallucinate.

Yes, there. You see? That blue-skinned person bending over him couldn't possibly be real. It had to be the ghost of the alien that Alexi had killed. Or an angel. But it seemed so solid, so detailed. Alexi was amazed at the amount of detail his imagination could create—right down to the snowflakes that were landing and melting on the alien's bald head.

The ghost's blue-black eyes became flecked with red as it chanted in a garbled tongue—the language of the angels, Alexi wondered? Maybe even his own personal guardian angel?

Alexi watched, entranced, as it raised its hands above its head, spindly blue fingers open to the sky. Something twined around them—a swirling mist that sparkled with points of energy. Then the creature lowered its hands to Alexi's wounded arm, and the sparkling mist flowed into the rent in his greatcoat sleeve like a snake down a hole.

Alexi's artery stopped pounding. The pain was gone. Suddenly filled with a surge of energy, he sat bolt upright.

"Who—"

13

"—are you?" Alexi asked. "A god?"

A fragment of historical trivia bobbed to the surface of Alexi's mind. In ancient India, deities were depicted as having blue skin. The creature whose midnight blue eyes bored into his own had flesh that was colored just like the gods in those ancient paintings. Except that it didn't have an elephant head or dozens of arms. And although it was sitting cross-legged, it wasn't perched on a lotus blossom.

No—the backdrop was even stranger.

It was daytime, and they were in the *taiga*, one of the expanses of forest that covered northern Siberia. The snow-covered landscape was thick with pine, fir, and spruce trees. Rising above them to the height of a twenty-story building was a gigantic pyramid made of gray stone with a sheen that was almost metallic. Utterly smooth and featureless, the tetrahedron balanced impossibly on its tip, its broad base high overhead.

Alexi and the blue-skinned alien sat in the inverted pyramid's shadow, on bare ground that had been sheltered from the falling snow. The tetrahedron loomed overhead. Alexi looked up at it nervously, feeling like a bug watching the heel of a boot about to descend. He shivered. He was afraid to move—afraid almost to breathe. Would a mere sigh send the thing toppling over on its side?

"What," he whispered, "is . . . *that*? And where are we? Did you transport me here?"

Absentmindedly, Alexi rubbed his arm. He expected to feel a torn greatcoat wet with blood. But instead his palm slid against the stiff fabric of a flak jacket. Then he remembered: He was wearing Soldatenkof's armored jacket. He'd been wearing it in the helicraft, when the alien had been about to slice open his . . . throat?

Alexi's hand rose to his neck. It was very much intact, his Adam's apple bobbing up and down as he swallowed his fear. He glanced at the weapon that was lying beside the alien, just within reach of its double-jointed arms. The wickedly sharp blade on the metal staff buzzed softly. The last thing Alexi remembered was the alien swinging it at him. . . .

No. That wasn't right. It didn't happen that way.

He touched his arm again. Ah. That was it. The alien had healed him, using some sort of godlike power to mend the wound in his . . .

His hand fell to his side. No. That wasn't the way it had gone, either. Now that Alexi tried consciously to think about it, he couldn't even remember what part of his body had been wounded. Or how it had happened. Or if he had been wounded at all. . . .

The alien's eyes flickered up briefly. Then they locked on Alexi's face. It peered intently at him.

"It's happening again, isn't it?" the alien asked.

Alexi nodded, even though he wasn't sure exactly what the question meant. Something was happening—something that was causing his memory to fragment into shards that were melting away like icicles in spring.

"It's fighting you," the alien said solemnly. "Good. Your idea will work, then. We really will be able to do it."

"What . . . ?"

"I can't stop," the alien said. "Not now. Just trust, Alexi. Trust and do. And hold on to . . . now."

Hold on to *what* now? Alexi wondered. He glanced down; his hands were empty. He wasn't holding anything.

Alexi didn't think the alien had misspoken. Its Russian was flawless. Its voice was couched at a moderate pitch, neither male nor female. Its vocal cords produced a slight crackling sound, as if its words were coming through a faulty electronic speaker. Yet when it began chanting in its own language, the staticky sound was gone.

Alexi thought of the Chinese shopkeeper he'd met in Moscow, and how the woman had spoken Russian with an English accent she'd picked up from the Brit who'd taught her the language. It was almost as if the crackle was an accent that the alien had picked up, after taking Russian lessons that had been broadcast over a radio.

Alexi studied the blue-skinned creature. Despite the cold air that was fogging its . . . it was completely naked. Sitting cross-legged as it was, Alexi could see that it had no genitalia. Unlike the other blue-skinned creature—the one Alexi had shot in Vladivostok—its chest was smooth, without nipples. And its skin was devoid of tattoos. The palms of its hands and soles of its feet were a paler blue, tinged with red—giving them a lavender shade. The same color as its tongue.

The alien's eyes were closed. As it chanted, Alexi took a better look around at the landscape, trying not to think about the tetrahedron balanced forebodingly overhead. There were no landmarks; the terrain here was made up of rolling, tree-covered hills. Closer at hand, the only thing that wasn't part of the natural landscape—besides the inverted pyramid—was a small wooden cross made of two pine branches that had been lashed together. Driven into the ground, the cross marked a mound of mud and snow: a grave.

The sight of it made Alexi overwhelmingly sad. He had

no idea whose grave it was; he couldn't put a name to the person who lay there. He knew only that the grave held someone who could have been his friend, had she lived. He tore his eyes away.

She?

Not . . . ?

The name was gone. Another one hovered at the edge of his consciousness: Raheek.

He stared at the alien's bald head. The name fit.

Alexi shifted. The ground was cold beneath him, even through the seat of the padded trousers he wore. And resting under his right knee was an uncomfortable lump. He moved his leg, and saw a pistol lying on the ground. A Pug—a Union army weapon. What was it doing there?

Alexi picked it up and turned it over in his hands. He cracked it open and saw that it was loaded.

Raheek's eyes flickered open. "Not yet," it said. "Wait."

Alexi snapped the weapon shut. What did the alien expect him to do with it? Was he supposed to shoot the alien? Shoot himself?

A sense of déjà vu settled upon him. As if his arm were moving of its own accord, his hand lifted the pistol. He touched the cold steel barrel to his forehead and blew air through pursed lips, softly mimicking the sound of a shot being fired. A bullet would be one way to sort out all this confusion. It even felt like the right thing to do. . . .

He laughed nervously. The last thought had been a joke—the whim of a crazy man. But it left him feeling slightly queasy, as if he had just drunk sour milk.

Alexi sniffed. What was that smell? Age . . . rot . . . decay . . .

He glanced over at the grave, wondering if a faint breeze was carrying the smell of the corpse it held. But she'd only just died a few . . .

The thought was gone.

The alien was still chanting, eyes closed.

"Raheek?" Alexi whispered.

The alien's eyes opened—and remained open, this time. Flecks of red were swirling within the blue-black irises. Raheek's skin was darkening to a deeper shade of blue, and now the darkness was bleeding off the flesh like black steam. Alexi thought he could see faces in that inky aura—faces of people long dead. His grandfather, his father, his mother . . . And others. Older, more ancient. More terrifying.

One of Raheek's hands fastened around Alexi's arm, just above the hand that held the Union pistol. The spidery fingers pressed into the inside of Alexi's wrist, making him aware of the pulse that throbbed there. Then Raheek forced the hand up until the barrel of the pistol was pointed at Alexi's head. Raheek's other hand was just in front of Alexi's mouth, lavender palm up.

Again, the sense of déjà vu. Of insurmountable fate. Of death whispering with gunpowder breath in his ear.

"Do it now!" the alien hissed. "Now—while I can still catch your soul!"

The torpor that had settled over Alexi as he'd struggled to sort out one crazy bit of unreality from the next suddenly broke. He struggled to his feet, yanking the alien who still gripped his wrist up with him. Flame roared from the pistol barrel as Alexi's finger tightened reflexively on its trigger. The bullet struck the pyramid overhead, ricocheting unscathed off its smooth surface.

The flattened slug of lead caught the alien in the chest. Raheek's grip on Alexi's wrist slackened, and the alien's mouth gaped open as it stared down at the purple blood that welled from the jagged wound.

"*Nyet* . . ." it whispered as it sagged.

Without understanding why, Alexi dropped the pistol and caught the dying alien in his arms. He had the horrified sense that he had just done something terribly wrong.

But he didn't know what. Or why.

The alien's blood pumped out of its chest, soaking the front of Alexi's flak jacket.

"Raheek," Alexi said softly. "I'm sorry."

It was a trick of the light—no more. But Alexi suddenly had a picture, in his mind's eye, of the tetrahedron teetering, tilting, racing down like a mountain falling triumphantly on his head. . . .

14

. . . is approaching your . . .

Irina panted out the words. She was breathing quickly, as if running. Cursing his helmet for the millionth time that day, cursing Soldatenkof sitting warm and cozy in the helicraft with his bottle of vodka, cursing the whole bloody war, Alexi glanced nervously around him for the growler they'd been sent to Tomsk 13 to kill.

There! A low, dark shape sprinting toward him down the gap between two of the bombed buildings. Alexi snapped the metal butt of the AK-51 to his shoulder, sighted down the barrel and . . .

Something—some sixth sense—made him lower the weapon at the last moment. It was almost as if he knew what he would see next. Not a growler, but a dog: a wolfhound, a purebred like the animals Alexi's grandfather had kept. The dog was scrawny, with matted fur. A ghost of its former, beautiful self. Running in terror from Irina, who had just tried to shoot it.

Alexi plunged a hand into the pocket of his greatcoat. He pulled out the tube of puréed sausage he'd been unable to eat earlier. Pursing snow-chapped lips, he whistled. The dog skidded to a stop, froze, and looked at Alexi with hungry eyes. Then its long nose twitched.

Alexi's feeling of déjà vu was still strong. He could feel it pressing down on him from above. He needed to get away from it. To hide.

"Come!" he shouted to the dog. "Treat!"

Alexi ran for the shelter of one of the bombed-out buildings, scrambling in through a hole where an entire window frame had been blown out. The wolfhound, following the scent of the sausage, leapt gracefully in through the hole behind him.

Squatting in the shadow of the building, Alexi stroked the dog's head, squeezing sausage out of the tube for it. The animal lapped it up, its tongue making loud smacking noises. Alexi prayed that it wouldn't bark.

Why the sudden urge to stay quiet?

Alexi looked around the interior of the building he'd climbed into. It was filled with dark shadows, its floor dusted with snow that had drifted in through the gaping holes in its thick cement walls. Was that a bare footprint in the snow, or just Alexi's imagination turning one of the dog's footprints into something larger? Was that a growler crouching in the corner?

One of the shadows shifted.

Alexi dropped the sausage tube and lifted his AK-51. Nothing. Just a shadow. It had only been a trick of his imagination. If there had been a growler there, crouching in the darkness, it would have torn out his throat by now.

Or his chest . . .

For a second, Alexi couldn't breathe. He fought to suck in air, as if battling a collapsed lung. Then his breathing returned to normal. Gasping in a shuddering lungful of air, he shook his head. A panic attack? Now—after so long in battle? It didn't make any sense.

Something had triggered it—some soldier's sixth sense.

Some threat. But the threat wasn't within the building. It was outside . . .

Irina's voice crackled over his helmet speaker: . . . *are you, Alexi? I can't . . .*

Alexi peeked out through the hole where the window had been. Irina stood just outside where he was hiding, her weapon at the ready. Her dark eyes swept the area between the buildings. Her lips were moving. Her voice was a broken whisper in Alexi's helmet speaker.

. . . *you, Alexi?*

The tension was unbearable. *Something* was about to happen. Alexi just didn't know what. Snow drifted down outside, settling on Irina's shoulders and helmet, flattening like tiny parachutes hitting the ground . . .

"Irina!" Alexi shouted. "Above you!"

The microphone in his helmet must have been working. Irina's head snapped back. Her mouth dropped open, even as she fought to bring up her weapon. The assault rifle in her hands spat fire, and empty cartridges fountained out the side in a tinkling counterpart to its roar. In that same instant, the chutter of a machine gun came from above. Bullets churned the snow at her feet to slush.

Then the slush became red. Irina was hit. Blood leaked out the bottom of her greatcoat as she slowly twisted to the ground. A bullet struck the visor of her helmet, puncturing a hole in it with a loud crack.

Alexi ducked. The wolfhound beside him lowered its belly to the ground and growled.

Silence. Then a soft thud and a whispery rustling. Summoning up his courage, sweaty hands gripping his assault rifle, Alexi dared a look through the hole in the wall. A Union soldier lay on the ground, his parachute still settling to the ground. A light machine gun lay smoking beside him, melting the snow. He was dressed in a dull silver bodysuit that had been riddled by bullets. Blood leaked from the holes, sliding off the water-resistant suit and dripping into the snow. As Alexi watched, the parachute settled over the body, gentle as a shroud.

From several directions at once, Alexi could hear gunfights erupting. There must have been more than one parachutist. But what was a squad of Union paratroopers doing there?

No time to wonder. *Leitenant* Soldatenkof was screaming. The radio transmission was broken with static, as usual, but Alexi could make out something about the helicraft. He could hear its engines revving and its rotors speeding up.

"Come on, dog," he shouted to the wolfhound. Then he scrambled out of his hiding place.

They ran between the buildings, man and hound racing each other toward the sound of the helicraft. The dog seemed to have adopted Alexi; it heeled beside him beautifully. Either that, or it was too exhausted and weak to run any faster.

Gunfire raged up ahead. And one by one, the familiar voices coming over the speaker in Alexi's helmet were falling silent. But Alexi was nearly at the helicraft, now. Just one more corner to round . . .

Suddenly all Alexi could hear was Soldatenkof's voice: *Get this helicraft into the air before—*

A sound overwhelmed all of the other noises. A strange roaring noise that sounded to Alexi like metal being torn apart.

The wolfhound suddenly was no longer running beside him. Alexi's mind only had a second to register the fact that it had skidded to a stop and was growling with hackles raised as he rounded the corner.

Alexi should have been looking ahead. Glancing back to figure out where the dog had gone had been a big mistake. He slammed headlong into the back of a figure in a silver bodysuit who was firing a machine gun in the direction of the helicraft. Tangled together with the Union soldier, Alexi fell to the ground.

He had only a moment's glance at the face of his enemy, but that one brief look sent a chill down his spine. How could it be? He *recognized* that face. Her features were burned into his memory: wide Korean face, snub nose . . .

But without the radiation blisters.

"Impossible," Alexi croaked. "I killed you in Vladivostok."

He scrambled away from her as if he were a crab and she a pot of boiling water. Amazingly, the woman did not shoot him. Then Alexi saw why: her weapon—a Pitbull assault rifle, by the look of it—had jammed. She was squeezing the trigger, but the rifle wasn't firing.

Yet.

Then Alexi saw what she'd been shooting at. Noticing the horrified expression on his face, she glanced over her shoulder.

The helicraft rotors whirred at top speed; the machine was seconds away from taking off. The pilot had turned around in his seat and seemed to be shouting at someone. Machinery whined, and Alexi could hear a wet crunching noise. In the rear of the helicraft, *Leitenant* Soldatenkof struggled to loosen the body of a Union soldier that was stuck in the cargo bay's wide door, preventing it from closing. Soldatenkof kicked ineffectually at the corpse, a look of frustration on his face. From the unsteady way he stood, Alexi assumed the officer was drunk. Too drunk to notice that the body wasn't the only thing keeping the cargo bay from closing.

As Alexi saw what the real problem was, his blood froze in his veins. Standing at the rear of the helicraft was a growler, its head nearly level with the rotor blades that flattened white hair against its muscled hide. One clawed hand had a death grip on the door, holding it open.

Alexi laughed—the cackle of a man driven to the brink of madness. "You've won your bet, Boris," he croaked. "It *is* as big as a house." Then he pulled the trigger of his AK-51.

The creature ignored the bullets that chewed their way into the helicraft beside it as Alexi fought to correct his aim. The thing was immense—three times the size of a gorilla, with tusks nearly a meter long that curved up over its shoulders. A single horn protruded from its jutting brow. The white hair on its body ringed its wrists and ankles, and hung in a tangled mat at its crotch. Muscles bulged as it strained against the motors that were trying to force the cargo-bay door shut. Slowly, the door was levered open.

In the same instant that Soldatenkof saw what he was up against, a second growler, equally as large as the first, bounded out from behind a building. This one had skin that was cracked and weathered, like the smoky glaze of flame-fired pottery. As it panted in the cold air, white fog whistled through its mouth like steam erupting from a broken pipeline. Alexi directed his fire at it, but the bullets literally bounced off its glossy black hide.

The growlers worked together like a team of soldiers, as though silently communicating with one another. As the white-tusked growler forced the door to the ground, the one with the weathered skin took a deep breath. Its chest expanded to impossible proportions, like the swelling chest of a pigeon about to call. Except that the results were anything but a pleasant coo. With a hissing roar that made a fragment of broken window glass next to Alexi rattle in its frame, the growler let loose. A searing mass of scalding steam shot out of its mouth, filling the interior of the helicraft.

Alexi could feel the wet heat from where he stood. Inside the cargo bay, *Leitenant* Soldatenkof gave a strangled scream. The pilot of the helicraft lasted slightly longer; he managed to get the cockpit door open and tumble to the ground as the steam seared his lungs.

Alexi's AK-51 fell silent. Smoke curled from its barrel. He didn't know whether it was out of bullets or had jammed, like the Union soldier's weapon—but he didn't want to take the time to find out.

Realizing the *leitenant* was dead, Alexi shivered. A dead officer meant a dead squad. But he had more immediate things to worry about. The growlers were both looking in his direction.

Alexi exchanged a startled glance with the Union soldier. A possibility entered his mind. Perhaps he was dead, like her. A ghost.

But then why did his stomach feel so loose? Ghosts didn't need to relieve themselves. And why did he see his own terror mirrored back at him in the Union soldier's eyes, if she was a ghost, too?

In the same instant, they both turned and ran. Behind them, the growlers let the hatch on the rear of the cargo bay spring shut against the corpse, and bounded after the humans.

Alexi and the Union soldier had been enemies. Now that neither had a functional weapon to fight the growlers with, they were rivals in a footrace. Whoever lost would be eaten.

Or scalded . . .

Or . . .

Cold stabbed into Alexi's lungs as he ran. He no longer cared about the deadly gamma radiation the air held. The Union soldier was gaining on him.

Alexi reached out, grabbing for her as she passed him. His fingers locked on her arm. He pulled, felt her stagger . . .

And then they were both down on the ground in a tangle, throwing punches and kicks at one another. Fighting to get away from his adversary, Alexi looked up—into the gaping, steam-filled mouth of the glossy black growler. The creature was at least three meters away, but it loomed as large as a monument, as unnerving as a statue of Stalin. Behind it, the white-tusked growler stood back to watch the fun. The hot steam gusting from the first growler's mouth suddenly sucked back into its lungs as it drew in a breath that inflated its chest like a balloon. . . .

Alexi closed his eyes. He knew he was dead.

Funny—he thought the growler that killed him would be smaller. . . .

The Union soldier screamed. In the same moment, Alexi felt an unmistakable presence in the air just ahead of him. Not a growler, not a human, something . . . other.

He opened his eyes.

A wall of shifting energy had sprung up in the air between the two human soldiers and the growlers. Within it swirled shifting, ghostly forms that looked vaguely human, but with starvation-thin bodies and strangely double-jointed arms like the alien that Alexi had shot. They wove back and forth, mouths open in a silent scream, forming a barrier between the humans and the growlers.

Alexi scrambled backward on hands and knees, and saw that the Union soldier was doing the same thing. He found the apparitions even more terrifying, somehow, than the growlers. So, apparently, did she.

On the other side of the ghostly wall, the growlers bristled like dogs with their hackles raised. The one with the curved white tusks took a step backward, then broke and ran. The other one glanced over its shoulder, then fled after the first.

The unnerving, ghostly barrier winked out of existence. In its place, a patch of blackness formed. A skinny blue hand with pencil-thin fingers poked out of the darkness, pointing toward the helicraft.

"Quickly," it said in Russian. "Get in your craft. The growlers are everywhere—an entire adult pack has returned for the young. We must leave."

The darkness shrank down to a point and disappeared. A second later, a blue-skinned hand was beckoning from inside the helicraft.

Alexi stared at the helicraft, dumbfounded. Had the blue-skinned creature really teleported before Alexi's astonished eyes? He glanced at the Union soldier to see if she was going to follow the creature—wondering if she even understood Russian. It seemed that she did. She sprinted for the helicraft and heaved herself in through the open cockpit door.

It also seemed that she knew how to fly a helicraft. The engines revved at a higher pitch. The helicraft lifted, settled, began to lift again . . .

A roaring noise filled the street behind Alexi. Glancing over his shoulder, he saw that the white-tusked growler was circling around the building in an attempt to attack from the rear. After several heart-stopping seconds, Alexi finally got his feet to move. Sprinting for the helicraft, he hauled himself up onto the rear of it just as it left the ground. He wormed his way in through the half-open cargo-bay door, and sprawled on the floor inside. Through the opening, he saw the ground fall away below them as the helicraft rose.

The white-tusked growler leapt in fury, trying to reach the helicraft as it soared away. The helicraft gave a lurch as the Union officer sent it skidding sideways to avoid the growler's grasping hands, and Alexi was tumbled in a heap against one wall of the cargo bay. Soldatenkof's scalded body flopped over on top of him.

A stray thought entered Alexi's mind: It was a good thing that it was just a body landing on him, and not a heavy canister.

Filled with . . .

The thought was gone.

15

Forest. Knee-deep snow. Footprints: a trail in the snow ahead. Flakes drifting down from an overcast sky. AK-51 slung over his shoulder. Stomach cramping with hunger.

Alexi sighed. He'd been walking for an hour, endlessly putting one foot in front of the other . . .

He jerked to a halt. Oh Christ. It had happened again. Another blackout. He had absolutely no idea where he was—or what time it was. He glanced at his watch. One question answered. It was seven in the morning. But of what day? There was no way to know.

Someone nudged him from behind. Alexi turned and saw the Union soldier who had piloted the helicraft away from Tomsk 13. She wore Neo-Sov combats over her silvery gray bodysuit and a Russian *ushanka* cap. Alexi said the first thing that came into his mind. It wasn't logical—but then, neither was anything else.

"You're not shivering? Why not?"

"You stopped to ask me that?" the woman said in irritation. "Are you stupid—or just deaf? I already told you; it's a therm suit."

"But why the combats?" Alexi asked. "And the *ushanka*?"

"Protective camouflage. I *am* behind enemy lines." Her voice grew more brusque. "And I'm behind you—with a Pug pistol in my pocket. And that's where I'm staying. Don't get any ideas about asking me to take the lead. Now move out, Corporal."

Alexi cocked his head. "You're an officer, aren't you?"

The woman's eyes narrowed. Alexi could see her weighing the merits of giving information to the enemy. "What makes you say that?"

He shrugged. "Just a guess." He wondered whether she'd shoot him if he refused to go on. He decided not to find out.

He turned around and continued trudging in the direction he'd been going before. He stared at the trail in the snow, trying to make sense of it. The person who had made it must have had tremendously long legs, judging by the spacing of the steps. He had gone this way once, then returned, then gone back again. And he'd had bare feet . . .

A piece of the jigsaw snapped into place in Alexi's mind: bare feet equals Raheek.

And Raheek had killed Alexi in the helicraft . . .

The Adam's apple bobbed up and down in Alexi's throat as he swallowed. No—Raheek hadn't stayed with them in the helicraft. The alien had gone on alone, last night. It had wanted to locate the place where the meteorite fell. . . .

But why? The answer was missing from Alexi's mind, like a piece gone from the puzzle. A piece right at the center of it, without which the greater picture could not be resolved.

Alexi wondered if he had just imagined the detail about Raheek looking for the meteorite, after seeing a falling star during the fighting in Vladivostok. Things had been crazy then; perhaps Alexi's mind had fixated upon that anomaly and woven it into a false memory. . . .

There was one way to find out. The Union officer behind Alexi would know where they were headed and what was going on. But how to ask her, without causing her to suspect that he was up to something? The armored jacket Alexi had taken from Soldatenkof would protect his back from a bullet, but his legs were unprotected, and his head was an even more inviting target.

Alexi sought for a place to start and found a name. Although he couldn't remember having asked the woman's name, it was lodged there. Just as Raheek's was.

"Juliana?" he asked. "What do you suppose we'll find when we get . . . ah . . . to where we're going?"

"A big hole in the ground," she answered. "And it's Captain Ko, Corporal. Not Juliana."

"I'm sorry?" Alexi asked. "What did you say about a hole in the ground?"

"An impact crater," she said tersely. "That's what we'll find."

Ah. So they were headed toward the place where the meteorite fell, after all.

"What does Raheek expect us to do once we get to it?" he said.

"Figure out a way to disarm it, I suppose."

Disarm it? After a moment's puzzled thought, Alexi hazarded a guess: "The 'meteorite' is really an unexploded bomb?"

"That's what Raheek says it is." Her voice sounded deliberately noncommittal. "If the alien is right, we'll be standing at ground zero when it goes off. Are you ready to die for your planet, Alexi?"

"To die for my country, you mean," Alexi corrected her. Funny, that her Russian had slipped up. Other than the one mistake, it was flawless.

"Neither one of our countries will exist anymore, if Raheek is telling the truth—if the meteorite really is capable of destroying the Earth."

Alexi shook his head. What in heaven's name was she talking about? Their conversation was starting to sound like the plot of one of the century-old children's science-fiction stories from the library of the school where Alexi used to teach. Alexi mulled over what to say next. But no matter how he worded the question in his mind, asking how, exactly, a meteorite would be capable of blowing up the Earth sounded silly.

Just as silly as following bare footprints through the snow in a Siberian forest.

Behind him, he heard the Union officer's sharp intake of breath. He looked up from the trail they were following— and saw an impossible sight. A short distance ahead, a three-sided pyramid with gray walls rose above the tree line to the height of a skyscraper. Except that it wasn't behaving as a pyramid should. Instead of resting firmly on its base, it was balancing on its point. Or so Alexi assumed, since the point of the tetrahedron was hidden by the forest.

He turned to see if Juliana's mouth was also hanging open, and found her consulting what looked like an over-size wristwatch. A series of maps flashed across it, gradually changing scale to show Asia, the Neo-Soviet Union, Siberia . . . At the same time, green letters followed by numbers flashed on an otherwise blank screen. The alphabet was English, but Alexi had used English-language maps of Europe and the Union enough times in his history classes to know what the letters spelled: LONGITUDE 100 DEGREES EAST, LATITUDE 67 DEGREES NORTH.

Alexi nodded to himself, envious of the Union's sophisticated equipment. The "wristwatch" was a Global Positioning System unit. Despite the fact that many of the satellites which supported that system had fallen from the sky or gone missing during the Change, there were obviously enough still left in orbit for the Union soldiers to track their position via GPS.

Alexi looked back over his shoulder at the tetrahedron. Had it really fallen from the sky? Why hadn't it burned up or spalled apart on impact? And why in hell was it balancing on one point? Had it driven itself into the dirt?

A thought occurred to Alexi: The trees should have been lying down. If the tetrahedron really had been the meteorite he'd seen streaking across the Vladivostok sky, it should have flattened the forest for kilometers around. Just as the Tunguska meteorite did, nearly two centuries ago. . . .

Alexi stared at the coordinates on the GPS. Then he blinked. No. It couldn't be.

It was. A flash of one of his history lessons came back to him. The pyramid was poised at the exact spot where a meteorite had fallen to earth in 1908. The meteorite had come streaking down in a giant fireball as bright as the now-vanished sun. It flattened trees in a thirty-kilometer radius and knocked down a trapper who was standing on the porch of his cabin eighty kilometers away.

When the scientists of the day struggled to the desolate spot in Siberia where the meteorite had struck, they found hundreds of dead reindeer—and a big hole in the ground. The meteorite—estimated to be more than sixty meters across when it first entered Earth's atmosphere—had spalled into a multitude of small fragments that finally exploded, just before striking the earth. That was why no pieces of it were ever found.

A second meteorite hitting exactly the same spot on Earth nearly two centuries later was statistically impossible. Boris would have offered odds of a billion to one against its happening—and lost his shirt.

Or would he? Alexi toyed with an equally impossible thought. What if there had been just one meteorite? If it had somehow existed in two places in time at once? Perhaps it had thrown the explosive energy of its landing back in time. That could explain why the tetrahedron was intact. . . .

Once again, a feeling of déjà vu settled over Alexi. He'd had these same thoughts earlier—had drawn the same conclusion once before . . .

Alexi shook his head to clear it. He couldn't believe the crazy paths his mind was wandering along. It was his own place in time he should be worried about—not the meteorite's. The blackouts were really starting to get to him. He had no idea where he'd wake up next, what impossible thing would confront him when he did . . .

Gunfire erupted from somewhere up ahead. Close: no more than a few meters away.

Alexi whipped the AK-51 off his shoulder. The Union officer pulled a pistol from the pocket of her combats. They pointed their weapons in the direction from which the gunfire had come—and at the same time kept a wary eye on each other. They were still enemies, after all. . . .

Out of the corner of his eye, Alexi saw a patch of inky darkness appear behind him. Raheek stepped out of it. After all of the crazy events of the day, Alexi never even thought to ask himself how that was possible. Magic, he told himself. The world had gone crazy, and magic had become possible.

The alien was still naked, despite the cold. But not shivering. A crease of bright purple marked its hip. Light glowed under the alien's overlong fingers as it held them to the wound in its side. Even as Alexi watched, the wound knitted together. Bright flecks of red danced in the alien's midnight blue eyes.

"There is an automated weapon, twenty-eight paces ahead," it told them. "A weapon of Earth, a short distance from the crystal. Go no farther, or you will cause it to fire."

Crystal? That was the first time he'd heard anyone use that word to describe the meteorite. But it fit: that perfect tetrahedral shape, those smooth glossy sides . . .

Alexi slung his assault rifle back over his shoulder. No soldiers to fight, then. No one but a crazy man would be soldiering here, in the freezing cold of a Siberian *taiga*. Of all the useless places in the world that weren't worth defending, this one topped the list.

Unless, of course, the crystal was valuable. Alexi looked over Raheek's bald blue head. The balancing tetrahedron didn't look like a diamond or any other precious stone—it had almost a metallic sheen. But it might be worth a few rubles, just the same.

No, wait. It would be worth something because it was a bomb—one capable of destroying the Earth, if the Union officer was to be believed.

"Can we circle around the weapon?" she asked Raheek.

The alien waved its fingers—a gesture Alexi assumed to be equivalent to a head shake.

"*Nyet*," it said. "A ring of these weapons completely surrounds the crystal. They are buried in the ground. They were not here last night."

"They're dug in?" the Union officer asked. She looked thoughtful. "Does the weapon have jets around its circumference, and a rotating top that telescopes up and down with a gun barrel protruding from it?"

The alien touched a forefinger to its chin. "*Da*."

"It's a combat drone then. One of ours." She glanced thoughtfully up at the sky, her head cocked as if she were listening. "If our side has ringed the landing site with drones, our airborne troops can't be far behind."

Alexi looked up at the tetrahedron. "Landing site?" he asked. "Do you really think that thing is a spacecraft?"

"I don't know what it is," she said. "It could be a bomb, like Raheek says, or a spaceship, or . . . anything. But whatever it is, it's going to be in Union hands, soon enough."

She looked meaningfully at the alien, who stood silently watching the two humans. "Raheek, as a Union officer, I can personally guarantee your safety—there's no need for you to fear our soldiers. You'll be treated by the Union with the same respect as an ambassador."

Then she turned to Alexi—and he saw that the Pug pistol was in her hand, its barrel leveled at his chest. "But you, Corporal Minsk, are a prisoner. Drop your weapon. Now!"

Alexi suddenly wished he hadn't been so quick to assume they were out of danger, just because they had not yet entered the range of the automated combat drone. The Union officer was still very much his enemy. Slowly, he raised his hands and let the strap of his AK-51 slide from his shoulder. The weapon fell into the snow.

The blue-skinned alien began to lay its blade-tipped staff down in the snow, meekly following Alexi's lead. But as soon as the Union officer glanced back at Alexi, it whipped the weapon up in a flashing arc. The blade smashed into the Pug, slicing the barrel in two and tearing the weapon from her hand.

The Union officer stared at him in shock. She backed up a step and raised open hands to plead with the alien. All the while she kept one eye on Alexi, who lifted his AK-51 out of the snow. "There's no need for hostilities," she told Raheek. "Our side isn't at war with your people. We can—"

"Be silent," Raheek said. "I have no time for the squabbles of your race. We must get to the crystal. Now. You will lead us past the weapon."

Her eyes widened. "I can't," she said. "The drone won't recognize me as a friendly. It's no more discriminating than a land mine—it's programmed to shoot at anything that moves. If I had my assault suit, I could walk right through that defensive ring. But without it . . ."

"Where is your assault suit?" Alexi asked. But he already knew the answer: according to a now-distant memory, the suit was irradiated and lying in a street in Vladivostok.

With Juliana's body beside it.

16

"—sounds like trauma-triggered repression to me," said Nevsky.

Alexi stared at the soldier who sat next to him. He and Nevsky were naked, sitting on cedar benches in a small, steam-filled room. Alexi clutched at the bench with both hands, his heart pounding. For a second or two he had a wild hallucination: The steam—it was coming out of the mouth of a gigantic black monster, scalding the flesh from his bones . . .

He gulped in hot air, his knuckles whitening. But even as he sought to bring the monster into focus in his mind, the image of it drifted away into the swirling clouds of steam that filled the room.

Nevsky shook Alexi's shoulder with a sweaty hand. "*Tovarish!* Are you all right? You're very pale, and your pupils are dilated. Do you need to leave the *parilka*?"

Alexi blinked away the last wisps of the ghost that had occupied his mind a second before. "I . . ." He looked around. They were sitting in a *parilka*, a bathhouse sauna. Hot rocks crackled on an electric heater, and a ladle and a bucket of water mixed with sweet-smelling eucalyptus oil hung nearby. Sweat poured down Alexi's body and his skin tingled and was red in patches. The gold cross that had been his mother's—and his grandmother's, and his great-grandmother's—lay against his bare chest, the hot metal searing it. He leaned forward so it swung away from his skin and looked down at the floor. Strewn across it were the birch branches that bathers used to switch themselves with, to get their blood flowing. The wire frames of his glasses were equally hot, but he bore it without complaint. The thought of being half-blind inside a swirling mass of steam was just too unnerving. . . .

He and Nevsky were alone in the sauna. He had no idea how he'd gotten there. The last thing he remembered, he'd been sitting beside Nevsky on the bench in the back of the helicraft. . . .

"I'm fine," he lied.

Nevsky's next question caught him by surprise. "No you're not. You've had another blackout, haven't you?"

Alexi glanced sideways at Nevsky. The former nurse looked more like a patient now, with his eyebrows gone and only clumps of hair remaining. His skin was blotchy—but not just from the *vennki* they'd switched themselves with. A radiation blister had erupted on one shoulder, and his hands were shaking.

"Did I tell you about the blackouts?" Alexi asked.

Nevsky nodded. "We were just talking about it. You asked what could be causing them, and I said they might be occurring because your mind is repressing a traumatic incident. Something that is impossible for your conscious mind to cope with."

"Ah." Somehow, Alexi didn't think that was the answer. He remembered with vivid clarity every detail of the battle in Vladivostok, with all of its gruesome horror. If there was anything he'd like his conscious mind to suppress, it would be the image of the irradiated Union soldier who had crawled out of her heavy-assault suit and died before Alexi's eyes. The look on her blistered face as she realized that she was dying haunted him still.

But why? Alexi should have found Boris's rocket-seared corpse much more disturbing. . . .

Except that Boris wasn't dead.

With a trembling hand, Alexi reached for the tin mug of tea that sat beside a thermos on the bench. He sipped from it, trying to steady his crazy thoughts. The taste gave him something concrete to focus on: bitter black tea, sweet sugar, and a dollop of blackberry jam lying in a sticky lump at the bottom of the mug.

"Where are we?" he asked.

"In Novosibirsk," Nevsky said. "On our second day of leave after the fighting in Vladivostok." His eyes searched Alexi's. "You do remember Vladivostok, don't you, Alexi?"

Alexi nodded. "I remember it. And shooting the alien. And flying out by helicraft. But that's where it stops. The next thing I knew, I was . . . here. In a bathhouse in Novosibirsk, thousands of kilometers to the east. A city I haven't been to since I was a child."

"Fascinating," Nevsky said. "You remember the city—where it is, when you last visited—and yet have forgotten how you got here."

Then he grinned. "Well, the vodka would account for your losing your memory of last night, but the alcohol would have been out of your system by this morning. You've been perfectly lucid all day."

Oh yes. Now that Nevsky mentioned it, Alexi could call up hazy memories of yesterday's drunken binge. Of the theater, and the church—and the guardian-angel hallucination that too much vodka had induced.

"Not even a hangover," Nevsky continued. He touched a hand to his temple and winced. "Not like the rest of us. But then—you aren't . . ." He glanced away before continuing. "Your immune system isn't compromised."

"Da, I know," Alexi muttered. "I'm not sick like the rest

of you." Then he laughed. "Too bad being ill doesn't make us unfit for duty, *da*?"

He kept the rest of his thought to himself: that the blackouts would be just one more excuse for the bureaucrats in Moscow to refuse to transfer him away from the rad squad.

"Is there anything I can do to stop the blackouts?" Alexi asked. "Any medication I can take?"

Nevsky shook his head. "Not that I can get my hands on."

Alexi sighed and wiped away a rivulet of sweat that was trickling down his temple. No hope then. He'd have to tough this one out.

They sat in silence, brooding and listening to the crackle of the hot rocks. Then Nevsky got up and used the ladle to toss water on them. Steam billowed into the air, and the temperature instantly increased. Hot though he was, Alexi luxuriated in the feeling of being clean—a rare luxury, for a soldier. The grime that had accumulated over the days of fighting in Vladivostok had wormed its way into his pores. It felt good to sweat it away.

"Do you remember anything of what we were talking about earlier?" Nevsky asked as he settled back on the bench. "We were having some fun, ranking the other members of the squad in the order of who we'd take a bullet for—who we'd actually throw ourselves on an unexploded grenade to save. Do you remember who was at the bottom of the list?"

"Soldatenkof?" Alexi asked tentatively.

Nevsky guffawed and clapped Alexi on the back. "He didn't even make the list!" He chuckled a moment more before continuing. "At least, not unless you were counting saving his life to avoid a court-martial, and thus saving the lives of all of the squad. No, last on the list was Irina—at least, that was my vote. But you had some reservations. You thought she was pretty enough to be second-to-last on the list."

"I did?" Alexi asked incredulously. "She's not that pretty—she's just the only woman in any of the squads who still has a full head of hair. *Nyet*—I must have been thinking of someone else."

Someone who wasn't pretty anymore, now that her face was blistered.

Alexi pushed that thought from his mind. The truth was, he didn't care enough for any of the members of the squad to take a bullet for them. Even if all of them were about to be torn to pieces with a frag grenade, he wouldn't throw himself on it for them. *Nyet*. The only one Alexi was interested in keeping alive was himself.

Now it was his turn to chuckle. Just a couple of days ago, Alexi had resigned himself to dying. Not in some heroic gesture like Nevsky was suggesting, but simply in the quickest and most painless way possible, for the peace and quiet it would bring.

He closed his eyes and leaned back against the wall, feeling the sweat slide down his body. He was glad that he hadn't carried through on his decision. Or rather, it was a good thing dumb luck had saved his hide, to be more accurate. Sitting here in the hot, humid womb of the *parilka* was as good as dying and going to heaven, any day.

He let the hiss of the steam lull him to sleep. . . .

17

Cold. He was freezing, despite the blankets he'd wrapped around himself. Darkness surrounded him, and the metal wall behind him was slippery with ice. Alexi fumbled for his glasses inside the heavy flak jacket he wore, then put them on, hooking the wires over his ears.

He was inside the helicraft, which was on the ground, silent. The only light came from the cockpit, which was illuminated by fading emergency lights in the instrument panel.

Alexi walked to the front of the helicraft and peered out through the cockpit windows, which were starting to dust over with falling snow. Outside, everything was dark. The helicraft was in a clearing in a forest, without a building in sight. Above, the sky was an inky black found only in the wilderness, away from the haze of city lights. The constellations of the Changed sky shone brightly overhead. There were fewer stars than there had been before. And all of the constellations were different.

Alexi sighed. So many mysteries. So far away . . .

Something stirred in the cargo bay. Alexi crept cautiously back, and in the fading light saw a figure curled up on the bench opposite the one he'd been sitting on. The Union officer—Alexi recognized her face under the *ushanka* cap. Her blankets had fallen onto the floor, but she didn't appear cold, despite the fact that she wasn't wearing much—just a thin pair of combats over a one-piece bodysuit. Alexi touched a hand to the dull silver fabric. It was warm—as warm as an electric blanket set on LOW. No wonder she wasn't cold.

Alexi shivered and breathed a fog of air onto his chapped hands. In her sleep, the woman rolled over on the bench, so that she was facing him.

No—not in her sleep. Her eyes were open, and one hand held a Pug pistol.

"What do you want?" she asked in accented Russian.

Alexi spread his hands to show her that he was unarmed. His AK-51 lay on the floor behind him.

"You're so warm," Alexi said. "And my hands . . . I thought . . ."

Where had that ludicrous idea come from? As if an enemy soldier would let him place his hands on her back.

"It's difficult to sleep when it's so cold," he finished lamely.

Sleep. Was that what he'd been doing during his last blackout?

"I thought we could talk," he added.

The Union officer sat up. "Why?" she asked in a suspicious voice. "I'm not going to give you any information, other than what you've already got. My name and rank: Captain Juliana Ko. Nothing more. And if you're thinking of warming your hands on my therm suit, you can forget it, *Leitenant*."

Leitenant? Alexi frowned, then remembered that he was wearing Soldatenkof's armored jacket. He must have put it on after climbing aboard the helicraft, sometime during his blackout. He was glad he didn't remember what Soldatenkof's body had looked like—probably pretty horrible, like the boiled beef they served in the mess, back at the induction center.

Funny, that the Union officer should have been fooled by Soldatenkof's jacket. Alexi thought she'd gotten a good look at him back in Tomsk 13, when they'd collided with each other in the street. She must have failed to notice his corporal's chevrons, in all of the confusion.

Alexi toyed with the idea of pretending to be an officer. But the thought left a sour taste in his mouth. Officers were petty-minded psychopaths, human excrement that seemed somehow always to float to the top of the military ranking system. Bad enough that Alexi was wearing Soldatenkof's jacket. At least the growler's breath had steamed away the stink of the *leitenant*'s sweat. Now all the suit smelled of was boiled meat.

The smell put a smile on Alexi's lips. At least the *Leitenant* was dead. That was one bright spot in an otherwise questionable day. Or night, actually.

"I'm a corporal," Alexi told her. "Corporal Minsk. But I'm not that formal. The others in my squad just called me Alexi. You can, too, if you like."

The Union officer took a moment to digest this new information. "You can call me Captain Ko, Corporal," she said.

Alexi settled on the bench beside her. He gestured at the silvery bodysuit she wore. "Nice suit," he said. He resisted the urge to lean closer to her, to try and soak up some of the warmth it was generating. Despite the fact that she was an officer—something that normally would have caused him to keep a cautious distance—he felt drawn to this woman. It was as if they had been friends in another lifetime. And yet he had only just met her.

And she was the enemy. Or so he kept having to remind himself.

She said nothing, merely stared at him in the semidarkness. But at least the Pug pistol was in her lap, now. She still held it—but it wasn't pointed at Alexi's chest.

An uncomfortable minute or two of silence passed.

"You don't like officers much, do you, Corporal?" she asked at last.

Alexi shook his head. "Not much. They're as bad as the *Gosavtoinspektsia*. And they shoot for the head, not the windshield."

"The what?"

Alexi chuckled. Despite her officer's aloofness, he'd managed to snag her attention. "The *Gosavtoinspektsia*— the traffic police. They make their living by pulling over motorists for made-up traffic violations. If you don't pay the fine, they shoot out your windshield. Or your tires."

She gave a skeptical snort. Obviously she'd never driven in Moscow.

"If you want to ask me questions, go ahead," Alexi told her. "I don't have any secrets. I'll tell you all about the rad squad. My comrades are dead now, anyhow. Words won't hurt them."

"What's 'rad'?" the Union officer asked. "The designator for your unit?"

"Rad is short for radiation," he answered. Then he explained how conscription worked, and how the bulk of the Neo-Sov army would collapse without its monthly issue of radiation pills.

"That's obscene." Her voice had an edge to it, as if she didn't believe what she was hearing. "No wonder your army's morale is so bad. You Sovs are hardly worth killing. Your soldiers are dead men and women already. They've got nothing to fight for."

"Except their next rad pill," Alexi said. "And another month of life."

They sat for a moment more before she spoke: "I volunteered."

"*Da*," Alexi said. "So did I."

"To get the pills?" she asked.

"*Nyet*. I wanted to go into space. But they assigned me to the rad squad. I didn't realize that extreme astigmatism fell into the same medical classification as radiation poisoning."

"Astigmatism? But that's easily fixed by laser surgery. They've known how to correct it for more than a century."

"That's true," Alexi said. "But just try to find a clinic that has the equipment—and that doesn't have a kilometer-long waiting list, with *boyars* at the front of the queue. I might as well waste my time waiting in a bread or milk lineup."

"Declaring war on the Union was a stupid thing to do," the Union soldier said sternly. "Just look at where it's left your country. Irradiated, unable to feed itself, and without the resources to do simple eye surgery. What the hell were you thinking, starting a war with us?"

Alexi bristled. "It wasn't me who started the war," he said. "I was still teaching high school—not even a soldier yet—when the nuclear bombs were launched at your country. I didn't—"

Her angry voice cut him off. "You didn't push the button that launched the nukes, so you're not responsible, right, Sov?" she gritted back. "It was your *country* that launched the first strike, and the target this time around just happened to be my country, instead of China. But I took the attack personally. And let me tell you why."

The Union officer's eyes glinted in the faint light that was coming from the cockpit. "I was night skiing on Mount Baker, taking a break after defending my thesis, when the war began," she said. Alexi thought he heard a catch in her voice. Her next words confirmed it.

"My lover was in Seattle. I had a perfect view of the bomb flash. I'd already seen the Maw appear in the sky a few minutes earlier. I thought it was a nearby star gone supernova and that its heat had caused the city to combust spontaneously. I couldn't understand why I wasn't burning up, too.

"Everything was chaos, after that. It was three days before I learned that Seattle had been the target of a nuclear attack by the Neo-Soviet Union. Three days of wishing that I was dead, too. I decided to kill myself—and found some pills in an abandoned pharmacy. I counted them out on the counter, and broke open a vending machine for a can of soda. But then I looked at the pills, lined up in neat little rows, and I changed my mind."

Alexi couldn't help but ask the obvious question. "Why?"

"I decided that if I was going to die, I might as well do it in service to my country. And take out a few Sovs, first. My only regret was that my assault suit didn't let me do it up close and personal."

The Union officer's cold eyes challenged him across the cargo hold. The Pug was pointed at him again. At first, Alexi wasn't sure what to say. He couldn't tell her about Tatyana—the ache was still too fresh. His sister's memory was still an empty hole in his heart.

He decided instead to tell his own story of where he had been when the war began. Everybody in the world could remember exactly where they were when the Change happened. Alexi had told his story so many times he could recite it in his sleep.

"I was in Omsk when the Change came," he said at last. "It was early in the morning, and I was taking a class on a field trip to the World War II memorial in the park," he said. "A bit ironic, since World War III was about to start. One of the students noticed that the sun had disappeared. I told her not to be ridiculous—that it was just hidden behind the clouds. The Maw had not yet risen that day, so the sky didn't look any different—yet.

"When we got back to the school, the principal made a

broadcast. That was when we heard that our nation was at war."

"And then?" she prompted.

Alexi sighed. "And then I went back to my lesson," he said. "Remember that we'd just been through a war with China—war was something my students had grown up with. It wasn't until the Maw rose that afternoon that I realized that something even more momentous had occurred. That was when the chaos started to happen. People screaming in the streets, looting, the priests all preaching that this was the Apocalypse—it was a full week before order was restored and the schools were opened again."

A few seconds of silence. "The war meant nothing to you, then." Her voice was bitter. "It left you untouched."

Alexi could have contradicted her. But for some reason, he remained silent. Despite his sister's death, he had no reason, really, to fight. Or to die. No thirst for vengeance burned inside him as it did for her. He knew that dying wouldn't bring anybody back.

"I didn't lose a lover to the war, it's true," he told her. "But I did lose something I treasured. A year after the war began, they shut down all of the senior schools. Several of my former students were fourteen years old—just old enough to go into the army. I was offered a job at a primary school, but there didn't seem to be any point. What good is it to teach children, to watch their eager minds blossom with ideas, when you know a bullet is going to smash all of that knowledge away as soon as they reach their teens? And so I drifted for a year. And then finally signed up myself."

After a moment's silence, the Union officer spoke in a quiet voice. "Our schools are still open," she said. "But the draft begins at sixteen."

Alexi smiled. She was starting to open up to him, to speak to him as one ordinary person did to another, rather than as an officer to an enemy corporal. He suspected that she had something in common with him—unlike the members of his squad: a love of learning that had been cut short by the war. Had they both been wearing the same uniform, they might have been friends.

Or even lovers . . . Which reminded him of something. Some common ground.

"You said you'd just defended a thesis on the day the Change occurred," he said. "You were a university student, then?"

"Computer science," she said. "In Seattle."

"With your lover. A fellow student?"

"*Nyet*. A professor."

"I see. A teacher, like me."

She spun on the bench to face him. The pistol trembled in her hand. She was a hair's breadth away from pulling the trigger. Alexi wondered what he'd said to provoke such a reaction.

"Nothing like you," she spat. "He was a patriot who believed in his country. If he'd lived . . ."

If the fellow had lived, Alexi thought, he'd have met his end some other way. That was the long and short of it. In the five years since the Change and the beginning of the war, all kinds of new ways to die had been invented. Only the lucky survived.

But she had one thing right: Alexi was no patriot. He loved his country—the land, its people, their history—but hated its government. And no wonder—his breeding had run true. When Alexi had traced his family tree, he'd found dissidents and deserters on every branch. They'd served in Russia's many wars, over the centuries, but only after being conscripted. Alexi had been the first, ever, to volunteer for military service.

"I'm sorry about your boyfriend's death," Alexi said. But it was a lie. He didn't feel sorrow about anything. Three months of brutal basic training at the induction center and nearly three years in combat had blunted all emotion. It was difficult to feel anything, any more.

He didn't even care that the tentative truce they'd begun to build had so suddenly shattered.

He crossed to the other side of the cargo bay, folded down the ice-cold bench, and sat on it. His teeth immediately began chattering. "Go ahead and sleep," he told her. "I'll just sit here until . . ."

He paused. What *were* they waiting for? Alexi wasn't sure.

A glowing circle of green appeared on the Union officer's wrist as she consulted an oversize wristwatch. The glow briefly illuminated her face, revealing the tear that was trickling down one cheek.

"The alien has only been gone an hour and a half," she said. Her tone had changed: She was speaking to him as an officer once more.

"There are still more than five hours until dawn," she added. "We'll wait until then. If Raheek isn't back by first light, we'll try to find it on our own."

Raheek. The name conjured up the image of a blue-skinned alien with a bald head. The alien had left the helicraft to find . . .

To search for . . .

The Union officer lay down on her bench, setting the pistol down beside her. She patted it with one hand.

"I'm a light sleeper," she warned Alexi. "So don't try anything."

Frustrated, Alexi chafed his hands together and blew on them in the darkness. His last clear memory of the alien was of its hand, gesturing from within a cloud of utter darkness as it told them to use the helicraft to flee Tomsk 13. He didn't remember the flight here—or anything that had happened since then. That was all part of the blank that stretched between now and then. But something told him that Raheek would be back soon. And when the alien returned . . .

The minutes ticked by. Alexi didn't even bother trying

to sleep; he was too cold. He found that he was rubbing his throat with one ice-cold hand. He shivered, and unfastened the armored jacket just enough to slip the hand under his armpit instead. On the opposite bench, the Union officer lay curled in a nice warm ball, snug inside her therm suit with the blankets untouched on the floor. He listened enviously as her breathing deepened into sleep. Typical bloody officer. Nice and cozy, while he sat here shivering in the dark.

Christ, but it was cold. He scooped her blankets off the floor and hugged them around him. The Union officer hadn't stirred. He stared at her through his fogging breath, wondering if it would be possible to overpower her and steal the therm suit. But even though she was sleeping, one hand still lightly gripped the pistol that lay on the bench next to her. And the therm suit was too small and slender to fit Alexi, anyway.

He glared at it, envious of the enemy's advanced technology. The silvery material was as thin as a layer of cloth; the wires that kept a warming current circulating through it must have been hair-thin, and the computer chips that regulated its temperature as flexible as tinfoil. He wondered idly if the electromagnetic pulse of a detonating rad grenade would be enough to disrupt the suit's circuitry.

The thought gave him an idea. Rising from his seat, he shuffled over to the emergency kit that held the squad's meager first-aid supplies. The metal box didn't contain much—just a few rolled bandages, some tape, and a plastic bottle with dried-up iodine crusting the bottom of it. But it wasn't the supplies that Alexi wanted. It was the canister itself.

Wrapping cold-numbed fingers around the metal box, he eased it away from the wall. Then he tiptoed silently to where the Union officer slept. Holding the magnetized side of the box toward her, a centimeter or two above her therm suit, he ran the box up and down her body. Then he tiptoed back to his side of the cargo bay, stuck the first-aid kit back on the wall, and sat down to wait.

It didn't take long. Within a few minutes, the Union officer shivered. Then she reached down to find her blankets—the ones Alexi had taken. She sat up, tugged off the suit's gloves, and began patting the suit with her hands. She swore softly in English.

Alexi raised his eyebrows. "Is something wrong?" he asked innocently. He held out one of the blankets. "Do you need this?"

She stared at him, a thoughtful look on her face. She was just about to answer when a faint noise came from the rear of the helicraft. They both looked in that direction. To Alexi's ears, it had sounded like a scraping noise, as if someone were trying to brush away the snow that had fallen on the cargo-bay door. The door opened a crack.

The Union officer raised her Pug pistol. "Raheek?" she called softly. When there was no answer, she pointed the pistol at the slowly opening door.

"No, don't!" Alexi cautioned. For some unknown reason, it was suddenly very clear to him that they must not make any threatening moves when the alien was around—and that shooting at it would be a fatal mistake. Especially when the alien was capable of magically teleporting itself before the bullets could hit. The metal pole that it carried as a weapon might look archaic, but its blade was wickedly sharp. . . .

Alexi's hand rubbed his throat.

A cold breeze gusted in through the crack in the cargo-bay door.

"Raheek?" the Union officer asked again. She rose to her feet.

The door fell to the ground with a crash. In that same instant, Alexi saw what was framed in the open doorway. Not the blue-skinned alien he'd been expecting, but an enormous creature with tusks that curved up over its back and grasping hands tipped with razor-sharp claws. Three times the size of a human, it filled the open hatchway completely, its mouth open in a snarling grimace.

Then it roared.

The sound hit Alexi like a physical blow, turning the blood in his veins to slush. *No!* his mind screamed. *No! We left this creature behind in Tomsk 13.*

The Union officer's scream blended with his own. The Pug pistol in her fist barked flame. The growler ignored the sting of the bullets, hauling itself into the cargo bay where the humans cowered, a malicious grin on its ugly face. With two fast sweeps of its hand, it tore gaping holes in Alexi's chest, claws grating against suddenly exposed ribs. Numbed by the pain, Alexi sank to the ground.

The Union officer lasted only a moment longer. The growler's teeth fastened around her leg, severing it at the thigh. Screaming, she fell on top of Alexi.

Feebly, his consciousness flowing out as quickly as the blood from his chest, Alexi draped an arm across her. This time, at least, neither one of them was meeting death alone. . . .

18

Alexi ran for the helicraft, the wolfhound sprinting beside him. The motors were revving up, and Soldatenkof screamed static in Alexi's ear. In another moment or two the helicraft would take off, leaving Alexi stranded here in Tomsk 13 with the growlers. . . .

Alexi skidded to a halt. What was wrong with him? The helicraft was just around the corner. Why was he hesitating? It would take off without him, leave him standing here like a fool, his feet frozen to the spot like a man in a dream where his legs will not move . . .

The wolfhound had also skidded to a stop. It crouched at the corner of the building, nose low to the ground and hackles raised. Then it nervously bared its teeth and whined.

Gunfire erupted just around the corner. A pistol—but in the hands of friend or foe? It had a slightly higher pitch—usually a sign of a Union weapon. But Alexi couldn't be sure. Boris would have offered high odds on there being other Union paratroopers around here somewhere. . . .

Alexi jogged back the way he had come, the dog trotting obediently at his heels. He'd circle around and come at the helicraft from the other side. Then he saw an open doorway, and a patch of light coming through a hole in the far side of the building. And through this hole, a blur of silver that was the helicraft rotor. He decided to cut through the ruined building; it would be quickest. He pushed the door open wider and stepped into the building . . .

And stopped short when he saw the pile of canisters inside it. A dozen or more of the things were stacked in a neat pyramid, like tins on a grocery shelf. Tucked into the gaps between the canisters were fragmentation grenades. Lying at the base of the pyramid was a soldier in an MVD uniform, a grenade clutched in one rot-bloated hand.

The upper half of the soldier, to be more precise. Something had chewed away the lower half of his torso, one tiny bite at a time.

The stack of canisters needed only a single frag grenade tossed into the center of it to set it off. And the canisters—each stenciled with a single word in faded white letters—TABUN—together contained enough nerve gas to wipe out an entire city.

The room was large, and housed what looked like a heating system. Ducts led away from two squat boilers near the pile of nerve-gas canisters. The wolfhound had trotted over to one corner of the room and was pawing at some gouges in the floor near a vent, nose to the cement. Then it growled, and the fur along its spine rose in a sharp ridge.

From outside the building came a loud roaring that had a hollow reverberation, as though the sound were echoing inside a tin can. The sound sent a shiver through Alexi. He was suddenly very glad he wasn't any closer to whatever was making that noise.

Alexi stared at the pyramid of nerve-gas canisters and frag grenades. Any sane man would back away from such a lethal sight. But Alexi felt strangely drawn to it. Slinging his AK-51 over his shoulder, he lifted one of the canisters from the pile. He cradled the canister in his arms like a baby, one hand stroking its rust-pocked metal. The thing was heavy, and it was against every rule of common sense to carry it around a battlefield. Even if a bullet didn't puncture it, the canister would slow Alexi down, make him an easier target for any Union paratroopers who might be lurking about.

But for some reason, he couldn't set it down. Some inner voice told him to obey the strange compulsion he felt to get it on board the helicraft. He shrugged. You never knew when a canister of nerve gas would come in handy.

The helicraft rotors were still turning over. For some reason, it hadn't taken off yet. He struggled across the rubble-strewn floor toward the opening in the wall that led to the helicraft. Sweat poured down his body as he struggled to carry the heavy canister over the debris. He set it down for a second, and shucked off his greatcoat. There. That was better. The icy air bit into his skin, offering some relief. He'd come back for the coat in a moment. He slung his AK-51 over his shoulder and grunted as he picked up the heavy canister again.

Outside the building, Alexi heard strange sounds: the *leitenant*'s strangled screams and the hiss of what sounded like a steam pipe rupturing. And more gunfire: a long burst that stopped abruptly.

A moment later, he clambered out of the building with the canister in his arms, and saw a strange sight. The pilot lay dead outside the open cockpit door, and the cargo-bay door was straining to power shut, the body of a Union paratrooper preventing it from closing all the way.

Still holding the canister, Alexi reached awkwardly up to pull the lever that would open the helicraft door. With a whir of machinery, the door fell open and the body of the Union soldier fell out. Alexi climbed into the cargo bay.

The first thing that greeted him was the smell of hot, boiled meat. The whole cargo bay stank of it. Then Alexi saw the source: Soldatenkof's body. It lay in a sprawled heap, the flesh bubbled with watery blisters. The eyes had turned a solid, rubbery white, like eggs left too long on the boil. Soldatenkof had been scalded to death. But how?

A vodka bottle lay on the metal grating beside the corpse. Alexi nudged it with his boot, saw that it was empty.

"Good riddance to you, *Leitenant*," he told the corpse. "But you could have saved a drink for me, you greedy bastard. Especially since you've condemned me to death by dying yourself."

He knelt—funny that the floor was so warm—and strapped the canister into place against one wall. He didn't want it rolling around when the helicraft took off. The thing was heavy and could crush a man's chest.

When he stood up, he bumped his helmet against the wall. The visor slammed shut—and stuck. Cursing as it fogged up, Alexi undid the chin strap and pulled the helmet off. No sense keeping it on anyway. Either the helmet speaker wasn't working at all anymore—or everyone else in the squad was dead.

It had taken only a moment to strap the canister to the wall, but Alexi was already freezing cold. The sweat in his hair was starting to chill, now that he'd taken his helmet off. The moist warmth that had lingered in the cargo bay when Alexi had come aboard had vanished. He needed to collect his greatcoat.

More importantly, he needed to find another pilot to fly the helicraft, now that the pilot who had flown them in to Tomsk 13 was dead. Funny, though—Alexi was certain one would come along soon enough. . . .

He peered out through the still-open cargo-bay door, and saw something moving inside the building in which he'd found the nerve-gas canisters. Not wanting to leave the dog behind, he whistled for it—but the whistle died on his lips as he saw what responded: a growler. The thing was about the size of a chimpanzee, with exaggerated muscles and metallic spikes radiating out of its spine. It emerged from the building, hunkering along on feet and knuckles like an ape. It blinked—and then its beady eyes focused on Alexi.

Although it was the first time Alexi had ever seen one of the creatures, it seemed almost familiar to him. Too familiar. The look in the creature's eye was pure hunger; the saliva dripping from its mouth sizzled when it splattered into the snow. The growler sprinted toward the helicraft, the claws on its feet leaving deep gouges in the cement, its eyes locked on Alexi's.

Alexi gulped, one hand clutching his chest, and slammed the button that would close the cargo-bay hatch. The door shut with only a second to spare. The growler slammed into the door, leaving a series of dents in the metal as it ran right up one side of the helicraft and down the other.

Alexi ran to the front of the helicraft and slammed the pilot's door shut. He listened—but heard nothing. The growler was probably gone, but he wasn't about to open either door again or venture outside for his coat. Not now. He'd wait here for the helicraft pilot.

Who was lying dead in the snow outside. Alexi looked out the window at his corpse. Stupid idea. There was no one to fly the helicraft, to help Alexi escape from Tomsk 13. Alexi faced the equally grim prospects of either being torn to pieces by a growler like the rest of the squad or freezing to death as he waited inside the helicraft for Neo-Sov reinforcements. And once those reinforcements came and found Soldatenkof dead, Alexi would be court-martialed and shot.

Alexi walked back to the cargo bay and began pacing back and forth to keep warm. He was wearing nothing more than his combat shirt and padded trousers. If the growlers didn't get him, he'd freeze to death.

He stopped to look down at Soldatenkof's body. The stench of the scalded flesh was disgusting, but the armor itself was intact. The pants would be much too small, but the jacket just might fit. And if Alexi could pass himself off as

Soldatenkof, even for a little while, he might be able to buy himself a reprieve from his death sentence. . . .

Alexi stripped the jacket off. Bits of flesh came away with it. He wrinkled his nose in disgust as he shook them out.

What to do with Soldatenkof's body? Tossing it outside in the hope that a growler would eat it was one possibility; it would be easier for Alexi to pass himself off as Soldatenkof if the *leitenant*'s corpse wasn't present to contradict him. But with Alexi's luck, the growlers wouldn't like the vodka-and-sweat stink of Soldatenkof any more than humans did.

Alexi instead dragged the corpse back to the storage lockers in the rear of the helicraft. He tried one, but the door was stuck. Odd—Alexi didn't see any lock on it, but it was as if the locker had been welded shut. It probably held supplies that common soldiers weren't allowed to have—more vodka for the *leitenant*, perhaps? He opened the locker beside it instead and pawed through the clothing it held, spilling a pair of dirty combats and an *ushanka* onto the floor. Then he stuffed the body inside. It was a gruesome task; the scalded flesh was slippery under his hands.

As he was closing the locker, a cold draft of air blew in from the front of the helicraft. Someone—or something—must have opened the cockpit door. Alexi spun around, his heart pounding. But it wasn't a growler; it was a human climbing into the cockpit. A woman, wearing the silver-gray bodysuit of a Union paratrooper.

An enemy soldier.

But she seemed to know her way around a Neo-Soviet helicraft. Or she was a quick learner. She immediately settled into the pilot's seat and began manipulating the controls. The helicraft rose—then sank suddenly and tipped to one side—then rose smoothly again into the air as the woman became more familiar with the controls. Alexi flattened himself against one wall of the cargo bay, praying she wouldn't see him.

At the moment, the Union paratrooper was busy flying the helicraft. Alexi didn't dare disturb her—not until they were higher in the air and she had better control. He thought briefly about confronting her, trying to force her to fly to a location of his choice—but he had no leverage. He didn't know how to fly one of these things. If he shot her, he was a dead man himself.

There was a chance that the situation would improve once they landed. But for all Alexi knew—especially given the fact that Union soldiers had parachuted into Tomsk 13— there might be Union-held territory close by. Which meant Alexi would become a prisoner. If the enemy thought he was an officer, perhaps he'd be worth keeping alive.

He flattened against the wall of the cargo bay a second time as the Union soldier—a captain, judging by the wide rank bands on the sleeve of her bodysuit—looked out of the cockpit's side windows. As he saw her face in profile, Alexi felt his knees go weak. The officer looked like the woman he'd killed in Vladivostok—the one inside the bright green heavy-assault suit.

Alexi must have been mistaken. It couldn't be the same woman. The assault suit had been painted with the single stripe of a *leitenant*, and this woman had a captain's rank on her sleeves. The soldier inside the assault suit must have been no more than a look-alike—a sister or cousin of this woman, at most.

When the officer turned her attention back to the controls, Alexi picked up Soldatenkof's jacket. Wrinkling his nose at the smell, he pulled it on and did up the fastenings.

The Union officer's attention was divided between the view out the cockpit window and the controls, with their Cyrillic lettering. She didn't see the patch of darkness that coalesced just behind her in the cockpit—or the blue-skinned alien that stepped from it.

The creature's head slowly turned. Right, to look at the Union officer. Left, to look at Alexi, who stood rooted to the spot in amazement. Then it walked back into the cargo bay, the blade-tipped staff in its hand gently thumping on the metal deck.

Alexi's first impulse was to grab his AK-51. But for some reason, he didn't shoot. And not just because a stray bullet might hit the woman who was piloting the helicraft. Something in the alien's eyes made him hold his fire. Some hint of compassion for Alexi, a mere human. He had a flash of himself lying in the snow, of the alien looking down at him. He let go of the assault rifle with his left hand, and rubbed his upper right arm. It had developed a sudden ache, like the phantom pain of a missing limb. Except that it was still very much intact. The AK-51 rattled as his right hand began to tremble.

At first, Alexi thought the alien was also wearing a bodysuit, like the Union paratroopers. Its body was smooth, hairless. But then he realized that it was naked. And utterly alien—with its double-jointed arms and complete lack of nipples or genitalia. Alexi's mind skipped over pronouns—he? she?—and settled upon the word *it* instead.

The tall, blue-skinned alien had to be a Zykhee—a member of the alien race that had attacked *Novyy Proezd 30*. A brutal race that had killed every human it encountered. The same race as the tattooed alien Alexi had killed in Vladivostok. But for some reason, Alexi couldn't wrap his mind around the concept of this *particular* alien being his enemy.

Its dark blue eyes bored into Alexi's.

"You know where the meteorite fell," it said.

Meteorite? Alexi's thoughts whirled as he struggled to keep up. What meteorite?

In the cockpit behind the alien, the Union officer's head whipped around. Her eyes widened as she saw the alien.

The alien glanced at her over its shoulder.

"And you," it told her, "will take me there."

The helicraft slipped to one side, and the Union officer

returned her attention to the controls. "I won't be taking anyone anywhere if I don't get this thing under control," she gritted.

Alexi saw her looking with determination at the compass, fighting with the unfamiliar controls to keep the helicraft on a heading. He could see that she already had a destination in mind. Probably the rally or pickup point for her paratroop squad.

The alien's attention was completely focused on Alexi.

"I don't know what you're talking about," Alexi told it.

"You will," the alien said. "The holy flame burns brightly in you."

Alexi suddenly remembered where he'd heard those words before—in the *sobor,* in Novosibirsk. This was the creature that appeared to him there—the one he'd drunkenly mistaken for a guardian angel.

"I'm no priest," he told the alien. "I'm a soldier. And before that, a history teacher."

The alien ignored his protests. "We knew the meteorite would strike your planet, somewhere on this continent, closer to the pole. We would have monitored its impact point precisely, had our ship not been disabled by your attack. When we were forced to land upon your planet, we thought all was lost. But then the ancient souls whispered to me that a human would lead me to the site. And I found and followed you. Now look inside yourself and tell me. Where did the meteorite land?"

Alexi just stood, blinking. This was crazy. The alien seemed so expectant, so . . . intense. It looked at Alexi like a religious zealot staring at an icon of the Christ child—like someone fervently expecting a mute painting to speak. But Alexi was no savior. He was just a soldier. Just a man—without any flames inside him, holy or otherwise.

But the alien expected him to say *something.*

"The only meteorite strike in this area that I know of

was the one near Tunguska," Alexi said slowly. "But it was—"

The alien's hands tightened around its staff. "Where is Tunguska?"

Alexi shook his head. "I was going to say that it can't be the one you're looking for. It struck the earth more than a century ago, in 1908."

The alien leaned toward Alexi. "Was the meteorite itself found?"

"No. That's what made it so memorable. There was an enormous blast, but no pieces were ever found. Some scientists actually suggested that a microscopic black hole—or a chunk of antimatter—had struck the Earth. But they ultimately decided that the meteorite must have vaporized explosively, just meters above the Earth."

The Union officer was listening intently. "Thanks for the history lesson—but I don't think it's what the Zykhee wants to hear," she told Alexi. Then she turned to speak to the alien. "The Union forces can help you to pinpoint whatever it is you're looking for. Our moon bases monitor—"

"Silence." The alien ignored her. Instead its eyes bored into Alexi's. "The meteorite protected itself from harm by throwing the explosive force of its impact back through time. That explosive energy emerged in the segment of time you number one thousand nine hundred and eight."

Flecks of red danced inside the dark blue irises of the alien's eyes. Its voice was slow and hypnotic. "Where . . . is . . . Tunguska?"

"I don't remem—"

Alexi's mouth was suddenly dry. He felt a strange tickling in his temples, and the air in the helicraft cockpit grew hazy. The shimmering whorls of air looked almost like human faces—faces whose expressions urged him to think back, to remember a lesson he'd given long ago. . . .

Like a forgotten name that suddenly springs to mind, the information popped into Alexi's head.

"The Tunguska meteorite landed near the Arctic Circle," he said. "I don't remember the exact latitude, but the longitude was an easy one. A nice round number: 100 degrees east."

"Good."

Alexi's vision suddenly cleared. He blinked, feeling like a student who had just been praised for getting the correct answer to a question he hadn't even studied. He lifted his glasses to rub his eyes.

The alien turned to the Union officer. "Do you understand the coordinates that were just given? Can this craft reach that location?"

"It could," she said. Then she tapped a finger against the fuel gauge. "But only if you don't plan on getting back again. That's kilometers from any town—right in the middle of the Siberian wilderness."

"It is the middle of everywhere," the alien answered solemnly. "And of every when. You will take me there." Its eyes bored into hers. The flecks of red were gone, but the gaze was every bit as hypnotic and intimidating as before.

The Union officer stared at the alien a long moment, then nodded. "I'll take you there," she whispered. Then she turned the helicraft onto a new course.

19

"We're losing altitude!" the Union officer shouted. "The rotors must be icing up. And it's getting dark. If I don't find a clear spot in the trees to put the helicraft down in the next few minutes, we're dead."

Alexi twisted around in the copilot's seat and peered out the cockpit window. The ground below was a vast expanse of snow-covered forest. Not a clear spot in sight.

But that didn't disturb him nearly as much as the blue-skinned hand that rested on the back of his seat.

Or the fact that another big chunk of time seemed to have gone missing.

He looked up into the face of the alien. The creature held the blade-tipped staff in one long-fingered hand and stared impassively out the window.

"We must reach the impact site," it said.

"We're not going to make it," the officer answered.

The helicraft drifted down toward the trees. Its engines were revving at a higher pitch, as if straining to carry a load . . .

"It's the growler," Alexi said suddenly.

Both the alien and the Union officer glanced at him

sharply. The officer turned her attention back to the helicraft controls, but the alien continued to stare at Alexi.

"What do you mean?" it asked.

"I don't know," Alexi said. But he felt twitchy. As if he should be doing something. Something back in the cargo bay . . .

Alexi undid his seat belt and rose from his seat. As the helicraft bucked and wove its way through the air, he staggered back across the unsteady floor of the cargo bay. Something compelled him to drop to his knees on the floor and fumble with a small hatch on the belly of the helicraft that was normally used for dropping butterfly mines. With chilled fingers he undogged the ice-cold hatches that held it shut, then wrenched the hatch open.

Cold air whistled in through the manhole-sized opening in the floor. Bracing himself on hands and knees, Alexi lowered his head out through the hole to peer outside. . . .

And found himself eyeball-to-eyeball with a snarling growler.

The thing had wrapped its arms and legs around the helicraft's landing gear. It clung there, muscles bulging, oblivious to the cold wind that was whipping its fur. Alexi recognized it at once by its curving white tusks: the growler from Tomsk 13. The one that had wrenched open the cargo-bay door while its companion scalded Soldatenkof and the pilot to death. The same one that had—no would—kill Alexi. Unless . . .

Still holding on to the landing gear, the growler twisted its body around. A clawed foot lashed out at Alexi, raking the belly of the helicraft near his head and leaving a jagged gash in the metal. Alexi yanked his head back inside.

"Juliana!" he screamed at the cockpit. Funny—when it came to a crisis, the name just sprang naturally to his lips. "There's a growler hanging on to the helicraft's landing gear!"

The answer was a muttered cursing as the Union officer

continued to fight the controls. The growler's violent motion had unbalanced the helicraft, causing it to slip to the side. The sudden sideways motion threw the blue-skinned alien sprawling into the copilot's seat.

Alexi grabbed for the hatch and tried to swing it shut. In the same instant, the growler's hand punched up through the opening. It flailed about, hooked claws seeking to rend and tear, like a cat that has thrust its paw into a mouse hole. Then a claw caught on the hatch, ripping it from its hinges with a loud screech of tearing metal, and tossed it against one wall. The hatch sailed into something that gave off a hollow metal sound, followed by a sloshing noise.

Alexi's eyes widened in horror as he saw the object that the hatch had struck: a metal canister about the size and shape of a beer keg that was strapped to one wall with a one-word, stenciled inscription in blocky white letters: TABUN. The nerve gas.

The canister was old—probably a relic of a previous war, like Alexi's AK-51. It was speckled with rust and ready to burst a seam if it was dropped. Whatever had possessed Alexi to carry it on board? He must have been crazy. The nerve gas inside it was enough to wipe out an entire company. If the canister burst, the helicraft would be filled in seconds with the fruity smell of the Tabun as it evaporated. A split second later, that sensation would be followed by progressively less pleasant ones. First by the complete shutdown of Alexi's respiratory system, then paralysis, then an explosive overload of his sweat, excretory, and salivary glands as his heart went into overdrive and then ground to a stop like a car driven headlong into a brick wall.

It wouldn't be pretty.

The growler's curved claws were flailing within a meter of the fragile-looking canister, gouging holes in the floor beside the storage lockers. Then the muscular hand fastened on Alexi's helmet, which had been rolling across the cargo-bay floor. One claw punctured its heavy steel like a spike going through foil. Then the hand closed into a fist, crushing the helmet like an aluminum can.

Alexi's AK-51 slid across the floor. He grabbed it and struggled to his feet. A roaring noise and smoke filled the cargo bay as he fired a burst at the arm. One bullet ricocheted and struck the canister of nerve gas with a hollow thud. Instantly, Alexi stopped shooting.

Raheek ran back into the cargo bay, weapon raised overhead. In a motion so fast that it was a blur, the double-jointed alien whipped the staff around, its blade tearing a line down the growler's overmuscled arm. Steaming in the cold air, drops of greenish blood sprayed onto the floor of the cargo bay.

The growler's hand retreated through the opening in the floor. Then Alexi heard a tearing noise underfoot. Part of the floor bulged up suddenly, as the growler's fist punched into it from below. Claw tips punctured the bent metal, and the floor began to shake violently. The creature was literally tearing its way into the helicraft.

Alexi and the alien looked at each other.

"Do something!" Alexi shouted. "Use your magic!"

The helicraft began to sink toward the ground. The growler's weight and the iced-up rotors were dragging it down. In another minute or two, they'd be on the ground. And assuming they survived the crash, they'd be faced with a rage-crazy growler tearing its way into the helicraft.

The alien began to chant in its own language. A flicker of red sparks ignited in Raheek's midnight blue eyes. Its long-fingered hands rotated empty air, as if sliding across the surface of a ball. With a sudden rush of air, a sphere of light with swirling energies trapped inside it popped into existence between them—and grew. In the space of a heartbeat it was the size of a basketball. Terrifying faces swirled within it, and a shrieking that turned Alexi's limbs to rubber echoed in the cargo hold.

In the last moment, Alexi was forced to look away. He

sagged against one wall, holding up a hand to shield his eyes from the howling ball of energy. Out of the corner of his eye he saw it streak out through the hatch on the floor.

An anguished roar came from below. All at once the helicraft surged upward, making Alexi feel as though his stomach were trying to sink into his boots. He sprang for the hatch, knelt next to it, and cheered in triumph as he saw the growler fall.

But the ground wasn't very far below. During the struggle with the growler, the helicraft had sunk to within about twenty meters of the treetops. Instead of splattering against the ground, the growler simply caught a branch with one massive hand and swung itself down, branch by branch, to the base of the tree. Completely uninjured, it began moving along the ground, loping after the shadow of the helicraft. After a second or two, the shadow drew ahead of the growler. Powerful though the growler was, it couldn't keep up with the helicraft. But that didn't mean it wouldn't catch up when the iced-up rotors forced them to land. . . .

Alexi ran for the cockpit.

The Union officer grinned at him. "Good job!" she shouted. "No wonder the helicraft was so sluggish. But I still have to set her down. The temperature's dropping; it's getting dark. The rotors will ice up completely, and we'll crash if I don't."

She gestured at the ground. "There's a clearing a few kilometers ahead. I think we can make it. But it will be tight."

"Turn around!" Alexi shouted. "We have to go back and finish it off."

She gave him a look that told him what she thought of his idea. "Forget it!" she said. "If we turn around, we'll go down in the trees."

"You don't understand!" Alexi shrieked. With an effort, he forced himself to speak clearly and get his racing emotions under control. But it was hard to sound rational when premonition was pummeling his pounding heart. If there was one thing he was certain about, it was that failing to take out the growler now would be the death of them all.

"I have . . . a premonition about these things. A soldier's sixth sense. I can . . ." He practically wept with frustration. How to explain, without sounding utterly foolish?

The alien laid a blue hand on the Union officer's shoulder. "Turn the helicraft around," it said. "Alexi is correct."

"But—"

"Turn it around!"

The command was as sharp as a gunshot. Amazingly, the Union officer obeyed. She banked the helicraft in a tight turn. But her lips pressed together in an angry line.

Alexi ran back to the cargo bay. Now he was blessing himself for stowing the nerve-gas canister on board. He wasn't such an idiot after all; Tabun had its uses.

He rolled the canister on its rim, poising it beside the opening where the hatch had been.

"Hover just above the growler," he shouted back to the cockpit. "And after I get this thing out through the hatch, fly away as fast as you can."

From the cockpit, the Union officer gave him the thumbs-up sign. After a second or two, the growler appeared below, framed in the ruined hatch. As the helicraft came to a hover above it, the growler leapt nearly six meters into the air, flailing with claw-tipped hands. Alexi rolled the canister over the rim . . .

And watched it fall.

It landed no more than five meters away from the growler. The canister burst open, showering the ground with a spray of greenish liquid. Then a gas began to rise.

The growler spun around, gave a deafening roar at the approaching gas—then suddenly went rigid. In less than a second, it collapsed in a quivering heap.

The helicraft was losing altitude again. Now its rotors were stirring up the evaporating nerve gas. The gas rose lazily toward them in deadly wisps, like thunderheads in an angry sky. . . .

"Get out of here!" Alexi said, waving his arm frantically.

Without realizing he was doing it—not that it would save him, anyway—he held his breath until the cloud of gas-poisoned ground slid out of view. Only then did he breathe a sigh of relief.

The helicraft tipped violently to one side.

"Buckle up!" the Union officer shouted. "We're going down. And it's not going to be a smooth landing!"

Alexi scrambled forward, throwing himself into the copilot's seat before the alien could claim it. With trembling fingers, he snapped the buckles shut and braced himself as the ground rushed up at them.

20

Minsk, you useless excuse for a soldier! Did you hear what I said?"

Alexi blinked as the flashlight mounted on the *leitenant*'s helmet glared into his eyes. It was dark and the Maw was high overhead; it had not yet set. Alexi had been looking at his watch—his hand still held the button that illuminated its face. He glanced at the time. It was 10:08 P.M. Strange—he could have sworn it had said something closer to nine-thirty, just a moment ago.

He looked down into Soldatenkof's glaring eyes. The vein in the *leitenant*'s temple was throbbing—never a good sign. "Sir?" Alexi asked.

"The Hotel Versailles, Corporal. The battalion's temporary headquarters and weapons depot. Run back there and fetch some grenades." He slapped a hand ominously on the pistol holstered at his hip. "Understood?"

Alexi nodded rapidly. "Yes sir!"

He turned to go—then realized he had no idea where he was. At some point during the long, exhausting battle for Vladivostok, his mind must have taken a brief nap—without letting his body know first. The last thing Alexi remembered clearly was taking out a heavy-assault suit with a rad grenade he'd found lying in a sewage-filled basement. And now the squad was down by the waterfront, near the Monument to the Fighters for Soviet Power in the Far East. The gigantic statue of World War II-era soldiers loomed over them, moonlight throwing an eerie shadow of long-dead soldiers on the paved square.

Boris, Nevsky, and Piotr sat with their backs against the monument, and Irina was wrapping a roll of gauze around a gash in her left calf—which explained why she hadn't been designated as runner. Vanya was bent over a broken water fountain, vomiting his dinner into its dirty bowl. It looked as though he'd gotten another bad batch of antiradiation pills.

Boris looked up and correctly interpreted the look of confusion in Alexi's eyes. He jerked a thumb at the road beside them. "Just follow *ulitsa* Svetlanskaya," he said. "The hotel's at the end of the road."

Then he turned to Nevsky and whispered in a voice that was deliberately pitched so that Alexi could hear. "One hundred rubles says he doesn't come back."

Alexi chuckled. Maybe he *wouldn't* come back. Maybe he'd just keep walking, all the way to Moscow. Nobody would think much of his disappearance. After all, soldiers went missing in battle all the time. Just like . . .

He pushed the thought away. Tatyana wasn't just missing. She was dead. She had to be. A whole year had gone by. If his sister had deserted, she would have contacted him by now.

It took him several minutes to get to the Hotel Versailles. At several intersections, he saw other squads of Neo-Soviet soldiers from the Battalion of Death moving through the city. But although explosions and gunfire could be heard in the distance, there wasn't a Union assault suit in sight.

As he jogged along, Alexi used the microphone in his helmet to radio the battalion headquarters. No sense getting killed by friendly fire. When a message finally came that the password had been heard and understood—five times, and he could keep quiet now—Alexi was at last satisfied that his helmet mike was working, and they knew he was coming in.

The hotel was palatial, with a sweeping drive. It took several long minutes for Alexi to pick his way between the anti-assault-suit explosive caltrops that were scattered across the broad pavement. Inside, the lobby was wide and deep, with a vaulted ceiling. Before the war, the hotel must have been quite something. Alexi could easily imagine a room there costing his monthly teacher's salary. But now the hotel roof was pocked with holes from the fighting, and its plush rug was ankle-deep in broken glass, splintered wood, and chunks of plaster. The only "guest" was the Neo-Soviety military, whose soldiers had fortified the hotel against attack with sandbags. And they were neither paying for—nor appreciating—what remained of its beauty.

Part of the building was being used as a medical dressing station. Alexi wound his way past rooms filled with wounded soldiers on stretchers. He knew he was getting close to the supply depot when he passed a room in which soldiers were hurriedly breaking apart wooden crates and unpacking the mechanical parts and weapons they contained. Alexi paused a moment, watching and trying to figure out what the parts would be, once assembled. Then the soldiers lifted a mechanical arm from one crate and what looked like a hollow head from the other. On the front of the head was a red star and the words URSA 1. Alexi suddenly realized what it was: a heavy-assault suit, half again as large as those the Union had. A Neo-Soviet model, big enough for two soldiers: a pilot and gunner.

Alexi breathed a sigh of relief, knowing that the rad squads would finally be getting some heavy-duty reinforcements. Assuming, that was, that the heavy-assault suit was assembled before the battalion was wiped out to the last grunt. And assuming, of course, that the damned thing actually worked.

One of the soldiers who was unpacking the crates looked up—and with a startled glance stepped forward to close the door Alexi was looking through. In that same instant, someone jostled Alexi from behind—a soldier carrying a machine gun. And he didn't look happy.

"Where are you supposed to be, soldier?" he asked curtly. If looks could kill, Alexi would have been dead already.

"I . . . I'm looking for the supply depot," Alexi stuttered. "My commanding officer sent me to fetch more grenades."

"Right." The soldier jerked his head, indicating a hallway to Alexi's left. "This way."

Alexi was briskly marched to what he'd been looking for all along: a supply sergeant. He was a squint-eyed fellow with a receding hairline. He sat behind a desk covered with neat piles of paper, staring at Alexi like a penny-pinching grocer watching a suspected shoplifter from behind his counter. Behind him, two Uzi-toting privates stood guard over the boxes of ammunition, neatly folded uniforms, and packages of freeze-dried foodstuffs that filled the room.

Alexi gave the fellow a wary salute. Noncommissioned officers could be even bigger bastards than officers—just give them a little power and watch it go to their heads.

"Corporal Alexi Minsk of the Sixty-sixth Rad Squad, Sergeant," he said. "*Leitenant* Soldatenkof sent me to collect some grenades."

The supply sergeant stared at Alexi for a long moment. "Radiation or fragmentation?" he asked.

Alexi hesitated. Soldatenkof hadn't specified which type. If Alexi brought back rad grenades, the *leitenant* might suspect him of plotting to use one against him and take the preemptive measure of correcting Alexi's misguided initiative with a bullet to the brain.

"Frag grenades," Alexi guessed.

"How many?"

Alexi shrugged. How many did the *leitenant* want? How many could one man carry?

"Fifteen?"

"They come in units of one dozen."

Alexi sighed in exasperation. "A dozen, then."

In one of the dressing-station rooms that Alexi had passed on his way in, a wounded soldier started screaming. Over and over, the woman begged someone not to amputate her foot. Outside, the sound of explosions drew nearer. The chandelier tinkled, and plaster dust drifted down from the ceiling.

The two privates guarding the stores glanced at each other uneasily, worried perhaps that a Union assault suit was coming their way. But the supply sergeant ignored the screams and explosions, intent upon the papers he shuffled on his desk. He thrust one of them at Alexi without looking up.

"Fill out this requisition," he said.

Alexi looked at the paper and frowned in disbelief at the multitude of lines to be filled out, boxes to tick, and sections to be initialed or signed. Surely the supply sergeant didn't really want him to fill out his full name, rank, unit, type of materiél wanted, date, time . . .

He glanced at one of the guards, who gave a slight nod. The other guard rolled his eyes behind the sergeant's back, mocking him.

"*Pazhalsta*," Alexi said, pointing at a green metal box that was clearly labeled as containing frag grenades. "My *leitenant* will be angry if I don't get back quickly. Can't I just take that one?"

"*Nyet.*"

The supply sergeant held up a pen and waggled it at Alexi, quite content to wait until he took it. He watched every scratch of the pen as Alexi filled out the form, making him rewrite the request in proper military order: grenade, fragmentation, one dozen.

The sergeant stamped the form, placed it neatly on a pile, then waited until plaster dust from the recent explosion had stopped falling and blew the dust away. Then he rose to his feet and crossed to the boxes of grenades. Slowly and carefully, he removed a dozen grenades and lined them up in a neat row on the floor, their heads all pointing in the same direction. He closed the hasp on the empty case and set it to one side.

"There you go," he told Alexi. "One dozen grenades."

"Why didn't you just give them to me in the case?" Alexi asked incredulously. He winced at the screams of the woman whose foot was being cut off, just down the hall. "Are you saving the case for something? As a coffin for the amputated foot, perhaps?"

"You didn't say you needed a grenade case," the sergeant said through annoyance-pursed lips. "That will require a second requisition form."

"Never mind," Alexi growled. He reached into the pocket of his combats and pulled out a web bag. "I'll use this to carry them."

Silently cursing each and every one of the petty bureaucrats in the Neo-Soviet army to a slow, lingering death by infected paper cut, Alexi filled the web bag and hooked it to his belt. Then he left with his dozen grenades bouncing against his thigh.

As he left the hotel, he mentally labeled each of the grenades. Number one would blow the supply sergeant and his idiotic paperwork into a bloody mangle. Number two was for the recruiter who had promised Alexi a place in the military's space corps, if only he would volunteer. Grenades three, four, and five were for the admin clerks who had refused to reassign him away from the rad squad. And maybe if he set off numbers six through twelve all together, the percussive force would be enough to knock Soldatenkof unconscious inside his protective armored suit, ridding the squad of him once and for all, cracking the armor off him like a shell from a well-boiled crab.

It was just a fantasy, of course. Alexi didn't really want to condemn the rest of the squad members to court-martial and firing squad. But the thought reminded him of something, making him slow his stride along the street. Steam . . . armor . . . But then the tickle of memory was gone.

He paused to catch his breath and watch the show as explosions blossomed with red fire on the hillside. He was glad to be momentarily out of the thick of it, to be a spectator to the battle, if only for a little while. In the center of Vladivostok flashes of explosions lit up the night, and the chatter of machine-gun fire was a constant background noise. Helicraft rose into the air and settled again like fat black flies on a corpse, moving squads of rad soldiers from one part of the ruined city to another. The Neo-Soviets were trying to outmaneuver the handful of Union heavy-assault suits, but were failing miserably. The assault suits were tearing them to shreds. But here on *ulitsa* Svetlanskaya, a few streets up from what used to be the waterfront, all was quiet. Even the static in Alexi's helmet speaker had dulled to a faint hiss.

Why the Union forces had suddenly chosen to attack Vladivostok three days ago was anyone's guess. The city, once a bustling port that was home to seven hundred thousand people, had shrunk to a fraction of its former population in the past few years. When the Earth was drawn into the Maelstrom, the coastlines had altered overnight. The Change brought the sudden departure of Vladivostok's shoreline, sending the city into a downward economic spiral from which it never recovered. The last of the city's civilian population had left three days ago, when the fighting began. There was nothing of economic or military value left in the city, as far as Alexi could see.

According to the briefing Soldatenkof had given the rad squad before they were shipped out to Vladivostok, Command had no idea why the Union had chosen to send heavy-assault suits against the city—Vladivostok's feeble reserve militia was hardly worth such a show of force. Perhaps the Union's intelligence service had been led to believe that the city held something of strategic value. Or perhaps there was no strategic reason. Maybe the Union had just wanted a place to test out its assault suits, and had thrown a dart at a map to choose the location. That made as much sense as many other military decisions made down through history.

And those who ignored history were doomed to repeat it.

As were those who ignored the future. . . .

Alexi shook the strange thought out of his head. He found himself staring at the main entrance of a sprawling, multiwinged building whose sign proclaimed it to be the Arsenev Regional Museum. The heavy front doors had been blown off their hinges, and a mangled turnstile lay beside them. The darkness inside seemed somehow to beckon to Alexi. He hesitated, feeling the bag of grenades swaying from his belt. Soldatenkof's voice was just barely audible over his helmet speaker; the squad must have changed position. And Alexi didn't really want to find them, anyway. He'd much rather take a tour of a museum. Especially when there was free admission.

Alexi entered the museum and wound his way through its corridors. He glanced briefly into the wing that held taxidermy, but decided that looking at the moldy corpses of animals would be too depressing. He also bypassed the display of military memorabilia. The last thing he wanted to look at just then were relics of previous wars, each equally as idiotic as the war he was currently fighting. Instead he climbed the stairs to the second floor.

Much of the ceiling had collapsed. Moonlight poured in through jagged holes that were probably the result of a mortar attack. But the displays along the walls were still protected by overhangs of ceiling. One, a display of eggshell-thin Japanese ceramics, had miraculously survived intact.

Alexi brushed grime away from the glass front of a display case to get a better look at the elegant vases inside it. He leaned closer, eyes drinking in the creamy yellow porcelain with its vivid red dragons.

A face stared back at him in the glass.

Alexi jerked back in surprise at the reflection. The face was androgynous—long and oval, with strangely shaped eyes and a shock of unruly white hair. The person was not wearing a helmet or uniform—no military insignia to mark it as friend or foe. Just a strange white pattern on the cheeks, like a photographic negative of Maori tattoos.

Holding his AK-51 in the ready position, Alexi looked warily around. Nothing. He was alone in the room. Then a drop of something splattered down onto his helmet. In that instant, he realized that the display case had been reflecting the ceiling above him. He looked up . . .

The person who had been crouching on the roof of the museum leapt down through a hole in the ceiling. Alexi had only a momentary glimpse of strangely articulated limbs covered in intricate blue-and-white patterns as he brought his assault rifle to bear. The patterns started to shift . . .

Suddenly, up became down. Overwhelmed by vertigo, Alexi fell sideways onto the floor. He landed hard, his finger reflexively tightening on the trigger of his AK-51. Bullets roared from the barrel, smashing the display case.

Splinters of glass and broken ceramics tinkled down onto Alexi's chest/back/side/chest. His body thrashed about while his mind fought to figure out which way was up. Something in his peripheral vision—the figure that had jumped through the hole in the ceiling—fled from the room. It ran with a peculiar loping gait, staggering as if it were wounded.

As suddenly as it had come on, the dizzy feeling stopped. Alexi sat up, his heart racing.

What in Christ had that thing been? Only one thing was certain: Although it had a face, two legs and two arms, it wasn't a normal human. Was it a new product of the Neo-Sov mutant program—a skinnier version of the *Cyclops* perhaps? Or something the Union had cooked up? And why hadn't it attacked Alexi?

Alexi got to his feet again, but one of his boots slipped on something on the floor. Looking down, he saw a purplish liquid—less viscous than blood, but somehow suggestive of blood in the way it was spattered. The mutant that had jumped down from the roof had been bleeding, and had left a trail of bloody footprints behind.

Alexi followed it.

The trail led to an intact wing that held a display of rocks and minerals. Its centerpiece was a fist-sized moon-rock, brought back to Earth by the Neo-Soviet cosmonauts who had surveyed the sites for the first moonbases. After a quick look around the room told him it was empty, Alexi crossed to the moonrock display. Glancing back over his shoulder—and laughing at himself for doing so, when the museum was long since abandoned—he brought the barrel of his assault rifle down on the display case. Then he brushed aside the broken glass and lifted the moonrock out.

The rock was a grayish black, and heavily pitted. Alexi stared at it, marveling at the irony. Here he stood, holding in his hand a little chunk of the heavens. He'd enlisted in the army with a dream of entering space, with hopes as big as the Maw. And now the dream had shrunk to the size of the rock he held in his hand, and the hopes were as shattered as the display case that lay in shards at his feet.

Alexi turned and hurled the rock down the corridor.

His impulsive anger saved him. This time, he hadn't seen the mutant as it crept up on him. But he heard the crack of the rock colliding with its skull and the heavy crash of its body falling to the floor.

AK-51 trembling in his hands, Alexi crept toward the

spot on the floor where blood was starting to puddle. He could see the outline of the purplish fluid around the prone figure clearly, but the body itself was no more than a dim blur as the white tattoos shifted.

On a whim, Alexi lifted his glasses—but the figure remained as blurry as before. No—the blur wasn't a smudge on his lenses. Had the military researchers developed some sort of cloaking device that conveyed partial invisibility?

Alexi prodded the still form with the barrel of his AK-51. The blur looked human enough, although it was incredibly tall and skinny. The fellow seemed to be out cold, but Alexi wondered if he should shoot, just to be sure. His finger almost tightened on the trigger, but then something made it relax. A face floated into his mind: a face much like the one he'd seen reflected in the glass, except without the tattoos and white hair. A friendly face, one he could visualize encouraging him to . . .

The thought was gone. Alexi groped for the meaning behind it, but came up empty.

He backed slowly away from the blur that lay on the floor. As he reached the section where the ceiling had fallen in, near the Japanese ceramic display, the hiss in his helmet speaker became clearer. Piotr's voice staticked in and out.

. . . *see that, Boris? It . . . blue* . . .

Alexi's head came up like that of a dog on the scent. What was Piotr talking about? Some sixth sense told Alexi that it was important he find out more. He thudded a hand against his helmet, but the static didn't clear. Maybe if he climbed onto the roof, the reception would improve.

Scrabbling up the pile of rubble that led to the hole in the ceiling, Alexi climbed out into the crisp night air. The rooftop was a maze of vents, chimneys, and low dividing walls. And something else—something that looked like a gigantic metal spider covered in multicolored blobs of melted plastic.

The body of the thing was a donut-shaped tube as wide

as an oil pipeline, standing on five mechanical legs that folded in on themselves like accordions. Two of the legs appeared to be broken; the machine was leaning to one side, exposing the bottom of the donut, which was studded with what looked like mortar tubes of varying lengths. Circles of blistered metal ringed the end of each of these tubes, and the donut itself was covered in sticky-looking blobs.

Alexi walked around the machine slowly, wondering what it was. It looked almost like the diagrams he'd seen of the Union's combat drones, but bigger again by a factor of ten and without the turret-mounted weaponry. Or course, if it had been a drone, Alexi would have been dead the second he climbed through the hole in the roof. Fully automated, bristling with infrared, vibration, and low-light sensors, the Union drones would open fire on anything bigger than a cat that passed through their multiple fields of fire.

The roof tiles that the machine sat on had blistered and burned away, and the cement under them was cracked in a radial pattern, as if a fist had slammed down into it. The tubes on the bottom of the donut were obviously jets—and ones that hadn't worked very well, judging by the damage the thing's legs had sustained upon landing. Probably one of ours then, Alexi mused. The Neo-Soviets weren't noted for their quality control, even when it came to cutting-edge military technology.

He flicked on the light in his helmet for a better look at the thing. He didn't see any military markings on its surface—no lettering in either the English or Cyrillic alphabets. Between the blobs of melted plastic, which turned out to shade from red to orange to yellow, were smoother sections, some of which were engraved with an intricate pattern. The design reminded Alexi of the pattern he'd seen on the cheeks of the mutant that had jumped down into the museum.

There had to be a connection. Alexi could feel it in his gut.

Then it came together in his head. That wasn't a mutant he'd knocked out with an incredibly lucky toss of a chunk of moonrock. It was an alien. And this strange-looking vehicle was the craft it had come to Earth in. So *that* was why the enemy was so interested in taking Vladivostok. One of the Union's moonbases or patrol ships must have picked up the spacecraft as it approached the Earth, and noted its landing place. Or rather, noted its approximate landing place, since the Union soldiers in their heavy-assault suits didn't seem to have found the spaceship yet.

Alexi trembled like a man who had suddenly discovered he was holding a billion-ruble lottery ticket. If he reported the spaceship to Intelligence, he might at long last be reassigned to the military's space arm as a reward for finding the first scout ship of what might be an invading alien force. . . .

Nyet. It wouldn't happen. He'd get a pat on the head and be sent back to the line. He was only a corporal, after all—a corporal they'd deemed useful only as missile fodder, because of his poor eyesight.

Did Alexi really care that aliens had landed on Earth and might even now be setting out to conquer the planet? He sighed. Not really. Aliens couldn't possibly mess up the Earth any more than the humans already had. Especially this corner of the planet. Let them have the abandoned coastline of Vladivostok and the polluted wastes of Siberia. Let them have the whole of the Neo-Soviet state, for that matter. Nothing in Alexi's world would change.

Then he realized he was making an assumption: that the aliens were his enemies. What if they were potential allies instead? Maybe this was a different alien race than the one that had wiped out the Neo-Soviet deep-exploration ship *NP-30*. Perhaps if they were approached correctly, in a spirit of friendship, they could teach humanity all of the secrets of this strange new universe the Earth had been sucked into.

The more Alexi thought about it, the more certain he became.

He suddenly hoped he'd merely knocked out the alien, not killed it. Entire wars had been started over such incidents. He slung his AK-51 over his shoulder, making a decision. He would not tell Intelligence about the spaceship. He'd go back into the museum, find the injured alien, and try to convince it that he really didn't mean it any harm.

He turned and headed back for the hole in the roof just as a blue-and-white arm snaked up through the opening. Something metallic whistled through the night air, something that looked like a whirling metallic boomerang. It cut through Alexi's armored vest as if it were no more than a layer of cotton gauze, slicing a deep crease through the flesh underneath. The pain hit an instant later. Alexi looked down at the blood that sheeted out of his chest, at the exposed ribs that glistened wetly in the moonlight. Then the air left his lungs in a sudden rush. Shock numbed the pain.

He crumpled to his knees, looking up at the alien that stood over him, its strangely jointed arms folded across its skinny chest. The moon haloed its egg-shaped head, illuminating its long strands of unkempt hair and throwing its face into shadow.

"This . . . wasn't . . ." Alexi could only mouth the words; no sound escaped his lips. "We could . . . friends . . ."

As Alexi lay dying, a strange thought entered his head. The bald one. That was the alien he could trust. The others . . .

But the bald one had killed him, too. Would kill him, too. Would be killed by him, too. Unless . . .

21

When the door opened at the rear of the cargo bay, every nerve in Alexi's body screamed at him to fling off the blankets that covered him, grab his AK-51, and shoot. But it wasn't the slavering growler with enormous tusks so vividly pictured in Alexi's mind's eye that peered into the cargo bay of the helicraft.

It was Raheek.

A second vision flashed through Alexi's mind: of the blue-skinned alien holding the blade of its staff to Alexi's throat, preparing to slit it ear to ear. But even as Alexi threw up a hand to ward off the blow, that image faded like the first. It had never happened. Would never happen.

Alexi blinked the sleep from his eyes as the alien climbed into the helicraft. Two things immediately registered on his sleep-fogged mind: he was naked, aside from a pair of military-issue boxer shorts and wool socks—and the gold cross he always wore about his neck. Juliana lay under the blankets beside him, her bare feet resting against his leg. The light touch sent a shiver of warmth through his body.

Her therm suit lay in a crumpled silver heap on the floor. Alexi reached out and touched it with a finger. It was as cold as the metal it lay on. He remembered using the magnet in the first-aid kit to scramble its programming—a stupid trick that he regretted now, since it left her without any other way to stay warm. But after that, everything was a blank.

Looking down at Juliana's face, he felt a rush of emotion for her. In his mind she was no longer an officer, nor even just a fellow soldier. She was a woman. And a beautiful one. They'd shared something in the last few hours, but whether they'd been physically intimate, Alexi couldn't say.

Juliana's eyes opened. She sat up, and Alexi saw she was wearing the combats that she'd been wearing over her therm suit earlier. Perhaps nothing had happened. . . .

The way she blushed and glanced away from him suggested that something had.

Alexi cursed whatever was causing his blackouts. If his memory loss really was triggered by trauma, as Nevsky had suggested, this was one trauma he wanted to remember.

The blue-skinned alien used the end of its staff to tug the blankets away. "We are close to the impact site," it said. "A walk of less than one-twentieth of your planet's period of rotation. We will leave now that there is sufficient light and warmth for you."

Funny, Alexi could have sworn he'd already heard the alien say those words, once before. But this time the phrasing was just slightly different.

Outside the helicraft, a light snow was falling. The wind shifted, carrying a few flakes inside the cargo bay's open door. Shivering, Alexi pulled on his trousers and Soldatenkof's flak jacket. Juliana already had the *ushanka* pulled down over her ears, and held the blankets around her as she stood. Her teeth chattered as she looked around the cargo bay.

"I'm freezing." She looked ruefully at the crumpled therm suit, then at the alien, who was tapping its staff, clearly impatient for them to set off. "You might not need clothes to protect you from the cold, but we do," she told Raheek.

As Alexi laced up his boots, Juliana began rummaging through the cargo bay's storage lockers. Only as she started to turn the handle of one in the back did Alexi remember the gruesome cargo he'd hidden inside it.

"Wait!" he shouted.

Juliana looked back over her shoulder at him, one hand on the latch that would open the locker. "What's wrong?" she asked. "Are you worried there's another growler on board?"

"What do you mean?" Alexi asked.

She pointed at the locker next to it. For the first time, Alexi noticed the hole that was melted in the bottom of its door and the bullet marks that pocked the floor in front of the locker. He had no idea what she was talking about— something that had happened during one of his blackouts, perhaps? He remembered shooting at the arm of the growler that had been clinging to the bottom of the helicraft earlier, when it reached in through the hatch on the floor. But that hole in the locker looked like an incendiary round had hit it.

"Don't worry," Juliana said. "The growler is dead, thanks to your quick thinking, and the helicraft is clear."

Before Alexi could stop her, she opened the door of the locker in which Alexi had hidden Soldatenkof, and the *Leitenant*'s corpse fell out. Cold and stiff, it hit the deck of the cargo bay with a loud crash. A puffy finger broke off and skittered across the floor.

Juliana stared at the corpse without flinching. She'd obviously seen as much combat as Alexi had, to be unfazed by its sudden appearance.

"Who is he?" she asked.

"A coward," Alexi answered. "And my commanding officer. He was hiding in the helicraft while the squad was fighting growlers in Tomsk 13. But the growlers got him, anyway."

Juliana looked pointedly at the jacket Alexi was wearing. "And if he was in the locker all this time, how did you come to be wearing his jacket, Corporal?"

The edge was back in her voice. Alexi suddenly remembered that she, too, was an officer. And that she came from an army that treated its officers with respect. He wondered if looting an officer's corpse was cause for court-martial in the Union forces—or if the Union executed a squad when its officer died. Somehow, he suspected the answer was no.

Alexi deflected her question. "Soldatenkof's greatcoat is in the next storage locker," he said. "It should be small enough to fit you. And there are some spare combat boots."

"We must leave now," the alien reminded them. "Gather those supplies you need."

The voice was quiet, but it crackled in Alexi's mind like a command. He grabbed a backpack and began stuffing it with whatever might be useful: the few bandages from the first-aid kit, extra ammunition for his AK-51, the blankets, some tubes of the vile-tasting sausage paste, two frag grenades, the helicraft's emergency flares . . .

He couldn't shake the feeling there was something else they should be taking with them—something too important to be left behind. But he couldn't see anything else that he should add to their meager supplies. Eventually, he picked up Soldatenkof's empty vodka bottle, figuring it would come in handy if they needed a container in which to melt snow.

Beside him, Juliana pulled on Soldatenkof's greatcoat and laced up the boots. Then she bent over the *leitenant*'s corpse and started to unfasten the holster that held his pistol.

"Don't," Alexi said. "Leave it." The Viper was a weapon of discipline, as loathsome as a slave master's whip.

Juliana ignored him. She slid the pistol from the holster and pulled its magazine free. Then she tossed the weapon into a corner, where it landed with a clatter. "It only has one bullet left in the magazine," she said.

Alexi's eyes widened in surprise. If the *leitenant*'s ammunition had been that low, Soldatenkof would have been faced with the dangerous prospect of enforcing discipline entirely by bluff. Alexi glared at the frozen corpse. No wonder he'd stayed inside the helicraft. If the squad had known he'd only had one bullet left . . .

Juliana held up her Pug pistol, then shoved it into the pocket of her greatcoat. "I've still got my own weapon," she reminded him.

Alexi frowned. Why had she told him that? Was she letting him know that she, too, had the officer's favorite disciplinary tool? Or perhaps she wanted to remind him that she was still quite capable of taking him prisoner.

Just as she had when they had first sighted . . .

The thought vanished.

The alien didn't wait for Juliana to finish her preparations. Instead it descended from the rear hatch and disappeared into the forest that surrounded the helicraft. The creature hadn't said a word; it seemed to expect the humans to follow. Alexi and Juliana had to scramble to catch up to it. They plowed through the snow, following its footprints.

Within minutes, Alexi was sweating under the armored jacket he wore. The alien walked quickly, on long spindly legs, the butt of its staff thumping neat holes in the snow. Its pace had the humans nearly jogging to keep up.

Alexi walked between the alien and Juliana; he noticed that she had deliberately taken the rear. Whether that was because she felt herself more competent to deal with any attack from that direction or whether she didn't want Alexi at her back, he couldn't say.

He waded through the snow after the alien, trying to stretch his pace so he could use the same footprints in the snow. They wound their way through the forest, following the path Raheek had made earlier, and crossed a frozen stream. The snow was trampled, as if Raheek had tested the ice carefully before crossing. Good thing, too—just upriver, a hole had formed in the ice. Alexi guessed that spring was early in coming to Siberia if the thaw was beginning already.

As they walked along through the forest, he looked at the alien's narrow blue back. The creature stood head and shoulders taller than Alexi. It strode through the *taiga* without looking back, confident the two humans were following it. The alien was warm-blooded, that much was implied by the sweet-smelling puffs of air that came from its mouth as it walked. But it was oblivious to the cold. The snow that fell around its bald head and shoulders seemed to melt a centimeter above its skin and slide away without ever touching its body. Alexi wondered if it had some sort of protective force field shielding it or whether the effect was magical.

At first, it had seemed natural to be marching away from the helicraft, out into the snowy Siberian wilderness. In the hurry to get dressed and pack his gear, Alexi hadn't stopped to ask any questions. But now they tumbled through his mind. He knew that the alien was headed to the meteor impact site—it had insisted that Juliana fly the helicraft northeast after taking off from Tomsk 13. She was obviously useful in getting the alien to where it wanted to be. But what was Alexi's role in all of this?

The alien must have explained what was going on during one of Alexi's blackouts. That was how Juliana had known what its name was. Alexi hoped Raheek wouldn't become angry if asked to repeat itself. The blue-skinned creature had an aura of power about it, a fluid grace and confidence that suggested it could cut either of the humans down with its blade-tipped staff without effort or even conscious thought. And then there was the ball of howling energy it had conjured up out of thin air. Looking into its swirling depths had been even more terrifying than looking down the barrel of Soldatenkof's Viper pistol.

They trudged along for several long minutes before

Alexi worked up enough courage to break the silence. He wasn't sure how to address the alien, so he fell into a familiar pattern.

"Sir?" he said.

Silence. Alexi tried again—maybe he'd gotten the gender wrong. "Ma'am?"

The alien didn't turn around.

"Raheek?"

This time, the alien acknowledged him. "Your question?" it asked over its shoulder.

Alexi was going to ask what the meteorite was. But then the answer bubbled up out of his subconscious. Without ever having been told, he suddenly knew the thing was a weapon. He had a brief flash of a pyramid-shaped object . . .

The words seemed to come by themselves, as if someone other than Alexi were speaking them: "The crystal—how does it work?"

The alien spun around so quickly that Alexi nearly crashed into it. Raheek's blue-black eyes bored into Alexi's.

"How do you know the meteorite's structure?" Raheek asked, its voice a white-noise hiss.

Behind Alexi, Juliana had paused and was listening intently.

"I . . . ah . . ." Alexi swallowed. His hands sketched a triangle in the air. His forehead felt pinched, as if he were concentrating hard. Yet his thoughts were swirling, unfocused. The trees around him were a blur, as if his glasses had iced over. Yet Raheek's face remained in sharp focus.

"Well, by its pyramid shape, I guess," Alexi continued. "The tetrahedron is one of the basic crystalline structures that . . ."

He blinked, and the forest around him came back into focus again. His mind cleared. He felt like a teacher who had suddenly lost his lecture notes and wasn't sure what came next. The tidal wave of insight that had been about to flood his mind with information had ebbed away.

"Uh . . . What was I just saying?"

Raheek's lips opened and closed rapidly, making faint smacking noises. Alexi somehow knew that this was the alien equivalent of a smile.

Juliana looked back and forth between Alexi and the alien. Then her gaze settled on Raheek.

"You said the meteorite was a bomb," she told it. "One that had hit its target—Earth—and was about to go off. You promised to show it to us. But now it sounds as though Alexi has already seen it. Or that he knows what it will look like. Which makes me wonder if he was really guessing when he told you where it was."

It took Alexi a moment to figure out what she was suggesting. "If it's a bomb, it's not one of ours, if that's what you're implying," he said. "At least, I don't think so."

"Alexi is correct," Raheek said. "It is not one of your planet's weapons. It was built by the Shard."

"The what?" Alexi and Juliana both asked the question at the same time.

"The Shard: an elder species, with technology even more advanced than our own," Raheek answered. "They are a silicon-based life-form, with a hatred of all other creatures. Their weapons, their tools—even their own bodies—have crystalline forms. They regard carbon-based life-forms just as we would view a virus—as something to be eliminated. They wish to wipe the universe clean of us—both your species and mine."

"So it really is a bomb?" Juliana asked. "I thought it was a . . ." After a moment's thought, she asked another question. "Why did it target us?"

"The beacon," Raheek said. "Your species has the unfortunate habit of finding crystals beautiful and placing value on them. A group of your space travelers brought back to your moon a crystal that was actually a Shard transmitter. It served as a homing beacon for the bomb."

"Is this bomb really capable of destroying our planet?" Juliana asked.

The alien gave the hand flick that Alexi now recognized as an affirmative. "When the bomb activates, it will tear apart the very fabric of local space-time. Space will lose its coherency as one of its four dimensions—time—becomes chaotic. The atoms that make up this planet—and everything on it—will become unstable and break apart into their smallest atomic components. Where your world once existed, there will be nothing more than an infinite distortion of space-time, one in which matter occupies every possible moment in time that ever was, is, or will be."

Juliana gave Raheek a skeptical look. "How can a crystal do that?"

The alien gestured at the GPS on Juliana's wrist. "It is like the silicon-based circuits you use in your machinery," Raheek said. "Only on a much larger and more complex scale."

"It's a gigantic computer chip?" Alexi asked.

"Similar," Raheek answered. "But not exactly the same."

"Is there a way to scramble its code?" Juliana asked. "Depending upon how it's stored, data is susceptible to being erased. If the software that runs the thing is recorded using a magnetic format, the bomb could be disrupted with an electromagnetic pulse."

Alexi glanced guiltily at her. He wondered if she'd guessed how her therm suit had been disabled.

"I know of no way to affect the crystal," Raheek said. "Its programming, as you call it, is an integral part of its crystalline structure and cannot be tampered with by physical means. We Zykhee assume that all such attempts by other races failed, given that there now are a number of severe time-space distortions in our universe where planets once orbited."

Other races? Alexi stared in wonder at Raheek. In the

past few days, Alexi had come to accept the harsh reality of the growlers and the enigma of the blue-skinned Zykhee, who seemed to be both friend and enemy in one. Before the Change, scientists had searched in vain for a single iota of evidence of life elsewhere in the universe. Now, it seemed, the Earth was occupying a universe that was filled with alien species.

"There must be a way to disarm the bomb," Juliana insisted.

"That is what I hope to learn," Raheek said solemnly. "The Shard are certain to eventually seed our own system with these devices. It's only a matter of—"

"Of time?" Alexi asked, rejoining the conversation. He stared at Raheek, trying to remember something. The alien was trapped on Earth because . . .

An image came to him: a spaceship, crashed on a rooftop in Vladivostok. And of one of these blue-skinned aliens hurling a weapon that tore open Alexi's chest. . . .

Alexi pushed the second half of the thought aside. Ridiculous. He was alive, wasn't he?

Juliana glanced up at the sky, then at Raheek. "If we figure out how to disarm the bomb, how are you going to get home again?"

"My people will come for me," Raheek said. "But they will not risk another ship and crew until they are certain the bomb has been disabled."

Alexi picked up the logic thread. "If we don't succeed in disarming the bomb, and it goes off, you'll be killed along with the rest of us." He paused and stared at the forest that surrounded them. The Maw had yet to rise in the east, but light was filtering down through the snow-covered trees.

"There's one thing I still don't understand," Alexi continued. "Juliana is useful to you. She flew you here in the helicraft, and I'm assuming you're taking her with you now because she studied computer science at university and might be able to figure out the crystal's programming. But why me? I'm just a history teacher—"

"A history teacher who figured out that the bomb must have landed in the same spot as the Tunguska meteorite," Juliana interjected.

"Oh." But that had been Alexi's sole contribution, as far as he could see.

Raheek cupped Alexi's chin in overlong fingers—warm to the touch, despite the cold, Alexi noted—and forced him to look into its eyes. "There is something more about you," it said. "An answer, hidden in your subconscious. I sensed it, the first time I saw you. I knew you would lead me here. That is why I followed you."

"You followed me?" Alexi asked. Then the pieces came together in his mind. The impenetrable darkness he'd seen on the helicraft as it pulled away from Vladivostok, and again in the shadows of the ruined buildings of Tomsk 13, and the countless other times he had seen and dismissed it. It had been Raheek, using its magical powers.

Powers that had no rational explanation. But there seemed to be a pattern to the hypnotic properties of the swirling tattoos on the other Zykhee, and Raheek's own abilities: to make them see a cloud of inky blackness, instead of its own body; to heal; to terrify. A pattern that suggested that the aliens were capable of manipulating human minds.

"What are you?" Alexi asked. "Some sort of psychic?"

"The closest word in your language is mystic," Raheek answered. "I use the flame that is the essence of all and the darkness that is the void to shape the energies that surround us."

"What word would you use to describe what you do?" Alexi asked. "Psychic powers? Religious belief? Magic?"

"Sounds like mumbo jumbo to me," Juliana muttered. She caught Alexi's eye and nodded at the alien's staff. "It's probably an advanced form of tech. Think how your assault rifle would look to an ancient Roman. Like magic."

She stamped her feet and hugged the greatcoat closer to her. "It's too cold to stand here," she said. "Let's move out. I want to see this bomb. We can talk as we walk. I'll take point." Her eyes fastened hungrily on the forest ahead. Alexi could see that she was driven by her curiosity, needing a closer look at the bomb. If Alexi had a choice in the matter, he would have been traveling in the other direction—any smart soldier put as much distance between himself and un-exploded ordnance as possible. But if what Raheek said was true and the bomb really could destroy Earth, there was no place left to run.

Juliana trudged past Raheek and Alexi and continued on along the path that the alien had made in the snow on its first visit to the impact site. Within a few minutes, the flat gray base of the pyramid came into view over the tree line. Alexi, trailing behind the alien, paused to stare at it in wonder. But Juliana and Raheek pressed on. In a few moments, trees screened them from sight.

The snow was falling more thickly now, silently dusting the shoulders of Alexi's jacket and softening the trail of footprints in the snow. He glanced at the trail behind them, which was starting to fill with snow. Would they be able to find their way back to the helicraft? Alexi wondered if it even mattered. With no fuel, the downed craft was useful only as a shelter. If no rescue came—and Alexi had no rea-son to expect it to—they would eventually freeze to death or starve, shelter or not.

He glanced around at the stunted trees. The snow lay heavily on their branches, bending them toward the earth. Except for one pine whose branches were green against the sea of white. The trunk of the tree was scuffed, as if a deer had stopped to rub its antlers against the bark.

Amazing, Alexi thought, that wildlife still existed in Siberia. Even up here, far to the north of any urban centers, patches of black marred the snow. A number of the trees were stunted from acid rain—or acid snow, to be more accurate—and more than one showed the twin trunks that were a hallmark of pesticide poisoning. Alexi wondered if this part of Siberia had ever been used as a dumping ground for toxic waste.

The tree that was bare of snow was about ten meters away. Squinting, Alexi could see that a trail through the snow led up to it and away again. He walked toward the tree, toying with the idea of following the animal if the trail was still fresh. If they could shoot a deer, the meat would help them survive. Assuming the deer wasn't radiation-poisoned or filled with toxins.

The marks on the tree were too high for a deer to have made them. They looked more like teeth marks. And they were fresh; sap oozing from the wound in the bark had not yet frozen. The trail in the snow was also fresh; only a light dusting of the falling snow lay over it. But it hadn't been made by the hoofprints of a deer. Instead it looked almost like Raheek's footprints. Bare feet—only much larger. Bigger even than the footprints of a Cyclops. And clumped in widely spaced pairs, as if the person that made them had been hopping. Alexi had seen footprints like that once before—but where?

Gunfire shattered his reverie.

Running back the way he had come, he fumbled the strap of his AK-51 off his shoulder with cold-numbed hands. By the time he had brought his weapon to bear on the forest ahead, someone was already almost on top of his position. A blue-skinned figure, holding the limp form of Juliana in its double-jointed arms. A livid purple crease in the alien's side leaked lavender blood.

Alexi had a sudden, horrible premonition of what Raheek was going to say next. It felt as if this was a movie that Alexi had seen once before, as if the alien were speaking from a script.

"There is an automated weapon, sixty-three paces ahead," Raheek told him. "A weapon of Earth. Go no farther, or you will cause it to fire."

Alexi stared at Juliana. She hung limp in the alien's arms. The chest of her greatcoat was dark with blood. Red trickled down into the snow in a steady stream.

Alexi rubbed his arm. It had suddenly begun to ache, as if wounded. The pain triggered an almost-memory.

"Raheek," he said. "Use your magic. Heal her."

The alien set Juliana down. The snow crunched gently as her weight settled into it.

"I can no longer embrace her with healing energies," Raheek said. "She is dead."

Alexi shook his head. No. No. This was all wrong. This wasn't the way Juliana was supposed to die.

She wasn't supposed to die at all. . . .

22

Alexi paused, halfway up the slope of rubble. He glanced back over his shoulder, up at the night sky. The Maw hung over the skyline of Vladivostok, separated from the moon by the skeletal remains of a ruined building. Above them, a star blazed with a fierce red light. It was brighter than the other stars—the unfamiliar constellations that had sprung into being during the Change. And it seemed to have a faint bulge at one side.

Alexi couldn't shake the feeling that the star was watching him. That it had just noticed him, and would come streaking down to obliterate him if he didn't . . .

The thought was gone. An explosion rattled the ground beneath him, and the rubble he was crouched on shifted slightly. His glasses slid down his nose, and for a moment his surroundings became a fuzzy blur. Pushing his glasses back up his nose, he looked up to where Boris had heaved open the door to what used to be the ruined building's second story.

"Come on, Alexi," the big man shouted over his shoulder. "This will make a fine vantage point."

A sense of dread gripped Alexi, preventing him from

climbing any farther. Unable to speak, unable to articulate or even understand his fears, he shook his head and began scrambling back down the rubble.

"Hey!" Boris shouted. "Where are you going?"

Alexi didn't have time to explain. Someone was coming his way.

No, some *thing* was coming his way.

As he ran back the way they had just come, Boris's voice crackled over the speaker in Alexi's helmet.

. . . wish you luck, Alexi, but . . . rubles says you don't . . .

Alexi didn't know where he was running to. Or why. He gave a wide berth to the street where the heavy-assault suit had been downed—the one that was lying in a crater in the road, making the street impassable. The crippled assault suit had been the squad's objective. Unable to move its legs, it was a target the rad grunts actually had a chance of taking out. But elsewhere in the city, other assault suits were chewing their way through the Battalion of Death, helping it live up to its nickname.

After a couple of blocks, Alexi slowed to a walk. He was exhausted, after three days and nights of fighting with only brief snatches of sleep. The battle of Vladivostok had become one long, painful blur. The AK-51 was like a lead weight in his hand, and his armored vest was as heavy as a waterlogged blanket. He could barely put one foot in front of another. All he wanted to do was just sit down somewhere and rest.

But something drove him on, some sixth sense that he had to keep moving. He couldn't stop now, he thought, glancing up at the sky. Not with that beady red eye glaring down at him.

He found himself in a street outside Vladivostok's athletic stadium. The charred remains of a Chem Grunt lay in the street. The tanks on the soldier's back had ruptured, and their spilled contents had spread across the road and were on fire. Tiny blue flames flickered across the oily-looking surface. Alexi was just deciding whether to circle around the edge of the flaming puddle or cut through the stadium when he heard the unmistakable whir and grind of a heavy-assault suit approaching.

He ducked behind a burnt-out automobile whose tires had been melted into gooey black puddles on the cement. Which way was the suit coming from? It was impossible to tell; the entire city was filled with the sounds of battle. The chatter of automatic rifles and the dull *whumff* of exploding mortars echoed off the buildings, or was funneled by the rubble-strewn corridors of the streets, making it impossible to pick out the sound of the assault suit.

Alexi raised himself above the burnt-out auto for a look, but ducked back as quickly as he could.

Christ! The assault suit was closer than he'd thought. It had paused, standing arrogantly with its feet in the puddle of burning toxins. By the light of the flames at its feet, Alexi could make out every detail of the suit. The metal monster was a bright green, with *leitenant*'s bars painted on the shoulder and what looked like a yellow thunderhead— or perhaps a mushroom cloud—on its chest. An inscription had been lettered in vivid red across the thunderhead: VENGEANCE.

Funny, why would a Union soldier write her nickname in the Cyrillic alphabet? Was it actually a Neo-Soviet suit? Alexi had heard rumors that the Neo-Soviet Union was working furiously to develop its own version of the weapon, but had yet to see one in action.

Alexi took another quick look. No, those shoulder flashes were Union, all right. The soldier inside that suit was Alexi's enemy. As soon as she spotted Alexi, he was dead meat.

That thought made him pause. How had he known it was a woman inside the suit, when the mirrored faceplate completely hid the soldier's features?

No time to think about that now. This assault suit was heavily armed, with a machine gun built into one arm and a rocket launcher gyro-mounted on the opposite shoulder. By some miracle, the soldier inside it hadn't spotted Alexi yet, even though the suit was facing his hiding place.

The suit had been headed in the direction Alexi had just come from. Toward his squad. When it reached them, it would chew through them like a meat grinder. Alexi could even picture the way in which each of them would die. Boris would be blown right out of that second-story vantage point he'd chosen, someone else would be machine-gunned down from a fire escape, and the *leitenant* would shoot at least one of the squad members in a misguided fit of rage. Probably poor Vanya, Alexi thought. The musician had already been unlucky twice today, first by getting a bad batch of antirad pills and second by losing his favorite music tape—one he'd carried with him for nearly two years. And bad luck usually came in threes. . . .

Alexi decided that it wasn't his problem. Without rad grenades, there was nothing he could do to prevent the deaths of the others in his squad, anyway. He decided to save his own skin instead.

He heard the whir of gyros as the assault suit started moving. Or was that the sound of its machine gun swiveling in his direction? Whichever was causing the noise, it was time to get out of there.

Sucking in a lungful of air, he planted his feet like a sprinter at the starting line and made sure the strap of his assault rifle wasn't hanging free. The last thing he needed was for it to catch on something and slow him down. Then he bolted for the stadium.

Alexi hadn't been much of an athlete in school. During his three months of basic training in the induction center, he'd always been the slowest of the new recruits. The non-commissioned officer who had overseen his physical training had yelled himself hoarse, trying to berate Alexi into keeping up with the others. But Alexi's former gymnastics teachers and *praporshchik* would have been proud of him now. He flew like the wind over the short distance between the burnt-out auto and the front doors of the stadium, leaping the turnstiles with the grace of a hurdler.

A machine gun opened up in the street outside. Bullets spanged off the turnstile, sending its arms whirling round. As Alexi ran down the wide corridor that led from the entrance to the stadium's floor, he heard the crunching thud of running footsteps and the screech of metal as the turnstile was wrenched from its mounting. Christ save me, he thought. That assault suit is coming straight for me.

Why me?

Assault rifle held in one hand, Alexi took a tight corner, then clattered down a flight of metal steps. Too late, he saw that he was headed for the open expanse of the stadium floor. The rows of seats to either side of him offered a tempting hiding place, but their flimsy plastic offered no protection. The second the soldier inside the assault suit saw Alexi, a single burst of machine-gun fire would punch through those seats like paper. The assault suit wouldn't even need to use its rockets.

Alexi hit the floor of the stadium and sprinted across it. The artificial turf was pitted with crater holes and had been scuffed away by the force of the explosions that had heaved the bare concrete underneath. Alexi ran a zigzag course around these obstacles, ears cocked for the sound of the assault suit behind him.

Machine-gun bullets stitched a line of holes in the artificial turf just to the side of Alexi. And a crater was just ahead. To zigzag around it, Alexi would have to run into that deadly stitchery of lead.

Legs pumping, lungs on fire, body surging with adrenaline, Alexi leapt into the air. His jump carried him to the far end of the crater in the floor, just barely. The toe of his boot just caught the edge, then slipped.

Crashing to his knees saved him. Like a soccer player who had tripped over the ball, Alexi tumbled out of the way of the hail of lead.

In an instant he was back up on his hands and knees. He crawled under the nearest of the seats, shimmying in through the gap between the bottom of the bleacher and the floor. Dragging his assault rifle behind him, he rolled behind a concrete pillar that shielded him from the next burst of bullets. Then he got to his feet and ran.

Behind him, he heard the crunching footsteps of the assault suit as it thudded down the stairs. Alexi wound his way through the scaffolding that supported the seats over his head and found a door that led out onto a lower level of the stadium. As he wrenched it open, he risked a glance behind him.

Motors whining, the assault suit lurched into high gear and ran across the stadium floor. It crossed the crater Alexi had leapt with an easy stride, then crashed shoulder first into the hollow metal tubes that formed the scaffolding of the bleacher seats. Muscling its way through them, it smashed the metal tubes to either side like toothpicks.

Breathing heavily, Alexi ran up a sloping corridor, the assault suit hot on his heels. He saw a door and ducked through it, out onto the street.

The cold air gave him a burst of fresh energy. He ran the length of the block, and was about to turn right at the first intersection he came to. But something made him pause and reconsider. He was running away from the assault suit. But at the same time he had the strange feeling he was running *toward* something, as well. Without understanding why, he continued straight ahead.

Bad move. Seconds later, he heard the heavy footsteps of the assault suit behind him as it emerged from the stadium and pounded down the street.

Only the fact that the street was choked with rubble saved Alexi. The block was a long one, but the heaps of broken concrete and fallen utility poles gave him cover as he ran its gauntlet. The heavy-assault suit, unable to get a clear shot, held its fire. But it didn't give up the chase.

Panting with fear, Alexi turned right at the next intersection. He should have kept running, but his lungs were on fire, and he was starting to get dizzy. He was forced to slow to a jog. This street had less debris on it; Alexi could pay attention to what was behind him, instead of to the uneven ground underfoot. But instead of looking over his shoulder to see if the assault suit was still pursuing him, he glanced up at the sky. There—the faint whistling noise that he could hear above the explosions that rocked the rest of Vladivostok. It seemed to be coming from the red star that Alexi had seen in the sky earlier. The reddish glow had grown a tail, and was now larger than any other star in the sky. A meteorite, falling to Earth. It wanted Alexi to stop, to admire the spectacle that it made as it fell from the heavens. . . .

A chattering explosion of sound came from just behind Alexi. Machine-gun fire chipped a wall to his right.

Suddenly it didn't matter if his lungs were ready to burst. It was run—or die.

Alexi was in the middle of the intersection of two broad avenues, completely exposed. The only shelter nearby was a sprawling building on one corner whose front doors had been torn off by an explosion. Racing for its cavelike entrance, Alexi sprinted inside, his lungs on fire and his legs as weak and loose as spaghetti. Only as he staggered deeper into the building and saw shattered display cases on either side did he realize what it was. A museum.

He glanced back over his shoulder, out through the ruined entrance. The assault suit was still following him. It was running across the intersection even then, and within seconds would be inside the building.

Suddenly Alexi heard shouts and rifle fire coming from just up the street. The speaker in his helmet crackled to life. For some reason, it had become functional again, but instead of picking up Alexi's own squad, it had tuned in to the frequency used by the squad in the street outside. Alexi heard snatches of an officer yelling at his men and soldiers calling out to each other in panic as they realized they had blundered headlong into the heavy-assault suit.

. . . to your left, Mikhail. Watch . . .

. . . grenade at . . . before . . .

Alexi heard a *whoosh* and then the crumping explosion of a rocket. An explosion lit up the night.

. . . my leg, oh God it . . .

. . . fall back, you stupid . . .

That would be the officer. He sounded as bad as Soldatenkof. No surprise. They all did.

Granted a temporary reprieve, Alexi stood and sucked in lungfuls of air as he watched the battle unfold in the street outside the museum. The assault suit's machine gun droned in a steady chatter as the Neo-Soviet soldiers dived for cover; Alexi could see red fire strobing out of its barrel. Just behind the assault suit, one soldier was trying to creep across the street. Her Uzi was slung across her back and both of her hands were full. She carried a gas can in one hand and had a sack slung over her opposite shoulder. For the moment, the heavy-assault suit was busy mowing down the others in her squad. But in another second or two, it would turn and have her in its sights.

Alexi had a sudden premonition: She wasn't meant to die out there. But she would, unless Alexi did something. And quickly.

He suddenly saw a solution. Lying in the street a meter or two in front of the heavy-assault suit was an abandoned street vendor's cart. The bottom of the *pirozhke* cart still held a bulbous white propane tank. If there was any fuel left in it . . .

The soldier holding the gas can began to sprint across the street.

The assault suit polished off the last of the rad squad and began to turn in her direction.

And Alexi, contrary to all common sense, stepped back out through the museum entrance and fired a burst from his AK-51 at the propane tank.

The tank exploded with a sudden, hot flash of blue flame. Distracted by the blast, the assault suit whirled in that direction instead. The soldier ran into the museum, unseen. Now that she was closer, Alexi could see that she was very pretty, with shoulder-length brown hair and wide brown eyes.

"*Spahseebe*," she panted.

The speaker in Alexi's helmet had fallen silent again.

"The others in your squad," he said. "I don't think they made it."

"Not my problem," she grunted. Then her glance flickered to the corporal's stripes on the shoulder of Alexi's armored vest.

Outside in the street, the heavy-assault suit was turning in a slow circle, surveying the carnage it had created. One of its heavy metal feet stepped on the belly of a dead soldier, pulping it to mush. The mirrored plate that hid the Union soldier's face turned toward the museum entrance—paused—then slowly scanned away again.

Time to move.

As they fell back into the shadows of the museum, Alexi put out a hand to help the other soldier with the sack she carried, but she shook her head fiercely and pulled it away. All at once, Alexi realized what was going on. The woman didn't care about the dead soldiers outside because she wasn't part of that squad. She was on her own. And she didn't want Alexi to take the sack because it held something she didn't want him to see. She was a looter—and probably a deserter.

A sudden thought entered Alexi's mind: Why not join her? They could ride out of Vladivostok together and . . .

Ride? What a strange thought. On what?

The woman jogged down a side corridor. She seemed to know where she was going, so Alexi followed her. They turned a corner, and in the dim light that filtered in through holes in the wall and ceiling, he could see crouched shapes on either side. One of them—a huge figure twice the size of a man with arms extended over its head—shifted slightly as a distant explosion trembled the ground underfoot.

Alexi blasted it with his AK-51.

"*Nyet!*" the other soldier shouted. "It's only a stuffed bear! Hold your fire!"

Silently, Alexi berated himself. She was right. The figures on either side were nothing more than stuffed animals. Had he given away his position to the assault suit? He listened, but couldn't hear anything over the static in his helmet. He gave it a thump, and the static settled down some.

Cursing under her breath, the looter moved deeper into the museum, past a display of paintings. Alexi started to follow, then balked when he saw another shifting shadow. This one was as tall as the stuffed bear, but had spindly legs and stick arms that seemed to have been broken at odd angles. One of its hands seemed to have a chunk of glittering metal embedded in it—probably shrapnel from a frag grenade or bomb. Alexi squinted to get a better look—and in an eyeblink, the entire figure was gone. Where the thin animal had stood a moment ago, now there was only bare wall.

Alexi relaxed his grip on the AK-51 and backed away slowly from the spot where the shadow had been. Something about the taxidermy display had unnerved him, causing him to hallucinate. He had to get out of there.

The woman had disappeared around a bend. Instead of following her, Alexi wound his way back toward the main corridor and peered carefully down it toward the main entrance. The assault suit was still standing in the street, its neck craned as it looked up at the roof of the museum. Then it lowered its head and began moving toward the museum's shattered main entrance.

Alexi froze, praying that the assault suit didn't have infrared sensors. His camouflaged combats would help him blend with the shadows if he only held still enough. The urban camo pattern might even be enough to fool a soldier using low-light enhancement. He held his AK-51 at the ready in sweaty hands, prepared to make a final defense, even though he knew his bullets would never penetrate that thick metal skin. . . .

Suddenly gunfire erupted from somewhere behind Alexi. He identified the weapon at once by its distinctive sound: an Uzi. The looter was shooting at something. Damn her! Alexi had been a fool to provide that distraction for her by shooting the propane tank, and now she was giving away his position. But something else told Alexi that she'd done exactly what she had been meant to do, that she had some sort of destiny to fulfill tonight. And he knew with grim certainty what this destiny would include: death.

But hers—or his?

The assault suit's engines whirred as it sprang into a run—straight into the museum.

Alexi made himself as small a target as possible, and to his amazement, it worked. The assault suit ran right by him, its heavy feet shaking the floor as it passed.

Alexi jumped to his feet and started to run for the front door, then heard the assault suit returning behind him. He skidded to a stop. No. Out through the front doors wasn't the way to go. Out in the street, the assault suit would find him again. And that *thing* in the sky would be able to see him.

Instead he turned and ran in the other direction, up a staircase. He couldn't say why, but it felt like the right way to go. There was something on the second floor—someone who could help him . . .

Someone? The lack of sleep and food over the past few

days was catching up with him, playing tricks on his mind. Once again, he was starting to hallucinate.

As the heavy-assault suit thudded into the corridor below, Alexi reached the top of the stairs. Something slid away under his foot, a loose chunk of tile. Alexi sprawled, painfully twisting an ankle. He gripped the banister, hauled himself to his feet. Then he limped away as quickly as he could while the assault suit thudded up the stairs. He entered another corridor . . .

And found himself face-to-face with a ghost. At least, that was what it had to be. Standing nearly three meters tall, the human-shaped figure was impossibly thin, and impossible to see clearly. The only details Alexi could make out were its overlong arms—which somehow seemed to be articulated in the wrong direction—and the thick mane of hair that framed its head. Blurred and shifting, it was lit from above by moonlight that shone down through a hole in the ceiling. It stood utterly still, yet only one thing stood out clearly: the weapon it held in one hand. It was a glittering crescent of highly polished metal with a razor-sharp edge. Alexi blinked. Since when did ghosts arm themselves with what looked like a steel boomerang?

Alexi's training screamed at him to shoot the figure with his AK-51. But a sixth sense told him that if he did, he would die. Just as the looter had. His imagination filled in the rest of the picture: The pain of his aching lungs became a slash in his chest. Instead of gasping for breath, he was losing it through his torn lung in a rush. . . .

Alexi staggered past the figure on his twisted ankle, making no hostile moves. Pretending that he hadn't seen it, he slumped in the shadow of a display case. Here was as good a place to die as any. He couldn't go a single step more. He wouldn't. Staring through its glass sides, he peered around the delicate vase inside the case and watched for the heavy-assault suit.

It was already at the top of the stairs. It hesitated on the landing, the faceplate swiveling left and right. Then it saw Alexi.

No—it saw the blurry figure. Moving with machine-augmented speed, the soldier inside the assault suit brought the machine gun on its arm to bear. In that same instant, the blurry figure hurled the weapon in its hand. Alexi gulped in amazement as the boomerang sliced through the assault suit's chest in a spray of sparks, leaving a deep gouge in the heavy-gauge steel. But the soldier inside the suit didn't seem to be hurt, and her return attack was even more effective. Bullets punched into the blurry figure, sending a spray of purplish droplets into the air. In the midst of the hail of bullets, the blurry figure crouched and sprang into a leap—straight up through a hole in the roof.

The soldier inside the assault suit must have seen Alexi; he wasn't even trying to hide anymore. All he could do was brace himself for the machine-gun burst that would end it for him. He reached inside his combats for the cross around his neck and began to pray for a swift, clean death.

But the assault suit ignored him.

Instead it followed the figure that had leapt up through the hole in the ceiling, reaching up with heavy metallic arms and hauling itself bodily onto the rooftop. Plaster and concrete tumbled down into the room as the edges of the hole crumbled, but the ceiling held. Now the assault suit was on the museum's roof. Alexi heard more gunfire and the meaty sound of bullets striking flesh. And then, in the silence that followed, the sound of the assault suit walking across the rooftop. The lighting fixtures over Alexi's head trembled under its heavy tread. He wondered if the Union soldier was walking back toward the hole in the ceiling—if she would jump back down to finish him off. But the footsteps seemed to be receding from Alexi's position. Then they stopped.

Alexi listened to his heart pounding, wondering what would happen next. This might be his only chance to escape. He rose to his feet and tested his weight on his twisted ankle.

It wasn't too bad, just a slight sprain. It hurt, but he could still walk on it.

Up on the rooftop, everything was still quiet. The assault suit had stopped moving around. A thought struck Alexi: There was something above him, on the roof of the museum. Something that had completely captured the attention of the soldier inside the assault suit. Alexi had a brief premonition of a gigantic, crippled spider—and then the flash was gone.

One thing remained: the realization that, like any soldier who had found something of interest, the Union soldier above him would be radioing her commanding officer to come and have a look. Alexi had to get away from there. As quickly as possible.

He limped back down the stairs, using the banister to support himself. He had to get away. In his mind's eye, he pictured dozens of heavy-assault suits sprinting toward the museum. Like the tragic king in Shakespeare's play, Alexi would trade all of the Neo-Soviet Union for a horse.

Or a motorcycle . . .

Wait a moment. The looter had been carrying a petrol can. Which meant . . .

Alexi turned and limped in the direction she had taken. This time there were no menacing shadows. He passed the taxidermy exhibit, patting a saber-toothed tiger on the head as he went by, and entered a room that held a display of weapons from the second of the World Wars.

There. It was almost exactly as he'd pictured it—except that the angle he was viewing it from was slightly different and the pool of blood around the corpse was fresher and smaller. The body of the looter lay on the ground with her stomach and chest slashed open, the petrol can on the floor near her hand. And beside her, miracle of miracles, was a motorcycle.

Alexi grinned and snapped a salute at the dead woman on the floor. Somehow he knew that the ancient motorcycle would still start, once he filled it with petrol from that can. And that all he had to do was ride it out of here, then hook up with his squad again, once they reached the harbor.

Which they would in about an hour . . .

Alexi didn't even bother stopping to wonder how he knew that. He picked up the petrol can, filled the gas tank, and started up the motorcycle. He revved it, cringing at the roaring noise and wondering if the Union soldier in the assault suit could hear it, up on the roof of the museum. Then he roared out through the ruined front doors of the building.

On a whim, he turned the bike toward the battalion headquarters. He might as well pick up a few grenades on his way back to the squad. He had a feeling they were going to need them. . . .

23

Do you mean to tell me that you were the soldier I chased into the museum?" The Union officer's chuckle echoed against the metal walls of the cargo bay. "So you're the one I have to thank for my promotion."

She lay beside Alexi in the darkness, shivering under the layer of heavy blankets that covered them. Her back was to him, and when he reached out to touch her to make sure he wasn't dreaming, he heard the click of a pistol safety.

"Not so close, Sov," she gritted. "We're sharing the blankets for body warmth, and nothing more."

Alexi carefully drew his hand away.

He, too, was shivering. He'd stripped down to his boxer shorts and thick wool socks. The armored jacket he'd taken from Soldatenkof was too stiff to sleep in, and his trousers had been cold and damp with melted snow. His last clear memory was of using the magnet to scramble the programming of the computer chips in the Union officer's therm suit. He must have fallen asleep shortly after that. But he had the distinct impression that they'd been awake for the last few minutes, and talking about something.

"What promotion?" Alexi asked.

"None of your business, Sov," she said. "I shouldn't have said anything. It was just such a remarkable coincidence."

Alexi shifted position slightly. The grated floor of the cargo bay was digging into his hip. It was almost completely dark, save for the thin sliver of moonlight that angled in through the windows, up in the helicraft's cockpit. The faint light illuminated the Union soldier's discarded therm suit, which lay crumpled in a corner. Two wide, dark shadows marked the sleeve: captain's bars.

Something clicked into place in Alexi's memory.

"You were only a *leitenant* in Vladivostok," he said. "And now you're a captain."

He thought back to their meeting in Vladivostok, when she had chased him into the museum. The creature she had tangled with there had been too blurry to see clearly, but Alexi now knew it must have been a Zykhee. And she'd chased it up onto the roof . . .

"You found something up on the roof of the museum: an alien, like Raheek. How were you able to kill it? Or did you capture it? Didn't the tattoos affect you?"

She lay still, not answering him. But she was listening.

After a moment's thought, he guessed the rest. "They rewarded your find by promoting you to captain, and put you in command of a special ops squad. But why did that squad parachute into Tomsk 13? Did Union intelligence learn that there were aliens there, too, and not realize that they were just growlers? Did you think another Zykhee ship had landed there?"

Alexi recoiled as the cold barrel of the Pug pistol touched his bare chest. His lips were suddenly very dry. He must have guessed correctly.

"Don't shoot," he said carefully. "Think about it first. We're in the middle of the Siberian wilderness, and the radio in the helicraft is dead. You haven't answered a single one of my questions. And even if you had, who could I possibly tell?"

"The tattoos," she said in a sharp voice. "Tell me about them."

Alexi recognized an order when he heard one. He sighed. Just when Soldatenkof was finally dead and gone, here Alexi was, taking orders from another officer who commanded out of the barrel of a pistol.

"All I can tell you," he said carefully, "is that they don't work if you can't see them. When I lost my glasses, I was the only member of our squad who wasn't affected by them. All I could see was a blur."

The barrel's cold metal moved away from his side as she digested that information.

"I regret having killed the alien," Alexi said. "I get a sense that, had the Zykhee landed on a planet that wasn't at war with its own kind, they might have been our friends. Think of it: an alien race, with completely different technologies. Even magic. Who knows what secrets they could have shared with us. And maybe it's not too late. Perhaps—"

"You're a dreamer," she cut in. "The Zykhee are as hostile as the growlers. I don't trust Raheek any further than I trust you, Sov. But I want to see the meteorite."

Alexi sighed. "I don't care about the meteorite," he said in a tired voice. "I just want to go . . ."

He chuckled softly to himself. To go home? That was what he'd been about to say. But he didn't have a home. Not any more. The school where he'd taught was closed, they'd given his government-issue apartment away to someone else after he joined the military, his parents had died years ago, before the Change, and his sister had been reported missing in action, presumed dead, one year ago, after the Battle of Petrograd. Her husband hadn't given up hope that she would somehow turn up alive, but Alexi knew it wasn't going to happen. Petrograd had been left a smoking ruin after the tactical nukes fell. Tatyana wasn't going to rise from its ashes.

Alexi himself had never married. He'd hoped to find a family among the soldiers of the military's space arm and a new home for himself among the stars. When that dream had been grounded, he hadn't bothered making any close friendships among the grunts in the rad squad. He'd chosen to remain an orphan, instead.

And to stay in the military, rather than deserting, as so many of the other soldiers had. It had simply been the path of least resistance.

Alexi tugged the blankets up closer to his chin. His teeth were beginning to chatter. Beside him, he could feel the Union officer shivering. He wondered if anyone would mourn her if she froze to death.

"Do you ever wish you could turn back time?" he asked the darkness.

"What?"

"If I could go back in time, I'd go back to my childhood and stay there," Alexi said. "To the summer when I was twelve years old, the last summer I stayed at my grandfather's house on the shore of Lake Baikal. It was the last truly happy time in my life. Later that same year, my parents died. And my grandfather, too. Somehow I knew I had to make the most of that summer, that their deaths were just on the horizon, rushing toward me across the vast expanse of the lake. And at the end of the summer, when I was playing on the beach with my sister, my father . . ."

A lump rose in his throat. No. He wasn't going to tell her about *that*.

Alexi blinked, but his eyes were dry. Somewhere over the three years since signing up for the military, he'd forgotten how to cry.

Except that he *had* shed tears when Juliana was killed. But that hadn't happened . . . had it?

No, Juliana was very much alive.

Alexi hadn't ever been much of a crier. Even when he was a boy, when they'd told him about the deaths of his mother and father. Unlike his sister Tatyana, he'd already known that his parents were dead. In the moment that his father's ghost had appeared to him on the lakeshore, Alexi had come to truly understand what death meant, and with it came the realization that memory—and history—were the only things that kept the dead alive. Later that same day, he had decided to study history when he grew up and went on to university. It had been a defining moment in his life.

And a useless one. If only he'd chosen to study mathematics, like his father, he might have been accepted into the space arm of the military, back when he'd volunteered.

The Union officer seemed lost in her own thoughts. It was a moment or two before she spoke. "I wish I'd had a premonition of Tom's death," she said in a whisper. "I'd go back to the day the bombs fell. This time, I'd stay in Seattle."

Alexi turned toward her in the darkness. "You have nothing to live for, either," he said. "Do you?"

Her gun barrel touched his bare skin with a cold metal kiss.

"I wish I could kill you," she said.

Alexi's eyes flew open wide.

"I wish you didn't look so much like Tom."

Then she began to cry.

Alexi hesitated for only a second. Then he put an arm around her shoulder. She stiffened and stared at him for a long, aching moment, her dark eyes luminous in the faint light. In that instant, a secret knowledge sparked between them, a voice that whispered that neither one had much more to endure. Alexi shivered . . .

Then, ignoring the press of the barrel of her pistol against his chest, he kissed her.

24

Alexi braced himself as the trees rushed up toward them. They'd disposed of the growler that had been clinging to the landing gear, but the helicraft was still sluggish. He looked up, and saw that the mechanism that drove the rotors was coated with ice; the blades must also be iced up.

Beside him, the Union officer's lips were set in a grim line. She held the controls in a white-knuckled grip. Alexi felt his own lips moving, and realized that he was praying. He reached down to pull the straps that held him in the co-pilot's seat a little tighter. Just a bit farther and they'd be able to set down in the clearing. Just a little farther.

He couldn't watch. Instead he glanced behind to see how the alien was faring. But all he could see of Raheek was a cloud of inky darkness in the center of the cargo bay. Then the cloud shrank to a fist-sized hollow of infinite darkness—and disappeared with a loud pop.

The humans were on their own.

The helicraft lurched violently to one side as its rear rotor brushed a treetop. Then, before Alexi even had time to gasp, the Union officer jerked the controls. The helicraft plunged down with a sickening crunch into a clear space between the trees that was just big enough for its massive body. The floor underneath crumpled upward as something speared through it.

Alexi was thrown forward and to the side. His head cracked against the window beside him, and he saw stars. Above the helicraft, the rotors smashed into the branches, chopping into them and sending bits of bark, pine needles, and snow flying. The rich scent of pine sap filled the cockpit, along with the burning smell of engines pushed past their limits and the smell of melting plastic as something inside the control panel sparked. Alexi tried to reach for the fire extinguisher that was strapped down near his feet, but the sudden movement made his head pound. The Union officer slammed her hand against the controls, shutting them down. The burning smell faded away.

Alexi blinked away the stars that were still floating in front of his eyes and rubbed the side of his head. He winced as his fingers found a sore spot, and wished he'd never taken his helmet off.

Beside him, the Union officer sighed her relief. "Well," she said. "We made it. Now what?"

Alexi heard a clicking noise and glanced down. The radio's microphone had fallen from its cradle during the crash. It hung from its coiled cord, swinging back and forth against the base of the seat like a metronome. He picked it up.

"We could radio for help," he suggested. "But whose army would pick up the signal, yours or mine?"

"Not an option," the Union officer said. "Take a closer look."

Alexi did—and saw that a piece of the landing gear had broken away in the crash and thrust up through the control panel like a lance—right through the radio. Another meter to the right, and the sharp prong of metal would have pierced his seat instead.

"I see," Alexi said, thanking his luck. He dropped the microphone.

The Union officer undid her seat belt. She glanced up through the cockpit windows. "It's almost dark," she said. Then she glanced back into the cargo bay and looked startled. She turned to Alexi. "Where did the alien go?"

"I think it—"

Before Alexi could complete his sentence, the cockpit door beside him opened, nearly making him jump out of his skin. Raheek peered inside. Stupid move, startling a soldier. If Alexi had been holding his AK-51—which was back in the cargo bay—he might have shot the alien.

He almost had . . .

Or would . . .

The thought melted away, like the snow that was sliding off the rapidly cooling cockpit windows. It would be dark, soon. And cold.

Raheek thumped the butt of the blade-tipped staff in the snow. "We will leave now," it told Alexi. "I saw the impact site from the air as the craft descended. It is not far. We will continue on foot."

Alexi looked up at the sky. The stars—what few of them remained after the Change—were starting to come out. But most of the sky was obscured by cloud. And snow had begun to fall.

A wave of tension-release exhaustion swept over Alexi. He was bone-weary. And hungry. And more than a little tired of being ordered about. Especially by enemy officers and aliens.

"I'm not going anywhere," he told the alien, crossing his arms over his chest. "Not in this weather, and not in the dark. I'd get hypothermia before I'd taken a dozen steps. I'd die." He stared at Raheek's bare skin and shivered. "Aren't you cold?"

"The eternal flame warms me," the alien said.

"Yeah," Alexi said. "Right. Well, that won't do me any good."

The Union officer rose from her seat. "I'm ready to go," she said. "The cold doesn't bother me; I'm protected by my therm suit. Let the Sov stay here. He'd only slow us down."

Alexi was startled by the alien's response. Its blue-black eyes bored into the Union officer's.

"You are not required," it told her. One of its slender blue fingers tapped Alexi's chest. "This one is.

"But I do not wish to risk this human's death," it continued. "If this one is unable to travel until the light increases and the temperature rises, it will have to be so." It turned to Alexi. "I will locate the impact site myself, and return to show you the way. And then you will come. *Da?*"

"Sure," Alexi muttered, not really following the conversation, but seeing that he was expected to agree. "*Da.*"

The Union officer's response was to raise a pistol and point it at the alien. "You're not leaving without me," she said in a hard, level voice. "Take me to the site. Now."

The alien disappeared. Just like that. One moment it was standing in the doorway, and the next it had been swallowed by darkness. The Union officer cursed. She pushed past where Alexi sat and scrambled out of the helicraft. Alexi heard her stamping about in the snow outside, and more muttered curses. After a moment, she climbed back into the helicraft.

"The alien's gone," she said, shaking her head. "Not even a trail in the snow. It seems to be able to teleport. But how is it possible?"

Alexi shivered in the cold and shut the door. The Union officer settled back in the pilot's seat and stared at him a long moment. Then she raised one arm and tugged back the sleeve of her silvery body suit to reveal what looked like an oversize wristwatch.

"What's that?" Alexi asked.

"A Global Positioning System," she said. While he

looked at it, she raised the pistol that she still held. She stared at him with cold eyes.

"I need to know the exact coordinates," she told him.

"Of what?" Alexi asked.

"Of the Tunguska meteorite. You gave the alien only the approximate coordinates, but you can stop playing dumb now. The alien's gone ahead on its own, and there's no need to be afraid. You can tell me exactly where the impact site is."

Alexi blinked. "But I don't remember them. I only knew about Tunguska because of a lesson I gave years ago . . ."

She cocked the pistol. Suddenly, Alexi was very tired.

"Go ahead," he told her. "Shoot me if you like. But I can't answer your question. I don't—"

From somewhere back in the cargo bay came a hollow crumping noise, like the dull pop of a rad grenade going off. The Union officer glanced into the cargo bay with a wary expression on her face, the pistol in her hand still trained on Alexi. Perhaps she thought he had caused the sound as some sort of diversion. But Alexi was as baffled by the noise as she was. He peered past her to see what she was looking at.

One of the metal locker doors had started to glow. A round patch of metal, down near the bottom of the door, had turned a dull red and was beginning to bulge and sag. As the hot smell of molten metal filled the helicraft, the bulge turned into a hole with dripping edges. Something—an incendiary round, perhaps—had burned a hole right through the door. Alexi half rose from his seat, one hand on the handle of the cockpit door beside him. That was the locker he'd been unable to open earlier. If it was filled with incendiary rounds, the helicraft would turn into a fireball in seconds. But fleeing the helicraft for the Siberian night meant a slow, cold death by hypothermia. Alexi stared in horrified fascination, caught between fire and ice . . .

A hand about the size of a cat's paw reached through the

melted opening at the base of the locker. It was shaped like a human hand, but with long, jagged claws and burnished metallic skin. In the same instant, Alexi and the Union officer realized what they were seeing.

"Christ!" Alexi shouted. "It's a growler!"

As the creature burst from its hiding place in the storage locker, the Union officer fired her pistol. The crashing shots of the Pug filled the cockpit with noise as bullets punched holes into the locker and cargo bay floor. A few pinged off the growler's reddish black hide. The creature was small—no larger than a cat. Apelike in shape and a touch unsteady on its feet. An infant, Alexi decided. Was that why the adult growler had clung to the helicopter for so many long, cold kilometers? Had the infant cried to it in a voice the humans could not hear?

A jet of steam erupted through holes in the growler's back, although whether the holes were breathing tubes or bullet holes, Alexi couldn't say. All he knew was that the firepower of the pistol alone wasn't enough to take the growler down, tiny though it might be. He had to get to his AK-51.

Which was in the back of the helicraft, within biting range of the growler.

The creature blinked beady eyes and opened a mouth as wide as a snake's and filled with more teeth than an alligator's. It belched, and a dribble of what looked like molten lava dripped onto the floor and began melting the metal grating on which it stood. Heat radiated from it.

Alexi had the distinct impression that he'd better think fast—or die. But his mind fastened on a single thought and wouldn't let go.

Fire, Alexi thought. The thing's gut is on fire.

The tiny growler slapped a humanlike hand against its hide, reacting to the string of the pistol bullets. It blinked stupidly, then realized at last that the humans were the source of this irritation. Baring its fangs in a menacing grimace, the creature began ambling toward the cockpit, its knuckles scraping against the metal floor with screeches that made Alexi wince.

He did the only thing he could think of—he dived for the fire extinguisher.

Fumbling out the pin that held the trigger shut, he pointed the nozzle at the advancing growler with trembling hands. Then he pulled the trigger.

A cloud of white filled the cargo bay. Alexi strode forward, aiming the cone until it was focused on the growler's ugly, gape-mouthed face. Instead of retreating, the thing actually seized the nozzle of the fire extinguisher and worried it like a terrier shaking a rat. It was all Alexi could do to hang on, to keep squeezing the trigger. Then the fire extinguisher was torn from his hands. . . .

The growler fell over on its side. A single puff of sulfuric air puffed from the holes on its back, and then it lay still.

The Union officer came up behind Alexi and stared at the creature, her pistol held at the ready. "Nice work," she said. "I think you've killed it."

Suddenly the creature belched. White powder from the fire extinguisher bubbled out of its mouth, and its eyes moved.

Moving cautiously, the Union officer lowered her pistol to the creature's throat. The skin, which looked tough and shiny as metal everywhere else on the growler's hide, looked thinnest there.

"What do you think?" the Union officer asked. "You Sovs have more experience with these things than we do. Will a point-blank shot under the chin be enough to kill it? Or should I be worried about glands in the thing's throat that could deflate explosively and shower us with that red-hot saliva?"

A thought flashed through Alexi's mind: If she shot this infant, the adult growlers would take revenge for the killing of one of their young. The logical part of Alexi knew that mommy growler—or daddy growler, or whatever the thing had been that had clung to the bottom of the helicraft—was dead in a cloud of nerve gas. But there might be others around. In his briefing, Soldatenkof had said that they'd spread from Tomsk 13 across all of Siberia, even into Alaska. It would be a remarkable coincidence if the helicraft had come to rest near one of them, but coincidences had a habit of happening when Alexi was around.

"Don't shoot it," Alexi said.

The Union officer paused. "Why not? What's wrong?"

The infant growler was still motionless, except for its eyes. They flickered to watch Alexi. A faint growl bubbled from its open mouth.

Alexi had no sympathy for the thing. He knew how dangerous even an infant growler could be; he had watched as four just this size had torn to pieces . . .

Someone.

But he had an overwhelming urge to keep it alive, dangerous though that might be. Just like the canister of nerve gas, it could prove useful. For what, Alexi couldn't say. But then, he hadn't had any clear ideas in mind when he picked up the canister of Tabun. Just the same, driving need to keep it . . .

But not inside the helicraft. Even if an adult was hundreds of kilometers away, it could be closing in on the helicraft. It wouldn't be able to smell the wounded infant, but perhaps it could hear its silent scream. . . .

Alexi grunted. Where had that strange idea come from? It was a crazy notion, but he decided to listen to it.

He nudged the growler with his boot. It didn't move.

"I've had some experience with these creatures," he lied. "That's why they sent our squad to Tomsk 13. Let me deal with it."

The Union officer nodded and backed off, but kept her pistol leveled at the growler. She watched silently as Alexi tore the microphone from the cockpit radio and used the cord to bind the creature's legs. Then Alexi picked up the creature, letting it dangle from the cord, and opened the rear hatch of the cargo bay.

"Where are you taking it?" the Union officer asked.

"There's a stream nearby," Alexi said. "I'm going to chip a hole in the ice and drop the growler into it. That should force it into suspended animation, just like a cryotank."

"How do you know that?"

Alexi paused. How did he know it would work—or how did he know there was a stream nearby? He didn't have the answer to either question. "Follow me if you like," he told her. "Or stay here. I don't care."

Picking his way through the forest by moonlight, he set out into the falling snow.

25

"Let's move out," Juliana said. "It's too cold to stand around talking, fascinating though this conversation might be. I'll take point."

She trudged past the place where Alexi and the blue-skinned alien stood in the snow. Alexi started whispering to himself, then suddenly realized that he was counting her steps.

Five . . . six . . . seven . . .

What was the unlucky number? Alexi didn't know—he just knew there was one.

Ten . . . eleven . . . twelve . . .

Raheek started to follow Juliana. The pair of them would be hidden behind the trees soon.

The trees.

Alexi glanced to his right and saw a tree that was bare of snow, its trunk gouged by . . .

Without knowing why, he lifted his AK-51 and pulled the trigger, firing a short burst. The response was instantaneous: shouts from up ahead—and then Juliana and Raheek came running back, pistol drawn and blade-tipped staff held at the ready.

"What's wrong?" Juliana asked.

"There's a growler nearby," Alexi said. "A big one. Adult."

"How do you know this?" Raheek asked.

Alexi pointed to the tree. "It left a trail in the snow," he said. "And it chewed on that tree."

Juliana gave him a skeptical look, then trudged across the unbroken snow to the tree for a closer look. When she returned, she shook her head.

"I thought you said your eyesight wasn't very good," she said. "How could you see something so far away in such detail?"

Alexi couldn't answer. He hadn't seen it. He had just known.

Raheek hadn't moved. The alien stared thoughtfully at Alexi. "You have traveled this path before," it said. "And you will travel it again."

Juliana glanced nervously around. "Alexi can take point," she decided. "Since he knows so much about growlers."

Alexi nodded. Yes, it made sense that he go first. He knew . . .

Something that they did not, but that they would find out soon enough. And there was a surprise for him, too. He could sense it just behind him, as real as the weight of the backpack on his shoulders.

He set off along the trail, Raheek and Juliana following a short distance behind. He was still counting footsteps.

Thirty-three . . . thirty-four . . . thirty-five . . .

He glanced around at the snow, at the forest, somehow recognizing this spot. That tree, with the forked branch. This was where Juliana would draw her pistol and take him prisoner . . .

Nothing happened. They passed the spot and kept walking. He kept his eyes on the ground, once again counting the footprints Raheek had left in the snow. He didn't need to look up, even when Juliana gasped. He already knew what he'd see: a gigantic tetrahedron, balanced on its point in the forest.

Forty-six . . . forty-seven . . .

Alexi was starting to sweat. But not from the tension that was winding ever tighter inside him like a trap about to spring shut. His back was uncomfortably warm, under the flak jacket. The backpack didn't weigh much, but it certainly was making him sweat.

Fifty-seven . . . fifty-eight . . .

Was the backpack actually getting warmer? Or was that just Alexi's imagination?

Sixty-one . . . sixty-two . . .

Alexi jerked to a halt in the snow. Something was wrong. He'd never seen this part of the forest before—he was certain of it. Yet he had the soldier's sixth sense that danger lay just ahead. Was it a growler, hiding in the woods?

As if in answer to Alexi's thought, the silence of the forest was shattered by an unmistakable sound: a cross between a lion's roar and a buzz saw's metallic whine. Juliana and Raheek froze in their tracks.

In the second or two of stillness that followed, Alexi heard a faint whirring noise from behind the trees up ahead. In that same instant, he spotted a branch moving.

No—not a branch. The barrel of a machine gun, swinging their way.

"Take cover!" he screamed, and threw himself face forward into the snow.

Bullets whined through the air over their heads as the others followed suit. Chips of bark and pine needles rained down upon them as the machine gun cut a swath through the forest. Alexi crawled into the shelter of one of the thicker tree trunks, and shrugged out of the backpack. If that was a machine-gun nest, one of the frag grenades he was carrying would be just the ticket.

He reached in to pull one out, shouting in Russian as he

did so. There was a slim chance that they were being targeted by friendly fire. And if it wasn't friendlies up ahead— if those were Union soldiers behind that machine gun, shouting wouldn't hurt. They were already shooting at him, anyway.

"Cease fire, *tovarish*!" he called. "We're friendly."

Then he froze, as his hand slid deeper into the backpack. He'd been right—there was something warm in there. Something he recognized by its metallic but flexible feel.

With great trepidation, he pulled an infant growler from the backpack. The thing was still tied hand and foot with the microphone cord, but it was squirming. Tiny puffs of sulfuric steam seeped from the blow holes in its back.

Alexi stared at it in amazement. What idiot had put it in his pack?

Suddenly, Alexi knew the answer: he had. He just couldn't remember when, or why. And now, if his instinct about the growlers being able to communicate telepathically with one another was correct, this infant would be calling to all adult growlers within range to rescue it.

The roaring noise—closer now—confirmed Alexi's fears.

He left the infant growler in the snow and crawled back to where Juliana and Raheek were. They had fallen back and were crouched behind a clump of trees. As Alexi reached them, dragging his backpack in the snow, the machine gun fell silent.

"Who are they?" Alexi panted. He looked at Juliana. "Ours—or yours?"

"It has to be one of ours," she said. "An automated weapon. A long-range rocket drone, judging by that jet burn."

Alexi looked up at the spot she was pointing to. Just above the spot where the machine gun must be, the treetops were broken and scorched.

"I've got more bad news," Alexi said, glancing back at

the spot where he'd left the tiny growler. But he didn't need to tell them what it was. This time, the growler's roar was only a few hundred meters away.

Juliana blanched and turned to run. But Raheek caught her hand. "Stay still," it hissed. It wrapped its other hand around Alexi's arm, overlong fingers closing around his wrist. "Wait."

Alexi wasn't sure what happened next. Raheek began chanting, and suddenly the world blurred around them. A barrier of swirling, ghostly figures surrounded the three of them, howling with alien voices that turned Alexi's guts to water. Shuddering, he tore his eyes away. But then a sudden motion outside the barrier made him look up.

Trees fell to either side as a growler crashed through the forest. Beside him, Alexi felt Juliana quail at the sight—and felt a certain satisfaction, knowing that she was reacting with the same intensity of terror that he had first felt when confronted by her heavy-assault suit. The growler, which had a row of spikes down its back and a gigantic twisting horn emerging from its forehead, opened a gaping mouth that reminded Alexi of the tyrannosaurus models he'd played with as a child. Then the creature began to cough. Alexi clutched his chest, vividly imagining how the wad of phlegm would eat through his armored jacket and into his flesh. He had a horrible feeling that he, Raheek, and Juliana were about to die a terrible, lingering death. . . .

And then the howling of the barrier that surrounded Alexi intensified. Although Raheek was still holding his wrist in a vise-firm grip, Alexi forced his hands up to cover his ears and lent his own scream to the howling wail.

A tremble ran through the growler. It backed away. Then it spun on one heel and loped for the place where the infant lay.

The blue-skinned hand that was holding Alexi's arm began to tremble. "I can't . . . continue the barrier much . . .

longer," the alien moaned. The red flecks in its eyes were starting to fade. "If the growler . . . returns . . ."

Alexi had a sudden premonition that they were going to be fine. That everything was going just as he'd planned and that they would survive this.

Suddenly, Raheek collapsed. The magical barrier fell. Juliana's eyes opened—and widened in fear when she saw Raheek lying in the snow. They widened still more when the growler roared from just behind the trees, a sound that shook Alexi's guts like a water-filled bag. It hadn't run far.

"Don't worry," Alexi shouted over the ringing in his ears. "It's here to collect the infant. And when it goes after the little one, it will—"

Gunfire erupted. The growler roared a challenge back.

Alexi smiled.

Perfect. He'd left the infant growler lying just within range of the drone. And now the growler was attacking it. Alexi heard the familiar cough—and the splat of a wad of phlegm against a hard surface. In that same moment, he also heard the *whoosh-whoosh-whoosh* of multiple minirockets being launched. There was a terrific explosion . . .

And then silence. The only sounds were the faint cracklings of tree branches that had been set on fire by the blast. And the soft thud of chunks of growler flesh falling back into the snow.

Raheek groaned and sat up. Alexi extended a hand. The alien's double-jointed arm snaked out, and its hand fastened once more around Alexi's wrist.

Alexi looked at the inverted pyramid, which lay just a short distance ahead. "Come on," he told the alien. "I have a feeling the drone's out of commission now. Let's get a closer look at this bomb you've been telling us about."

26

A lexi stared at his reflection in the surface of the crystal. Its perfectly smooth gray wall was polished to a dull sheen. Snowflakes struck its sloped surface above and slid down the side. As they slid across Alexi's reflection, it wavered like an image on a faulty monitor screen.

Staring back at him were haunted blue eyes circled with dark shadows. In the past few days he had seen too much, had been forced to make too many decisions. He'd earned the yellow *leitenant* stripe on the shoulder of his newly acquired armored combat jacket, even if it wasn't an official promotion.

Alexi scratched the stubble on his chin. His whiskers were as fair as his hair, a birch white blond. The other soldiers in the rad squad had always teased him whenever he tried to grow a beard, asking if he was trying to look older than his students. But they wouldn't be teasing him any more.

Neither would anybody else, ever again, if this thing went off.

Alexi pondered the fickleness of fate. Of the six men

and women in his platoon, only he had survived. The rest were all dead now.

He laughed. Now. A funny word, that. It had become slippery in the last few days. A fish that slithered out of your hand whenever you grabbed it. In a very real sense, his comrades were still alive. Still fighting, and suffering, and dying . . .

And so was Alexi. But hopefully, that nightmare would soon end.

Alexi craned his head to look at the top of the structure. It balanced—impossibly—on its point like an upside-down pyramid. He blinked as the wind blew snow up into his eyes. The wall in front of him was a perfect equilateral triangle, rising from its pointed base to the height of a twenty-story building. A tetrahedral crystal, hard as a diamond. And like a diamond, it could be split, if only the jeweler knew where to place his chisel.

And that chisel was . . .

Alexi blinked as he suddenly realized that another chunk of time had gone missing. He looked down and saw Juliana attaching a vodka bottle to the base of the tetrahedron with white tape from the first-aid kit. A clear liquid sloshed back and forth inside the bottle, opaquing it from the inside. A harsh chemical smell rose from the mouth of the bottle. Alexi had smelled that odor somewhere before. He'd been in a close, dark place, and a growler had . . .

Suddenly, his breathing was ragged. His chest felt tight—he must have been breathing in fumes from the chemicals in the bottle. He took a step back and waited until his breathing became steady again.

"What are you doing?" he asked Juliana.

She winked at him. "Bomb-disposal work. Lucky for us that the growler vomited up the one thing that will do the job."

When she'd finished taping the bottle in place, she stood and took his arm. "Come on. It's nearly eaten through the glass. We don't want to be standing anywhere near it when it topples."

They jogged away from the tetrahedron, leaving the bare ground that it shadowed and wading into the knee-deep snow. Alexi was careful not to turn his back on the thing; he couldn't shake the feeling that the tetrahedron was watching him.

He nearly tripped over something that was lying in the snow, something soft and yielding. He looked down and was amazed to see Raheek. The alien was lying unconscious on its back, partially covered by a dusting of fallen snow.

Alexi looked up at Juliana. Without understanding how, he knew that she was responsible. "How—?"

Just at that moment, the alien's eyes fluttered open. At first they were as puzzled and uncomprehending as Alexi's. But then they widened in alarm. The alien struggled to sit up, then froze in place as the bottle attached to the inverted pyramid splintered with a faint cracking noise.

Raheek stared at the broken bottle. Then it looked up at Juliana. "You should have listened to me," it said. "But now—"

A loud hissing filled the air as hydrofluoric acid flowed from the ruined vodka bottle. The acid ate into the point on which the tetrahedron balanced, obscuring it with a cloud of vapor. Alexi and Juliana both tensed. Any moment now, the base of the inverted pyramid would shear off, causing the tetrahedron to fall . . .

And then the hissing suddenly stopped. There was no shuddering crack, no loud splinter of stone as the crystal split apart. No crash as it fell to earth. Just acid dribbling to the ground and a faint fog of vapor drifting gently around its smooth, unblemished point.

The acid hadn't eaten the crystal at all—just the glass bottle. Alexi stood, fists on hips, staring back at the structure. Why hadn't it . . .

A spot of color appeared on the surface of one smooth

gray wall, and a loud electronic humming filled the air. Alexi had only time to frown—

And then a jagged bolt of lightning lanced from the tetrahedron. Blown off his feet as the bolt hit his chest, Alexi's shattered consciousness somehow registered the fact that the lightning had forked in three, its other deadly tongues licking out at Raheek and Juliana as well.

Hurled through the air, chest on fire with burning agony, finger-sized bolts of lightning shooting out of his hands as the wash of high-amperage energy sought a ground, Alexi smelled burning flesh and ozone. He observed with dizzy wonder that he had been blasted right out of his boots. His vision purpled as his heart fluttered in his chest, its natural rhythm overwhelmed. He landed against a tree with a thud that would have produced a shock of agony had his mind not been occupied by one overwhelming, terrifying thought.

I am dying . . .

Juliana lay a few meters away, her neck twisted at an impossible angle, her eyes glazed.

I am dying . . .

The alien lay to the other side of Alexi, its blue skull cracked open and unpleasant-smelling smoke wisping from its charred brains.

I am . . .

Alexi's heart stopped. The thought in his head completed itself. But somehow it became a question, rather than a statement of fact.

dead?

27

They found the remains of the combat drone by the sizzling noise. The growler's highly corrosive acid had eaten right through the steel armor that protected the drone's turret, leaving a steaming, bubbling hole in the metal. The machine gun pointed up at the sky at a crazy angle, and exhaust still swirled inside the rocket tubes that had risen in neat columns on either side of the drone. The heat of the rocket's minijets had melted the snow, exposing the ring of soft earth that had formed around the drone when it dug itself in and that was now turning to mud.

Chunks of growler lay here and there, scattered across the forest. A viscous, almost-clear liquid had splattered over a wide area; the trees all around the drone were dripping with the stuff. Wherever it had landed, the bark and needles of the trees were eaten away. A heavy, acidic odor hung in the air.

The severed head of the growler lay cradled on a tree limb. Even though it was an alien—a monstrous creature—the thought of decapitation made Alexi shudder. And for good reason: had the drone torn one of them to pieces with its rockets, it might have been Alexi's head resting on that branch. Or Raheek's. Or Juliana's . . .

He prodded the growler head with the barrel of his AK-51, lifting the thing's lip and staring at the rows of razor-sharp teeth. A dribble of saliva slid from the monster's mouth.

Raheek caught Alexi's arm and gently pulled the barrel of the assault rifle away from the growler's head. Alexi saw that the metal was already beginning to pit. "Be careful," Raheek cautioned. "The glands will still be secreting acid. If the head falls, it will splash."

Juliana sniffed the air. "What kind of acid?" she asked.

Alexi suddenly realized where he'd smelled that particular odor before—why it seemed so familiar to him, even though this was his first encounter with a growler that spat wads of acidic phlegm. In the arts-and-crafts room of the high school where he'd taught, they'd used an acid with exactly the same smell to etch glass.

"It's hydrofluoric acid," he said.

Juliana stared at the dismembered growler, a look of disbelief on her face. "Impossible. How could the creature possibly have something so toxic inside it and still live?"

Alexi shrugged. "Our stomachs are filled with acid—just a different type." Then he jerked a thumb at his backpack. "If you don't believe me, I can prove it to you. There's a glass bottle inside my pack. Shall I stick it into the acid and show you how it gets eaten away?"

But Juliana wasn't listening to him. Instead she seemed to be lost in thought. She stared up at the tetrahedron. "Hydrofluoric acid," she murmured. "Glass . . . silicon . . ."

Raheek nudged Alexi. "Let us go," it said. "We haven't much time."

"I know, I know," Alexi said, not bothering to keep the skepticism out of his voice. "The bomb's about to go off and the end of the world is coming. And you expect me to do something about it, though I can't imagine what. Well, let's get it over with, then."

Alexi turned to follow Raheek, but Juliana caught his

arm. "That bottle," she said. "Give it to me. I want to see if your guess about what type of acid was in the growler's stomach was right."

Alexi hesitated, suddenly regretting having suggested the glass-etching test. He didn't want to give the bottle to Juliana. He had the sudden sense that, if he did, some terrible result would occur. But the worst outcome his imagination could come up with was her hands being burned by acid. And if she wanted to risk her own skin, so be it.

He shrugged off the backpack and dug inside it. He handed the empty vodka bottle to Juliana, but almost didn't let go of it. She had to tug it out of his hand. Still fretting, he closed up the backpack, then turned and trudged after Raheek. Soon the trees hid Juliana from sight.

Something still nagged at Alexi, something that made him stop and then backtrack to a point where he could see her again. She was crouched beside the growler's severed head, using a stick to ease its mouth open. With her other hand, she held the bottle under the trickle of corrosive saliva that dribbled from the mouth. He saw her wince—and jerk slightly—and assumed a drop or two of it had splashed onto her skin after glancing off the mouth of the bottle. But she ignored the pain, her expression set in a determined and thoughtful frown.

At the rate the acid was trickling, it would be quite a while before the bottle was full. Alexi wondered what she planned to do with it. Hurl it at the crystal like a Molotov cocktail, in a futile act of defiance?

Raheek called to Alexi, startling him. Not wanting to be caught spying on Juliana, Alexi hurried away through the trees. He found himself in a small clearing—and in shadow. He looked up and saw the tetrahedron towering above him. The broad base of the inverted pyramid, high overhead, was like an umbrella that stopped the snow from falling. The ground under Alexi's feet was almost bare of snow.

Raheek sat just outside the shadow the crystal cast,

cross-legged in the snow. The alien's staff lay across its knees. Staring at Alexi, Raheek patted down the snow beside it with a slender blue hand.

"Come," the alien called out. "Sit."

Alexi shivered—he was already wet, cold, and tired. He wasn't about to bring hypothermia even closer by sitting in the snow. Ignoring Raheek, he moved closer to the tetrahedron, studying its smooth gray surface as he entered its shadow. Was the thing really a bomb, built by an alien intelligence? Ever since the Change had drawn Earth into another universe—one filled with blue-skinned mystics and acid-spitting monsters—anything was possible.

Frightened though he was, Alexi felt strangely drawn to the crystal. He needed to be near it, to touch it, to be . . .

He touched the flawless surface with a fingertip. The crystal was as warm as flesh, as smooth as glass.

The thought tickled something in his memory. Glass could be etched. A silicon crystal could be . . .

The thought disappeared.

Alexi flattened his hand against the pyramid, then slid it slowly across the smooth surface. It seemed flawless, unbroken. But like everything else in the universe, the crystal was made up of atoms. And those atoms, made up of a nucleus, protons, and electrons—and all of the other subatomic particles—had spaces between them. Spaces like doors and windows . . .

Alexi suddenly shivered and drew his hand away. With a start, he realized where he was: in the middle of Siberia, next to a ticking time bomb—pun intended—with only an alien and an enemy soldier for company.

He walked back to where Raheek sat and looked down at the blue-skinned alien. "So," he asked. "What happens next?"

"That depends on you," the alien replied. "The answer lies inside you."

Alexi snorted. "Well, if it does, I don't know it."

"I can help you know it."

"With your magic?" Alexi asked.

"No," Raheek answered. "With yours."

Alexi raised his ice-cold hands to his lips and blew on them. His insulated combat boots and Soldatenkof's armored jacket were keeping out the worst of the cold, but his pants were wet and his hair was dusted with snow. Now that he'd stopped walking, the condensation on his glasses was starting to crystallize into ice at the edges of the lenses.

"I don't have any magic," he told the alien. "Not like yours. We call our 'magic' technology."

"That isn't the magic I am speaking of," Raheek answered patiently. "You humans also have another kind of magic—a truer form. You mentioned it once before, when you asked if I was a mystic."

"I did?" Alexi had to think about that one for a moment before the answer came. "You mean psychic powers?"

The bald-headed alien nodded, a look of satisfaction in its eyes.

"They don't exist," Alexi said.

"They do," the alien insisted. "And they are strong in you."

Alexi laughed out loud. "Sorry," he told the alien. "You must be confusing me with someone else. My great-to-the-power-of-twenty-grandmother, perhaps. She was a fortune-teller—and look where she wound up. Exiled to Siberia when she predicted the death of Peter the Great. Or so the family legends have it."

Alexi grinned. "Too bad she's dead. She'd be the one to talk to about psychic powers."

"That is an interesting suggestion," Raheek said in a thoughtful voice.

Alexi suddenly felt uneasy. "What do you mean?"

The alien's eyes stared up at him. The blue hands lifted from its knees, fingers twitching.

"The mystic power I used to call up the barrier that protected us from the growlers draws upon the eternal power of long-dead Zykhee souls," Raheek said. "My training allows me to shape the souls of my ancestors into a protective ethereal barrier that enemies—and creatures like the growlers—find terrifying. But I find the souls comforting. They embrace me like a protective parent, sustain my courage, whisper secrets to me . . ."

Raheek reached out with a sudden zigzag motion. Its long, steel-strong fingers wrapped around Alexi's wrist. "I have never attempted to call up the long-dead souls of another species," it continued, an intent look in its eyes. "But if I could, perhaps your ancestor could communicate with you and tell you how to awaken your own mystical power. And then you could tell me the secret of how the crystal can be defeated."

Alexi tried to tug his hand free. Out of the corner of his eye, he saw Juliana emerge from the forest. Perhaps she could help him talk some sense into the alien.

"I don't think your idea will work," Alexi told Raheek. "And even if it does, I'm not interested in trying. Even as a kid, I didn't like ghost stories. My imagination would run away with me, and I'd start . . ."

He suddenly realized what he was saying. A memory from his childhood flooded back to him. He'd start seeing things. Ghosts. Like the ghost of his father, who had come to him on the shore of Lake Baikal to tell his little Alexi that he and Mommy were dead . . .

"You must allow me to try," Raheek insisted. "Does the fact that the existence of your entire planet hangs in the balance not move you?"

"Why should I care about anyone but myself?" Alexi asked indignantly. "Look at this planet—it's a mess." He gestured at the black patches of soot-stained snow. "Even without the war, we were killing ourselves with radiation poisoning and pollution. What difference does it make if the whole thing gets blown away? Good riddance to it!"

Alexi decided then and there that he didn't believe a word Raheek was saying—any of it. The balancing tetrahedron was an amazing and strange artifact, it was true. Undoubtedly alien. But that didn't mean it was a bomb. If Alexi could get back to the downed helicraft and somehow repair its damaged radio, he could call for help. He had flares; another Neo-Soviet helicraft would come to rescue him. And Alexi's discovery of an alien artifact would almost certainly earn him the promotion he needed to finally be reassigned to the military's space arm. He just had to get away from the Zykhee—and then give Juliana the slip. . . .

Juliana was closer now, almost behind the alien. One hand held the bottle of hydrofluoric acid, the other, her Pug pistol. Slowly and silently, she raised the weapon above Raheek's head . . .

Alexi suddenly realized she was going to try to knock the alien out. And that she would succeed. And that somehow, this would lead not to the thing he most hoped for, but to the thing he most feared.

And no matter how he blustered and said he didn't care, he didn't want to die.

"Look out, Raheek!" he shouted, jerking the alien forward by the hand that still held his wrist.

Juliana's pistol swept harmlessly past the back of the alien's head.

"Damn you!" she shouted at Alexi. "That thing's an alien. We humans have to stick together against it!"

She danced back, leveling her pistol at Raheek. But just as it had before, the alien was suddenly no longer where it had been. One moment it was sitting cross-legged on the ground—and the next it was behind Juliana, staff in hand. The staff whipped around in a blur and Juliana's head fell from her shoulders. Her body collapsed twitching into the snow, turning it a mushy red.

Alexi stood, too shocked to do more than tremble. He'd seen hundreds of deaths in his years of combat, but somehow this one moved him more than any other. Hot tears trickled down his cheeks.

"She wasn't going to kill you," he whispered. "She only meant to knock you unconscious. You didn't need to . . ."

His words trailed off as he stared at Juliana's corpse. Where was she now? Had her soul flown to Heaven to join that of her dead lover? Alexi doubted it. He didn't believe in ghosts, or in life after death. That time he'd seen his father on the beach—on the day his parents had died—his sister Tatyana hadn't seen a thing, even though she'd been standing right beside him. It had just been a figment of Alexi's childish imagination.

Yet it was so clear in his memory. He'd seen his father out of the corner of his eye: a lonely figure standing on the beach. Alexi had at first turned to greet him, thinking that his father had come early to fetch them—but when he looked straight at him, his father had disappeared, just like that. Alexi had stood there, perplexed, as an oblivious Tatyana had thrown a stick for the dogs. Then, just when Alexi decided it must have been a trick of the light—perhaps the sun glinting off the lake water or a shadow cast by the trees—he'd imagined his father's voice, whispering in his ear.

Alexi, my son. I love you. The voice ached with a sadness that had found an echo in Alexi's heart. *Whatever you choose, whatever path in life you follow, I know that you will make me proud. Farewell, son.*

"Father!" Alexi cried out. "Don't go!"

Tatyana had stopped in mid-throw to stare at Alexi. The dogs had barked for a moment at the stick in her hand, then also turned quizzical eyes upon him.

And in that moment, Alexi had felt as if the whole of his future hinged upon what happened next. But with both his sister and the dogs staring at him as if he was crazy, he'd suddenly felt embarrassed.

"It's nothing," he'd told Tatyana. "Let's play."

And in the years that had followed, he'd convinced

himself that the whole incident had indeed been nothing more than his imagination. That he'd only imagined seeing his father's ghost.

Alexi stared at Juliana's body as the alien wiped the bloody blade of its weapon in the snow.

"We each have our destiny," Raheek said. "Hers was to die here."

No! Alexi silently protested.

"And we each have our duty," the alien continued. "Mine is to learn the secret of disarming the crystal, and carry that knowledge back to my race. And yours is to give me that knowledge."

Alexi stared defiantly at the alien. "And what are you going to do if I refuse?" he asked, anger choking his throat. "Kill me?"

Alexi's hand was still on the strap of his AK-51. Even though he knew he'd never be quick enough, he was tempted to whip the weapon off his shoulder and pull the trigger until the assault rifle was hot and smoking. His fingers whitened on the strap.

The alien stood motionless, staring at Alexi, leaning on its staff. Then it began to speak in a strange language. Flecks of red were swirling in the midnight blue of the irises.

Slowly, Alexi eased the assault rifle from his shoulder. He lifted the AK-51, wincing as his bare palm stuck to the ice-cold metal of the barrel. Jerking his hand free, tearing the skin, he shifted his grip to the weapon's wooden stock. His right hand wrapped around the grip, and his index finger settled on the trigger. The sweat froze, gluing his finger in place. All he had to do now was pull . . .

The blue-skinned alien stared down the barrel of Alexi's gun, calmly looking its death in the eye. Alexi hesitated—why hadn't the alien pulled its disappearing act by now? Was it just going to let Alexi kill it? Raheek continued whispering.

"What are you saying?" Alexi asked. "Your prayers?"

The air between Alexi and the alien began to shimmer. Fearing a magical attack, Alexi at last pulled the trigger—

And found himself shooting his own father. Wrenching the weapon up and to the side, he jerked his finger free of the trigger. Then he stared in amazement at the man he had not seen in more than twenty years.

His father was just the way Alexi remembered him: a slender man with a scholar's high forehead and receding hairline and old-fashioned books tucked under his arm. Like Alexi, he wore glasses, although his had heavy black plastic frames. He wore the same clothes they'd buried him in—his best blue suit. Except that it wasn't blue. Like the rest of him it was a pale, translucent white. Behind him, the air shimmered and swirled.

Alexi had to tip his head back to look up at his father, just as he had as a child. He found himself whispering a word: "Father." The ghost smiled down at him and reached out to tousle Alexi's hair.

Startled, Alexi took a step back. Tearing his eyes away from the apparition, he glared at Raheek. The alien stood with arms outstretched, chanting in an alien language.

"Stop it!" Alexi shouted. "It's a trick—one of your illusions. Stop it right now!"

Alexi, the apparition whispered. *Why are you so afraid? Don't you recognize me?*

Alexi pointed his assault rifle at Raheek. "Quit creating the illusion or I'll—"

I haven't seen you since you were twelve, Alexi. My, how you've grown. And wearing a soldier's uniform. I should have expected it, given your fascination with military history. Tell me, have you been a soldier all your adult life?

Alexi heard the trace of disappointment in his father's voice and couldn't help but answer. "I was a teacher before the war. Like you, Father. Except that I taught history, not mathematics."

Realizing that he was probably talking to thin air, Alexi

tore his eyes away. Embarrassed, he lowered his assault rifle. His hand crept into the open neck of the armored jacket he wore and found the cross that hung around his neck. Clenching it, praying for clarity, he tried once more: "Stop it," he gritted at Raheek. "Now."

Where is your sister?

Habit forced Alexi to answer, even though he didn't believe. "She's dead."

A frown creased his father's forehead. *She can't be. I would know.*

Closing his eyes, Alexi took a deep breath. Lies. His fingers rubbed the cross that hung around his neck like prayer beads, stroking the faceted stone set at its center. These were lies and illusions that the alien was creating for him. With his other hand, he raised his rifle into the air. He would fire a burst, end this madness . . .

Tell me—does she have the toy dinosaur still?

Alexi opened his eyes. "What?"

The one you gave her—that you pretended to let her win after your race with the dog. You were going to call the wolfhound to heel, just before the finish line, but instead you let it win. Even when she teased you for weeks about winning the bet, you never told her the truth. And now Tatyana must be an adult, like yourself. Does she still tease you about winning the bet?

"Enough," Alexi shouted at Raheek. "I don't know how you are able to read my mind, but you must stop. Now!"

The alien ignored him.

"Enough!" he shouted at the ghostly image of his father. It was hard to speak with such a lump in his throat. "Tatyana is dead, I say!"

And I say she is not. Listen to your father, Alexi!

Alexi blinked his suddenly stinging eyes. Could it be true? Who better than the dead to know? Perhaps Tatyana hadn't been in Petrograd when it was nuked. Perhaps she, like Alexi, had deserted the army. She might not have contacted her husband for fear of being captured. Or perhaps he knew that she was alive, and hadn't told Alexi. It was possible. Anything was possible . . .

And if Tatyana was alive . . .

Alexi glanced behind him at the tetrahedron. In that moment, he knew there was something worth dying for: his sister. But Raheek didn't seem to know how to prevent the time bomb from going off. And if an alien with mystic powers didn't know, how could Alexi? No, he was going to die. As was Tatyana—and the rest of the world. Alexi stared at the trampled snow beneath his boots, wanting to sink down into it and sleep forever in its cold embrace.

That's right, grandson. You are going to die. But don't worry. You'll live again.

Alexi's head jerked up when he heard the woman's voice. The ghostly image of his father was gone. In its place was a swirling wall of mist. With a face looking out at him from the center—the wrinkled face of a woman with a peasant's scarf over her long gray hair. Somehow, Alexi could feel that there were centuries separating them. Yet by her pale blue eyes and the set of her lips—and the silent communication that passed between them—he knew her: his long-dead ancestor. The fortune-teller.

The cross that hung around her neck—the same one Alexi's tense white fingers gripped—confirmed it. She'd had the cross made to provide a Christian disguise for the "lucky stone" that was set into its center, a gem that she said enhanced her ability to part the mists of time. The cross had been passed down through the family for generations, always to the eldest child—down to his great-grandfather, his grandmother, his mother, and at last to Alexi himself. Alexi had worn it faithfully into every battle—and was convinced that its luck had saved his life on more than one occasion.

He let go of the cross and reached out with his hand, as if to touch the ghost that stood before him.

"What . . ." He could barely speak. Somehow the words

whispered from his lips. "What do you mean, I'm going to die?"

By dying, you can give life to a world. By throwing yourself into the void, you can become a shield for your sister—a shield that will also protect countless unborn generations.

It sounded like a prophecy. Something about the way she'd worded it reminded Alexi of a conversation he'd had a few days ago with Nevsky. They'd been talking about throwing themselves on unexploded grenades or stepping in front of other squad members to take a bullet, talking about who they would die to protect. Back in Novosibirsk, Alexi's answer had been simple: No one.

He stared at the ghostly face. "You want me to throw myself on the bomb," he concluded. Then he frowned. "But what good could that possibly do? So what if I'm sitting on top of the pyramid when the thing goes off and time and space tears itself apart. What difference will it make?"

The fortune-teller laughed—a rich, full laugh that wasn't at all the cackle Alexi would have expected.

Silly boy. The answer is on the inside.

"What do you mean?"

Raheek grunted. Alexi glanced at the alien and saw what he assumed were lines of strain creasing its forehead. Raheek's blue hands were sagging as if drawn down by an invisible weight. The alien's knees trembled, and its breathing was labored.

"Tell me!" Alexi urged the ghost-woman. "Tell me what you mean! I don't understand!"

With a final grunt, Raheek let its hands fall to its sides. The swirling mist from which the ghostly face had spoken spiraled in on itself and disappeared with a soft sucking noise. Dropping his weapon, Alexi stumbled forward through the snow, arms outstretched. But his bare hands waved helplessly through empty air.

Raheek's eyes opened. "What did you learn?" the alien asked.

Alexi shook his head. What could he say? Advice of the fortune-teller notwithstanding, he was as puzzled by all of this as he'd ever been. His eyes fell on Juliana's corpse.

"I need time to think," he told the alien. He pointed at the decapitated body. "I'm going to bury her. When I'm done, I'll tell you what I learned. And not a moment before."

Raheek stared impassively at him. Whether the alien was angered by his defiance, Alexi couldn't tell.

"We have some time," it said. "We have this moment. And the one after that. And perhaps even the one after that. But our nows are precious and few. If you want your sister—and your planet—to survive, you had better not waste them."

28

Alexi smacked the palm of his hand against the smooth surface of the crystal. "She said the answer lay on the inside. But I don't see any way in. This thing looks like a solid block of stone."

"That is so." Raheek nodded slowly.

Alexi watched as the muddy handprint he'd left on the side of the tetrahedron slid down its flawless surface, like oil on polished metal. He turned his hands over and looked at his palms. They were grimy with earth.

A short distance from the tetrahedron was a fresh grave. Juliana's grave. Alexi wondered how he had managed to bury her—the ground was frozen under the snow. Then he noticed that the trees closest to the grave had gouges in the bark and broken branches. The faint smell of exploded ordnance hung in the air. He must have used his frag grenades to blow a hole in the ground and loosen the earth. But he had no memory of doing it.

He wiped his hands on his trousers. Somewhere in the distance, he heard a faint droning noise.

"What else did your ancestor say?" Raheek asked.

Alexi sighed. "Something about shielding my sister, and giving life, and being thrown into the void . . ."

"Stop." Raheek laid a hand on Alexi's chest. "The void is something that only a trained mystic can walk through. We attune our auras to it, darkness to darkness, and pass from one shadow to the next. It requires a lifetime of training and study. I cannot teach you this in the short time we have left before the crystal activates."

"Are you talking about the disappearing act you sometimes do?" Alexi asked. "It's a form of teleportation, right? I'm not sure I'd *want* to learn that. What happens if your coordinates are off and you materialize inside a solid object by mistake?"

The alien dismissed the question with a wave of its long-fingered hand. "It is not possible. A physical body cannot occupy the same space as a material object. The two are incompatible."

"So what happens, then?" Alexi continued. "If you aim for a spot that's already occupied by an object, do you get stuck somewhere in the middle and fail to materialize at all?"

"In that case the body would simply disappear. We do not know where it goes. Some mystics believe its atoms are simply annihilated, others think the body is expelled into another universe. But all agree on one thing: The soul survives. It emerges from the void into the shadow the mystic was trying to walk to for a brief moment, then goes to join those who have died before it in the Otherwhen."

An idea occurred to Alexi then—an idea that seemed to resonate with the moment, as if it had always been. "So if the soul survives, no matter what . . ." Suddenly there was a lump in his throat as he remembered the ghostly image of his father. He swallowed hard. "And if a soul can exist within a solid object . . ."

He stared up at the inverted pyramid that loomed over head. "Could a soul be sent by a mystic into the crystal?"

He was close—he could feel it. His hands were trembling and his heart was racing. Déjà vu had wrapped itself around him like a sparkling shroud.

"Impossible," Raheek said. "A soul is attached to the body. The two must travel together."

Alexi glanced at the freshly made grave. He forced himself to say the words. "But if the body were dead, the soul would be free to walk into the void, *da*?"

Raheek saw where Alexi was looking. "I cannot teach a dead human to void-walk."

"Not her," Alexi said. "Me."

"I cannot teach a living human, either."

"You might not be able to teach me to void walk. But perhaps you could give my soul a shove in the right direction." Alexi jerked a thumb at the crystal. "Right into the heart of the bomb."

"It is possible," Raheek said slowly. "In times of need, I have shaped and directed souls. I could send your soul through the void into the crystal. I am not convinced that it would have any effect. But I am willing to try."

Alexi suddenly realized what he had suggested: his own death. Now that the moment of inspiration had passed, he was starting to have second thoughts. Did he really want to kill himself? What if Tatyana wasn't alive—who would he be making this possibly futile gesture for? He couldn't think of a single person in the world that he cared enough about to die for. Was this all just a ploy by the alien, who had tricked him into saying the right words, into talking himself into this mad experiment?

Alexi shivered. He was suddenly very cold. He decided then that he'd been going in the wrong direction, all along. It wasn't he who was to throw himself on the bomb and save the Earth. Raheek could do it.

The thought warmed him considerably. Even the feeling of déjà vu disappeared.

"Tell you what," Alexi said. "Since you've got the ability to void-walk, why don't you try it? That way, you don't have to teach anyone anything. You can get inside the bomb yourself, and figure out a way to disarm it. And then—"

"And then I will be dead, and my mission will be a failure. I came here to learn about the bomb, not to throw my life away in an ill-thought experiment."

"You and me both," Alexi muttered.

That was when he noticed that the droning noise had gotten much louder. He recognized it now: a plane. And practically overhead. Undoubtedly military, up here in the middle of nowhere. The plane was probably on a reconnaissance mission. And the tetrahedron would be its objective. But was it Neo-Soviet or Union? It didn't much matter. The *taiga* stretched in all directions; there wasn't a clearing in which to land for kilometers. Alexi wouldn't be rescued or taken prisoner anytime soon. But help—or capture—would eventually come.

Alexi ran out from under the overhang of the inverted pyramid and looked up. The plane was a black cross against the cloud-white sky; Alexi didn't know enough about silhouettes to identify it as friend or foe. But he did recognize the circular white snowflakes floating gently down from the sky: parachutes—half a dozen of them. As the chutes drifted lower, Alexi spotted the by now familiar sight of therm suits. These paratroopers were Union special ops forces. Just as Juliana had been.

His soldier's instincts took over. He ran for the cover of the trees, a defensible position. He was careful not to go too deep. The ring of drones the Union had placed around the tetrahedron earlier was an invisible curtain of death, hidden somewhere in the forest. He chose instead to hunker down behind a fallen tree. He squatted in the snow, panting, his AK-51 in hand as the paratroopers descended into the forest around him.

Suddenly Alexi realized his mistake: the trail of footsteps he'd left in the snow would show them exactly where he was hiding. With six-to-one odds and his assault rifle low on ammunition, there was no way he'd win if it came to a fight. The best he could hope for was to throw down his weapon and speak two of the handful of English words he'd ever bothered to learn: I surrender.

Alexi glanced back at the inverted pyramid and saw Raheek standing under it. The alien's bald head was tipped back and its strangely articulated arms were raised, lavender palms up as if in greeting. One of the paratroopers who had been about to land on the inverted base of the pyramid spilled air from his chute, sending himself sliding down toward the forest. He landed gracefully, sinking to his knees in the snow. Then he pointed a Pitbull assault rifle at the alien and shouted something in English.

For a heartbeat or two, human and alien locked eyes. Then Raheek's hands tilted slightly. Alexi saw the Union soldier tense, then two screaming lines of neon blue energy erupted from Raheek's palms. They slammed into the chest of the paratrooper, throwing his body back like a man who had just been kicked by a horse. He crashed into a tree, hung there, then slid in a limp heap to the ground, the front of his therm suit smoking.

Gunfire erupted all around the tetrahedron as the other paratroopers, all but one of whom were on the ground now, opened up on Raheek. In defiance of all battlefield logic, the alien stood utterly still as bullets chuffed into the snow all around it—a perfect target. A swirling curtain of energy began to form around Raheek, partially obscuring the blue-skinned alien from view, and for a second time an intensely bright beam of energy streaked out toward the paratrooper who was still descending. But this attack missed, hitting the chute instead. The parachute burst into crackling blue-white flame and the soldier beneath it plummeted the last few meters to the ground, landing in a sprawled heap.

One of the Union soldiers—the officer, Alexi guessed—was shouting, trying to make himself heard above the rifle fire. He had landed just inside the trees and was running to-

ward Raheek, weapon held to the side and his free hand gesturing frantically. Alexi guessed, from his urgent tone, that he
was telling the others to cease fire. And small wonder. This
might very well be the first contact between the Zykhee and
the Union forces. Raheek was worth more to them alive than
dead. They'd want to capture him. . . .

Unless they already had a Zykhee captive. Which meant
that the crystal was their goal, and Raheek was merely
something that stood in their way.

Alexi ground his teeth. What was the alien doing,
fighting the paratroopers? Why didn't Raheek just void
walk out of here and let them take their objective? The alien
had already said there was nothing that could physically
harm the crystal. What did it care if the soldiers held it for
a while?

Except that it wouldn't be just a while. These paratroopers would be just the toehold. The Union wasn't
about to let an alien artifact go, and would invade this area
in force. Nor were they likely to be convinced to let Raheek try to figure out how to disarm the crystal. They'd
pack the alien off ASAP for interrogation. The time bomb
would go off—and Raheek would have failed in its mission.

Raheek had figured this out long before Alexi did. The
alien continued to summon up magic and hurl jagged streaks
of energy at the paratroopers. The blue and green lines of
force shot toward the Union soldiers in a screaming rush,
streaking through the air like rockets. A second paratrooper
died, her head exploding in a hot shower of blood and bone
as a bright blue beam of light lanced through it.

Now the odds were four to one—or three to one, since
the officer was still holding his fire and shouting. Or three to
two, if Alexi joined in the firefight. Undecided, he half rose
to a crouch from behind the fallen tree, his AK-51 at the
ready. Even if the therm suit provided the same protection as

armor, Alexi still had a clear shot at the Union officer's unprotected head. . . .

What the hell. The bomb was going to go off anyhow. Alexi was already a dead man. It was only a matter of time.

Grimacing at the irony of his thought, Alexi squeezed off a shot. The bullets from his AK-51 found their mark, tearing off the top of the Union officer's head. The corpse crumpled to the ground. . . .

In that same instant, Raheek went down.

Two of the remaining paratroopers turned and fired at the fresh target: Alexi. The third looked wildly around, unable to tell where the attack that had taken out the officer had come from. Bullets chunked into the trees next to Alexi, sending chips of bark flying. Cursing, praying that Raheek was still alive, praying that the few bullets he had left in his AK-51 would find their mark, Alexi returned the paratrooper's fire in short bursts. But the trees provided a thick screen between him and his targets.

One of the Union soldiers went down, but the paratrooper who had been able to locate Alexi earlier was moving into position. In that instant, Alexi recognized the weapon he carried as a sniper rifle. The Union soldier found a clear line of sight . . .

Alexi was going to die.

The paratrooper lifted the sniper rifle to his shoulder and aimed through the scope . . .

Alexi flung aside his AK-51 and threw his hands in the air. "Friend!" he screamed in English. "Surrender!"

The sniper squeezed the trigger.

Something hot punched through Alexi's forehead.

Alexi found himself floating in the air, looking down on his own body. A neat hole in the center of his forehead was just starting to seep blood. As he rose gently up through the trees, he saw one of the Union officers flipping over Raheek's body. The other paratrooper wound his way cautiously through the woods, toward Alexi's corpse.

Alexi was dead.

But his soul . . .

His soul was free to . . .

The crystal had unwittingly given him the power to . . .

Go!

29

Juliana jumped as Alexi shook her shoulder. Her hand jerked to the side, and the growler saliva that she had been collecting in the vodka bottle splashed onto her fingers. She dropped the bottle into the snow and whirled on Alexi, cursing.

"Why did you sneak up on me like that?" she spat angrily at him. Tears welled in her eyes. As the acid ate into her hand, the flesh began to redden and sizzle. Bright red burns blistered through the skin. Groaning, she plunged her hand into the snow, trying to wipe the acid from it.

"Prastitye pazhalsta," Alexi said. But he wasn't sorry. Not at all. Compelled by an urge he didn't understand, he had deliberately shaken the Union officer's shoulder so that her hand would be covered in acid. Now she wouldn't be able to use her pistol, or to . . .

Alexi used the toe of his boot to dig the vodka bottle out of the snow. Already the hydrofluoric acid was beginning to opaque the glass. The bottle held only a centimeter or two of growler saliva. Not enough to . . .

To what?

Alexi brought his heel down on the bottle, breaking it.

As the acid sizzled out into the snow he dropped his pack in the snow and fished the first-aid kit from it. There was little inside that would help, but at least he could cover the burns to Juliana's hand with a little gauze.

"What were you doing?" Alexi asked.

Juliana's face was pale with pain. "The crystal," she gritted through clenched teeth. "It's silicon. Hydrofluoric acid will eat through it. If we shear off part of its hardware, maybe its programming will . . ."

"It wouldn't have worked," Alexi said. "The crystal wouldn't allow it to."

He paused. That had been an odd thing to say. How could he be so certain? Raheek had said the silicon crystal was like a gigantic computer chip, and if there was one thing Juliana should know about, given her university education, it was computers. But somehow he knew her idea had been doomed to fail.

"Here," he said. "Let me help you with that hand."

He bandaged her hand carefully, taking care not to brush his fingers across the fresh blisters. When he was done, Juliana cradled her injured hand against her chest. But when Alexi offered her his arm, she drew back from him with an angry grimace and shoved her left hand awkwardly into a pocket.

"You did that on purpose, Sov," she spat, drawing her Pug pistol. "Don't touch me again. Let's move out—I want to find out what the alien is up to. And stay in front, where I can see you."

Alexi did as he was told. He wasn't too worried; he still had his AK-51 slung over his shoulder and Soldatenkof's armored jacket would protect his back. He didn't think that Juliana would be able to aim very well with her left hand, not with her injured hand throbbing. But he kept his hands where she could see them as they wound their way through the forest, not making any threatening moves.

Raheek was waiting for them near the tetrahedron. Alexi shivered as he passed into the triangle of shadow it cast. He had the overwhelming sense of a blank face staring down at him, watching his every move and preparing to squash him like a bug.

When they were close enough to touch the tetrahedron, Alexi reached out and slid the palm of his hand along the wall of crystal. It was smooth as glass, without even a hairline crack in its surface. And yet it had fallen in a fireball from the heavens and landed on Earth with the explosive force of a nuclear warhead.

An explosive force that it had directed back in time, through the Otherwhen . . .

Where had that word come from? Alexi jerked his hand away from the surface of the crystal.

"So," he asked Raheek. "What happens next?"

A wave of déjà vu rushed up at him, making his head spin. He had said those exact words once before. He had done all this—exactly—before. The forest, the crystal, Raheek . . . the only difference was Juliana. She shouldn't have been there. And there should have been a grave, just there in the forest.

Like a man in a lucid dream, Alexi sleepwalked through the same conversation he'd had with Raheek, sometime in the Otherwhen. They spoke of psychic powers, of Alexi's great-to-the-power-of-twenty grandmother who had been a fortune-teller. Of souls, and ghosts and duty. Ghosts came and talked to Alexi while Juliana stared in white-faced horror. And then Alexi and Raheek spoke of death, and of souls walking through a void. . . .

It all happened in fast-forward, like the proverbial life that flashed before a dying man's eyes. Except that it wasn't Alexi's whole life—just a small slice of it. A slice he'd viewed once before . . .

Time suddenly jerked back into its normal speed, leaving Alexi's mind spinning like a top. As the déjà vu feeling gradually wound down, he heard an aircraft droning through the sky. And in that instant he knew that he was going to die. No matter which path he chose.

"Do it," he said. "Take my soul and push it into the void. Throw me inside the crystal. If I'm going to die, I might as well die a hero."

Raheek protested, as Alexi knew the alien would. "It is possible to place your soul inside the crystal. But I am not convinced that it would have any effect. The mystic energy burns in you, but the flame is very small. How can one tiny intelligence possibly affect something as large as this?"

"Chaos theory," Juliana said.

Both Raheek and Alexi turned to look at her. She stared up at the crystal with a thoughtful expression.

"Computers operate on the principle of serial processing," she said slowly. "A computer can process information several thousand times faster than the human brain, but the flow of information through the system as a whole is highly regimented. A single error has a snowball effect; there is no margin made for self-correction. If we interrupt that data flow by sending into the crystal a human consciousness with its chaotic, parallel processing, the errors it induces could be catastrophic. The entire operating system could freeze up."

Raheek digested this a moment before speaking. "This is much more than just a computer," it reminded her. "It was built by a highly sophisticated alien race. The bombs that were encountered previously have demonstrated the ability to react to outside threats of varying natures. They seem to be capable of both self-awareness and learning."

"But they're made of silicon," Juliana insisted. "Here on Earth, silicon is made into a computer chip by doping it to endow it with either a negative or positive charge and then layering it like a sandwich to create millions of on/off switches. The flow of electricity through the system must follow specific paths. The bomb's programming must be the same. Which means it operates using a binary system—not a parallel system, like the human brain."

Raheek remained unconvinced. "Alexi is suggesting that his soul be sent into the crystal, not his brain."

Juliana threw up her hands in exasperation. "Everything in the human body operates on chaotic principles. Even when our hearts are beating at a constant rate, the heartbeat itself is not perfectly regular. What makes you think the soul won't be chaotic, as well?"

Alexi tipped his head to listen. The droning noise was getting louder. Wrapped up in their hypothetical argument, neither Raheek nor Juliana had noticed it. Alexi had the overwhelming feeling that death was just a few thousand meters overhead. . . .

"Quiet!" he yelled.

Both the alien and Juliana fell silent.

"We're running out of time," Alexi said urgently. "And the theory doesn't matter. We already know it will work."

Both Juliana and Raheek asked the same question at once: "How?"

"My memory lapses," Alexi said. "You must have noticed—both of you—that at times I've appeared disoriented and confused, that I've forgotten where I was or what I was doing. I thought they were blackouts—memory losses caused by fatigue, or drunkenness, or some new symptom of toxic or radiation poisoning. But now I know what they were."

Alexi slapped a palm against the tetrahedron. "My soul is inside the crystal, even as we speak. I've always been inside it, ever since it entered Earth's atmosphere—from the moment I saw it in the sky over Vladivostok. Somehow, I've been using its time-distorting mechanisms to jump around in time."

"Impossible," Raheek said.

"You'd get stuck inside a paradox," Juliana added.

Alexi tapped a finger to his forehead. "There's one other human element you forgot, Juliana: free will."

He paused and thought for a moment. "And there's an even more obvious clue," he added. "If the crystal's a bomb—and not only that but a smart bomb, capable of self-defense—how come it hasn't gone off yet? Why is it just sitting here, when at this very moment . . ."

Alexi suddenly had a flash of déjà vu. Of silver-suited paratroopers falling through the sky. Not in Tomsk 13, and not Juliana's squad—but here. Now.

He grabbed Raheek's arm with one hand and Juliana's good arm with the other. He forced her hand up until the Pug pistol was pointed at his head.

"Raheek, get your magic ready. It's time to hurl my soul into the crystal. And Juliana, as soon as Raheek's ready, shoot me."

They both stared at him, as if transfixed. Just beyond the triangular shadow that the tetrahedron cast, Alexi could see a circular shadow growing against the forest floor. . . .

"Do it!" he yelled. "Now!"

Raheek gestured yes with its hand, then immediately began to chant. The alien stepped back from Alexi, gesturing as it did so. A spiraling vortex of energy formed in the air between human and alien. Alexi stared into it, feeling the haunting call of death.

"I am ready," Raheek said.

Alexi stared at Juliana. The Pug pistol was pointed unwaveringly at his head, but her dark eyes were blinking. He hoped she didn't miss.

"Go on," he whispered. "Isn't this what you always wanted? Vengeance for the death of your lover—up close and personal?"

Juliana shook her head. A tear trickled down her cheek.

The pistol barked flame . . .

And in that same instant Alexi's consciousness was pulled forward into the swirling vortex that Raheek had created. Even as the paratroopers touched softly down behind the alien and leveled their assault rifles at it, Raheek cupped Alexi's soul in one lavender-colored palm and tossed him, as softly as a dream, into the crystal.

30

Alexi was drifting, flowing, swimming lazily through a space that had no sensation, through a time that had no duration.

So this is what it's like to be dead, he thought.

There had been a brief burst of pain as the bullet tore through his forehead, and then all of the sounds around him had begun spiraling inward as darkness closed in on him. His consciousness had tugged gently free of his bloodied, collapsed body and stared dispassionately down at it. And then it had begun fragmenting apart. Bright sparkles of light, disassociating from one another . . .

Something scooped up the tattered fragments of consciousness and kneaded them back together like a baker working dough. Lavender-colored palms, strong blue fingers. Then, like a double-jointed pitcher hurling a ball, those hands had whipped the spark of consciousness that was Alexi against something hard, smooth, unyielding . . .

A patch of darkness opened—a hole into the Otherwhen—and he was inside.

Alexi found himself flowing like water through a canal with walls of smooth glossy stone. The walls were vibrating, and as Alexi tuned in to those vibrations he could feel the bumps of individual atoms as he slid past them. They were clustered in fours, each a tiny tetrahedron. And then in fours, and in fours again—regimented, precise, like the hardware of a machine.

He joined the flow of electrons as they worked their way through the crystal from atom to atom, moving along at precisely defined angles and lines. Moving in perfect time, like a clockwork.

Except that this clockwork was not built to measure time, but to bend it until it broke. Inside the crystal, Alexi could feel the individual threads of time being pried out of their normal weave, then snapping as they lost their coherency. So far, the effect was contained within the tetrahedron—within the individual atoms of the silicon crystal. But it was straining to expand. . . .

A flaw in the mechanism held the effect back—a random element that had corrupted the process. The steady flow of electrons, the precise angles of deflection and movement from one atom to the next, was being thrown out of kilter. But what was that flaw? And where?

Rounding a corner, Alexi suddenly was confronted with the answer: He had been there before. And before. And before. It was as if he was looking into a mirror that was reflecting the surface of another mirror, set parallel to the first. Those mirrors reflected all of the possible nows that had, did, or would exist for Alexi. The blurred reflections of all of these possible nows stretched back to infinity, creating a folding that the crystal was unable to correct. . . .

Knowledge blossomed in Alexi's consciousness: The fact that he was inside the crystal was the only thing that was keeping the time bomb from going off. His very presence had introduced an element of chaos to the mix. He was the butterfly that caused a hurricane of skewed programming and thwarted effect. All he need do was stay inside the crystal forever—until the end of time—and the bomb would never go off.

Alexi contemplated the seemingly infinite number of reflected nows that could have been. In one of those sequences of nows, everything had gone smoothly. There had been no death, no wounds, no confusion, no jumping about in time. Raheek had found Alexi in Vladivostok, the Zykhee crew had repaired their ship, and they had made it to the impact site in time for Alexi's soul to enter the crystal before it had a chance to explode. But that thread had been lost among the myriad possibilities that could be.

Why?

Intuitively, Alexi knew that the answer was linked to the fact that the bomb had thrown the explosive force of itself striking the planet back in time to the year 1908. That must have been some sort of defensive mechanism, a way of cushioning the impact so the crystal was not damaged by the landing.

Alexi mused on that thought. If the bomb was capable of hurling explosive force back in time, was it also capable of freeing itself of an irritating "bug" in its programming by hurling that irritant back to another time?

For the briefest of moments—the tiniest fragment of time imaginable—the flow of electrons paused.

Alexi suddenly wished he hadn't had that thought. In the instant that the electron flow paused, he had the overwhelming sense that something was watching him, listening in on his thoughts. Absorbing them into itself. And that presence was malevolent in the extreme.

A realization dawned: He was not alone inside the crystal.

He was not . . .

The electron flow Alexi had been flowing along with suddenly sped up. Alexi was swept through a series of impossible angles that seemed to fold in upon themselves. He raged against the flow, but could do nothing to stop it. Then, at the center of the angles, a tiny tear appeared in the fabric of space-time: a wormhole. Alexi's consciousness was squeezed, compressed, compelled—and squirted through that tear. He found himself . . .

Back in Vladivostok. In a ruined building, on his knees, searching for his glasses. About to die.

Yes, he could see it now—literally, because he had found his glasses. The approaching heavy-assault suit, the flare as a rocket launched from its shoulder, the needle of death streaking toward him.

Even though he was in the moment—inside his body as it recoiled in horror from the whooshing rocket—he felt as though he were watching it all from a distance. He felt no emotion as his body was blasted nearly in two and hurled across the ruined building. Was he having a near-death experience? Had he become a ghost? But that wasn't right. His death lay far in the future, in a now when Juliana shot him. That was when his soul had left his body and had been hurled by Raheek into the crystal.

The crystal . . .

Even as he watched himself die, Alexi could still sense the crystal all around him, could feel the flow of the electrons that coursed through it. The awareness was deep, at the subconscious level. Some essential, invisible sliver of Alexi—the core of his soul—remained inside the crystal and was watching the Alexi of this other now go into shock and begin to die. . . .

And notice a "falling star" in the sky above Vladivostok: the fireball that surrounded the crystal that contained Alexi's soul.

The part of Alexi that was inside the crystal could feel the friction and heat produced by its descent through the outer atmosphere. But that didn't make sense. How could Alexi be inside the crystal at this point in time if his soul had yet to be hurled into the crystal by Raheek? That event lay far in the future.

Then Alexi realized what the answer must be. Had that part of Alexi that remained inside the crystal still been wearing that body, he would have used its mouth to laugh out loud.

The crystal had sent him back in time—to a now in which he was certain to die. The crystal had concluded that, when Alexi died in that now, it would be free of him. If it had worked, there would have been no Alexi to kill the Zykhee and be granted leave in Novosibirsk and assigned to fight growlers in Tomsk 13 and survive to fly north in the helicraft and die and enter the crystal. Alexi would have died back in Vladivostok, and that would have been the end of it.

But the crystal had made a fatal miscalculation. Only a tiny fragment of Alexi's soul—his consciousness—had been completely ejected into the Vladivostok now. The rest of his soul had also made the journey back in time, but not in space. It remained inside the crystal—which in that moment was hurtling toward Earth, just beginning to fireball its way through the outer atmosphere.

As a result, Alexi's soul now occupied every moment in time between the battle in Vladivostok and the current now. He had only to send his conscious mind back to rejoin it, in order to escape.

Alexi's body died as the wounds he suffered from the rocket's blast caused him to bleed to death. . . .

And like a flat stone on water, he skipped his conscious mind back across time and space, back to the crystal and the current now.

It hurled him back in time again like a petulant child. . . .

This time, Alexi was able to tap into a tiny fragment of memory from the part of his soul that remained inside the crystal. Avoiding the ruined building that the rocket was soon to tear to pieces, he went down to the street instead. . . .

Only to be killed by Soldatenkof.

As he died, Alexi wrenched his consciousness free once more. . . .

The crystal returned the volley. Back to Vladivostok,

where the heavy-assault suit killed Alexi a different way, with a machine gun.

Alexi yanked his consciousness back from his dying body a third time and was hurled once more by the crystal. Once again, he listened to the tiny voice that was a whisper from that part of his soul that remained inside the crystal, and avoided his own death.

But this time, the replay led to his killing Juliana with a rad grenade. Which meant that she would not be there to fly the helicraft or convince Raheek that the crystal's programming could be disrupted, or deliver the fatal bullet that set Alexi's soul free.

This time, when he returned to the crystal, Alexi could feel an emotion coursing through its silicon body. Like an artificial intelligence, the bomb was learning from its mistakes. It had already learned how to gloat.

Hovering inside its crystalline structure, Alexi could overhear its next thought. If it couldn't kill Alexi, the bomb would instead send him back to a time and place where Alexi would kill Raheek. Which would close, with utter finality, the door Alexi had used to access the crystal.

The bomb paused for a microsecond, thinking. Where to send Alexi next?

Alexi had to move. Fast. When the space-time wormhole opened, he did not wait for the crystal to push him in but instead dived through it before the angles could complete their intricate folding. He found himself back in Novosibirsk on leave. As his physical body stumbled drunkenly through the streets, into the theater and up onto the stage, Alexi watched himself from the darkened theater, from the seat beside Raheek.

Look here! he tried to tell himself. This alien can help you!

But even after he had stumbled in panic to the church, the Alexi that was physically in that now could not be made to understand. He simply did not have the necessary information. His consciousness was living its life out of order. Missing his memories of what had happened between Vladivostok and Novosibirsk, and with only a tickling of déjà vu provided by the memories of futures that might come, he stumbled through the now, unable to make sense of it.

Frustrated, Alexi abandoned that now and withdrew his conscious mind back inside the crystal. There had to be another way. . . .

The bomb seized the moment, tossing Alexi to a time when Raheek would startle him by returning to the helicraft, when the Alexi of that now would try to kill the alien and then would think that the alien was trying to kill him in revenge.

The Alexi of *this* now realized that Raheek had never intended to kill him, back when the alien had held the blade of its metal staff against his cheek. Raheek had merely been trying to use the weapon's mystic energies to jar Alexi's memories back into place—an alien version of electroshock therapy. Raheek knew that Alexi was the key that would unlock the bomb's secrets, even if the alien at that point still did not know how, or why. The last thing the alien wanted was for him to die. Although Raheek would change his mind later, when the right now came along. . . .

Once again, the crystal had erred in its choice of nows to send Alexi back to. The Alexi of that now had no memory of meeting Juliana and establishing a tentative friendship with her, and regarded her as his enemy. But at the same time, he learned that Juliana did not die in Vladivostok. And so he began to actively probe for these missing memories. In the process his consciousness forged connections with the part of his soul that remained inside the crystal, gathering hints and half memories that he could later use to alter the sequence of events.

That he *would* later use to alter the sequence of events.

Which meant that Alexi's conscious mind had been sent back through time to a now when it was possible to set things right.

Which was something the crystal never would have done.

Which could only mean one thing: It was possible for Alexi to jump around in time himself, without the crystal's aid. But how?

There had to be a force other than the crystal at work. One that lay within Alexi. . . .

He suddenly realized what it was. Humans had a limited power over time: They could send their consciousness back to the past, anytime they wanted. That power was called memory. It was imperfect, and imprecise. But it existed.

Why then could humans not send themselves forward in time?

Perhaps, mused Alexi, because they were still tied to their physical bodies—constructs that were forced to plod through time one step at a time, not skip through it as the human consciousness did.

But then another thought occurred to him: Humans *could* send themselves forward in time, by imagining the futures that might be. These glimpses were of what might be—not what must be. Even psychics who could foresee the future could, by the very act of their relaying this information to others, change it.

Psychics. The word stuck for a moment in Alexi's consciousness. That was what Raheek had implied Alexi was, when the alien had called him a mystic. Was there a genetic code that enabled someone to be a psychic, a code that had been passed down through the generations from Alexi's ancestor who had prophesied the death of Peter the Great? Or was there something else at work, some trigger that explained why only some human beings had "the sight"?

Whatever the reasons, Alexi had found the answer. The memories he needed—the keys to all of those other possible nows—were stored inside that part of himself that he called his soul. He had only to turn one of them . . .

As he concentrated, something clicked inside Alexi's

mind. His consciousness skipped back in time—precisely to the memory he was dwelling upon: the moment when his squad had been airlifted out of Vladivostok. He watched as the scene on the helicraft played itself out, as he learned who and what the Zykhee were. And that he had been the one to kill the Zykhee warrior and save his squad—and himself—from certain death.

Perfect! Now that he knew he could direct his consciousness to other nows, he would use this newfound skill to help the Alexi of a previous now use the information he had just acquired. He skipped back to Vladivostok, to a quiet moment in the museum—and by the force of will alone held the crystal at bay until the whispers of future memory told the Alexi of that now how to kill the Zykhee warrior that emerged from the submarine.

But he couldn't keep the crystal at bay forever. With a wrench, the crystal yanked his conscious mind away and threw Alexi elsewhen. This time, the destination was Tomsk 13.

Unprepared for that now, Alexi watched himself get killed by a growler in the underground corridors of the military research facility. At the last moment, as he lay dying, he pulled his consciousness free and sent it to the place where knowledge lay: in the briefing room, where Lieutenant Soldatenkof was explaining what a growler was.

The crystal tried again. But the Alexi of that when knew not to turn his back on the underground corridor. He squeezed past the collapse in the ceiling—only to be startled by the cryotanks filled with baby growlers that he found there. Terrified by the hatchlings' attack on Piotr, he turned and ran and died . . .

Alexi retreated from that now. Back in the crystal once more, he pondered his next move. The bomb was experimenting with him, sending him back to points where a decision could fork in two directions, both of them bad.

Alexi instead sought out a moment before the one he had just been cast into, a now in which a decision could lead to life, not death. His consciousness jumped back to Tomsk 13 again, but this time, he refused to go into the underground corridors. This time, he was above ground. Only to be mortally wounded. But Raheek was there to heal him, as Alexi knew he would be. . . .

Alexi could sense the crystal's growing anger. Had he still worn a physical body, this squeeze through the time-space wormhole would have left it battered and bruised. The bomb fired Alexi's consciousness into a now that lay just before the moment when Alexi's soul had entered the tetrahedron. In his panic at realizing that he was to kill himself—and his lack of the memory that told him why—the Alexi of that now accidentally killed Raheek.

The hop back to this now was a short one. Inside the crystal, Alexi and the bomb withdrew from one another like boxers retreating to the corners of the ring, silently contemplating each other. Alexi's physical body would have been breathing hard at this point from the strain. The bomb's physical body . . .

Was a crystal.

Alexi saw it now with absolute clarity. He wasn't battling an artificial intelligence—a silicon chip constructed by an alien race. He was locked into mental combat with a member of that race itself. What had Raheek called them? The Shard. Beings with bodies built from silicon, rather than carbon. Bodies made of crystal.

The tetrahedron was a gigantic, complex body that the Shard had built for itself. Like Juliana's heavy-assault suit, the silicon construct surrounded the Shard's consciousness. But unlike Juliana, the Shard was unable to take its suit off. Body and mind were one.

When the bomb went off, the Shard whose consciousness was inhabiting and controlling it would be destroyed. Just like the Japanese kamikaze pilots of World War II, it was willing to die for its country. Or planet.

Or universe.

For all Alexi knew, the Maelstrom and everything in this strange chunk of space that the Earth had been violently wrenched into during the Change was the Shard's home turf. And if it was, small wonder that the first overture of that race toward humanity was a hostile one.

Another thought occurred to Alexi. If he was here inside the crystal, present and conscious in this moment, he must have already won the battle. For him to exist in this now, he had to have survived all of the previous nows that the Shard tossed him to. No matter what deaths lay in those past moments, Alexi could avoid them—and would avoid them.

The thought gave him the courage to go on. There were a few loose ends to tie up, back in those other nows.

He sent himself back to Tomsk 13 and met Juliana and Raheek and got on board the helicraft. . . .

The crystal retaliated by sending him ahead to a now when Juliana took him prisoner. Based on what had come later, in other nows, Alexi knew that it would be only a matter of time before Union paratroopers came and took him prisoner and carried him far away from the crystal and claimed the bomb as their own . . .

But that now gave him a vital clue: the latitude and longitude of the "meteorite impact site." Alexi clutched it to his consciousness, determined to give this information to Raheek. But first he jumped back further in time, to the moment when Nevsky planted the seed of an idea in his mind: of a soldier throwing himself on an unexploded grenade to save his comrades.

And ahead to a moment when he and Juliana began to develop a tentative friendship, only to have that bond break when Alexi had made the mistake of comparing himself to Juliana's lost lover. In retaliation for her outburst, he disabled her therm suit. Which would lead to an interesting now, down the time line . . .

But there were other things to do, first. Alexi jumped his consciousness back to a now in which he found the can-

isters of nerve gas in Tomsk 13 and watched bemusedly as
he obeyed the strange compulsion that told him to carry one
on board the helicraft. Then he jumped ahead slightly in
time, to the point where he realized that a growler had attached itself to the bottom of the helicraft—and that the
nerve gas was the only thing that would kill it. After the
growler had been dealt with, Alexi was able to tell Raheek
the coordinates of where the "meteorite" fell.

The Shard's next attack caught Alexi off-balance. This
time, it sent him back to the battle of Vladivostok. Once
again, it presented him with a now that included a momentous discovery: the Zykhee spaceship that had been forced
to land in that city—thousands of kilometers from its intended landing site—after human ships attacked it during its
approach to Earth. Startled by this knowledge, Alexi died—
this time at the hands of the Zykhee who had stayed behind
in the museum to try to repair the damaged ship while its
companions sought another way to get Raheek to the Shard.

Alexi tore his conscious mind away and jumped it forward to a point where he learned three vital things: that the
bomb disrupted time; that an adult growler was in the immediate vicinity of the impact site; and that the tetrahedron
was surrounded by Union drones.

The cost was Juliana's life. But by jumping all the way
back in time to Vladivostok again, Alexi was able to lure Juliana away from the spot where she was killed. Away to the
museum on whose roof the Zykhee spaceship had landed.

Which led to her promotion . . .

Which led to her being put in command of the special
ops team that parachuted into Tomsk 13 . . .

Now Alexi was on the right track. He just needed to
jump to the now in which he discovered the baby growler,
and the now in which he used it to lure the adult growler into
range of the drone. . . .

But that led to the setback of Juliana trying to use the
highly acidic growler saliva to break apart the tetrahedron—

as Alexi found out when the Shard skipped him ahead to a now in which it killed all three of them.

Building on this tiny victory, the Shard hurled Alexi into the now in which Raheek killed Juliana—a now in which, even as Alexi wept over her grave, he learned from his dead ancestors the secret weakness of the Shard.

The Shard jumped him ahead—just a little ahead—to a now in which the Union soldiers killed Alexi before he could use that secret. . . .

Alexi threw himself back—just enough, to a point in time when Juliana was alive, and could be the one to shoot him instead.

Which brought his consciousness circling back, as he had always known it would, to this very same now.

It was Alexi's turn to gloat.

You can't defeat me, he told the Shard. *Part of me has been inside you since that moment when you first tossed me back to Vladivostok—when you first entered Earth's atmosphere. There's no escaping me—and others like me. As long as there are humans on this Earth, there will be someone who can defeat you.*

A thought echoed back from the Shard—a gloating note of triumph. *There was a time before humans existed on this planet?*

Fear rippled through Alexi's consciousness. He suddenly realized his mistake. The Shard could escape him. It only had to go back far enough in time, to the age of the dinosaurs . . .

With a ghostly echo of laughter that reverberated through the millennia, the Shard was gone.

Alexi found his soul suddenly cast free. With one last effort of will he cast his consciousness out, searching for the single defining moment that could change his life. . . .

31

U nidentified object in quadrant one-zero-nine.

The voice, even though it originated several thousand kilometers away at Moonbase Gagarin, was coming in loud and clear, squirted in laser-light pulses. For the millionth time in his three-year career with the space arm of the Soviet military, Alexi thanked Christ that he didn't have to deal with the outdated and faulty equipment that the Earth-based forces were issued. Especially in a critical situation like this one.

"*Da,*" Alexi answered. "My instruments have it."

He followed the red pulse as it blipped across the three-dimensional display on his console. At the center of the display was a blue dot representing Earth. Farther out, a white dot represented the moon. The red blip had come from just beyond the moon's orbit. Since the comets and meteoroids had been left behind with the other planets in the solar system when the Earth was yanked into the Maelstrom during the Change, there was a strong possibility that the red blip was a foreign object. Perhaps even an alien spacecraft, like the one that had nearly wiped out the *NP-30* ship. Alexi shuddered, wondering if the blue-skinned bastards had finally found Earth.

If it was an alien craft, it could be the last thing Alexi ever saw. Just three days ago, one of the Union's patrol ships had disappeared without a trace after firing upon an unidentified object. The garbled communications the Neo-Soviets had intercepted suggested that the bogey had been a ship of some kind—or at least an object that was capable of returning their fire. Whatever it had been, they'd lost it.

What do you suppose the object is? the communications operator back at the moonbase asked.

"I don't know," Alexi said. "But I'm about to find out."

Alexi called up mass, spectral, and reflective analyses of the object. His lips pursed when he saw the results. It was big: nearly a kilometer across. And according to the probable chemical breakdown that scrolled across his datascreens, it was made of a single element: silicon.

That alone was cause for alarm. If the object was pure silicon, it had to have been deliberately manufactured—probably by aliens, since Alexi couldn't think of a single reason why humans would construct such a thing. It certainly wasn't natural. On Earth, silicon only occurred naturally in combinations with other elements. And the asteroids that had occupied the solar system until the Change were made up of carbon, ice, and iron.

Alexi whistled softly into the wire-thin microphone that was taped to his jaw. The skin under the tape itched where his whiskers were growing out. He resisted the urge to scratch. Instead he concentrated on the mystery that lay before him. At last: something exciting. It was what he'd craved, ever since he signed up for the military's space arm. Exciting enough to make him forget the uncomfortable bloating that the zero G was putting his body through.

"Looks like an unidentified object," Alexi told the comm op. "Probably alien. And it's on a trajectory that will take it toward Earth."

Wish I was there to see it, too. The wistful new voice over Alexi's headphones was Vasily, another scout-ship pilot. He was on the other side of the Earth, performing a reconnaissance over the Union. *Permission to attempt an intercept?* he asked.

Nyet, the comm op told him. *Continue with your mission. Minsk will handle any intercept.*

Whatever the unidentified object was, it was minutes away from Earth. And Alexi's scout ship was the only Neo-Soviet craft standing in its way.

Alexi positioned his body over the pilot's seat and hit the control that powered up his directional thrusters. He drifted down into the seat as he began the burn that would point his ship in the direction of the object. He had more than enough fuel to go in for a closer look and still be able to return to base on the moon. His ship didn't have the firepower to do anything about the object—even if it was just an inert chunk of silicon, he couldn't hope to deflect it or break it apart. One of the Union's battle stations could do that, but the only one in this quadrant of space had been knocked out of commission by a Neo-Sov attack, ten days ago.

Alexi would only be able to observe and report. And to wonder if this might be a historic moment.

He let the thrust push him back into his padded chair, every muscle tense as his scout ship jetted its way toward the unidentified object. Already his mind was writing the entry that would appear in Neo-Soviet textbooks, once the war was finally over and school resumed. It wouldn't be as large an entry as humanity's first contact with an intelligent alien race—which at the moment was top secret; only the men and women of the Neo-Soviet space-recon teams knew that the Maelstrom was inhabited by more than just growlers. But it would be an entry, nonetheless. And Alexi's name would be part of history.

History. Alexi had to laugh at himself. He'd loved the subject as a kid, but where had it ever gotten him? No, he'd made an intelligent decision on the day when he'd decided to pursue a career in mathematics instead. With a math degree under his belt, he'd persuaded the military to surgically correct his astigmatism and allow him to join its space arm. And he had childish imagination to thank for it. That day on the shore of Lake Baikal, when he thought he heard his father's "ghost," he'd sworn to choose a life path that would make his father proud.

Alexi hadn't looked back since. The polluted, wasted husk that was Earth could blow itself to pieces, for all he cared. Except that Tatyana was still down there. A good Neo-Soviet soldier, she was still continuing the futile fight.

Suddenly, Alexi had the sensation that he was being watched. Which was ridiculous, given that his was a solo scout ship. Even so, he glanced around the confined cockpit. Nothing but his own shadow, cast by the lights on the instrument panel. Just as his logical mind had told him. But he still couldn't shake the sensation of unseen eyes, watching.

Something began to press uncomfortably into Alexi's chest. He glanced down and realized it was the gold cross that had been his mother's. Contrary to all rules and regs, he'd smuggled it into space with him and wore it every time he flew a mission. His mother had always claimed that it was lucky, or blessed—or something. The cross itself dated back to the 1700s, and the gemstone it was set with was said to be even more ancient. Alexi wasn't going to take any chances by leaving his lucky cross behind, even on missions when weight was calculated down to the last gram.

Realizing that the stone that was set into the face of the cross was what was digging into his chest, he flipped the cross over. The semiprecious stone—probably a piece of gray quartz, by the look of it—was a perfect tetrahedron. Probably the point of a larger quartz crystal. Its point was sharp enough, at two Gs acceleration, to leave a pyramid-shaped dent in Alexi's chest.

He lifted the cross to his lips and kissed it for good luck. The sensation of being watched grew stronger. And the presence was not a friendly one. It was dark, malevolent, destructive.

And confused.

Alexi still held the cross that hung around his neck, despite the fact that two Gs were making his arm as heavy as lead. He pressed his index finger against the crystal that was set at the center of the cross. Without understanding how, he knew that the object that was hurtling toward Earth was linked, somehow, to the pyramid-shaped gemstone.

Alexi's ship was closing on the unidentified object. But it was still too far away to register as anything but a blur on his instruments. He peered out the tiny cockpit window and spotted the object by its reddish glow against the velvety blackness of space. It had just begun to enter Earth's atmosphere, and the friction of its passage was creating a fireball. It was as beautiful as a sunset against the blue-and-white orb of Earth.

The object wasn't taking any evasive action, even though Alexi's ship was approaching it. It seemed to be headed straight toward Earth.

Alexi still had the sense that something was watching him—listening in on his very thoughts. He wrestled his paranoia down, then made his report, choosing his words with care: "*Leitenant* Minsk to Moonbase Gagarin. Unidentified object appears to be a hostile alien artifact. It has entered Earth's atmosphere."

As he spoke, his computer calculated the probable impact point: Siberia—just shy of the Arctic Circle. A desolate, lonely place, far removed from centers of population or anything of military importance. And far from Vladivostok, where his sister's squad was currently putting one of the Neo-Sov's new heavy-assault suits through its paces. But an object that large striking the Earth could throw up enough dust and debris to cause the "nuclear winter" that World War III had already come so close to precipitating. It wasn't quite as large as the meteorite that had wiped out the dinosaurs, sixty-five million years ago. But it was damn close.

"Probable impact site of the object is . . ."

His words trailed off. Struck dumb by surprise, Alexi could only blink in amazement. The object was gone. Just like that. One moment it had been just starting to fireball its way into the Earth's atmosphere, and the next it had disappeared.

A crazy notion popped into Alexi's mind then: The meteorite was running away from him. Just as it had when . . .

In that same instant, Vasily's voice erupted in Alexi's ear. *We've got another unidentified object!* he said in a voice tense with excitement. *It appeared out of nowhere, a split second after Alexi's transmission ended. Probable impact site is the Yucatán Peninsula. Estimated time until impact is—*

Vasily's voice dissolved in a strangled curse. *Christ!* he muttered. *Where in hell did it go?*

A crazy thought blossomed in Alexi's mind: It's gone back in time to destroy the dinosaurs. Which will allow mammals to inherit the Earth, and humans to evolve, and me to be born . . .

Alexi suddenly realized that he was laughing out loud. Some sort of cosmic joke had just been played out. And even though Alexi couldn't understand it, the joke was more delightful than any he'd ever heard. He felt dizzy, lightheaded—which was not a good symptom, up in space. He glanced in alarm at his instruments, but the oxygen supply was still constant, and the ventilators were whirring. It must have been an attack of nerves, then.

But as those jitters settled down and his laughter subsided, an even stranger feeling came over him. It settled over Alexi, as immovable as the heavy press of thrust-induced G forces. He had the overwhelming sensation that he'd played out this confrontation once before—in another lifetime, perhaps. And it had all started with the fireball—but he'd seen it from a different angle.

There. His imagination supplied the image. He'd been down on the Earth, looking up into the evening sky. An infantry soldier in a war-torn city, with a battle raging around him. An angry red streak had appeared in the heavens, midway between the moon and the Maw . . .

As suddenly as it had washed over him, the feeling was gone. Realizing that he had been silent too long, that the comm op back at the moonbase was shouting frantic questions in his ear, he returned to the here and now. His training taking over, he began methodically to plot and report the last known position of the unidentified object, which appeared to have somehow teleported itself to the other side of the Earth—and then out of this universe entirely. He ignored the questions in his mind: what, how, why?

Just as he ignored the tiny voice in his soul that knew the answers.

About the Author

Lisa Smedman is also the author of four novels set in the Shadowrun™ universe, has written a number of adventures for several game systems including TSR's Ravenloft® line, and has published short science fiction and fantasy stories in various magazines and anthologies. Formerly a newspaper reporter, she now works as a freelance game designer and fiction writer. When not writing, she spends her time organizing literary conventions, hiking and camping with a women's outdoors club, and (of course) gaming. She lives in Vancouver, B.C.

VISIT WARNER ASPECT ONLINE!

THE WARNER ASPECT HOMEPAGE
You'll find us at: www.twbookmark.com then
by clicking on Science Fiction and Fantasy.

NEW AND UPCOMING TITLES
Each month we feature our new titles
and reader favorites.

AUTHOR INFO
Author bios, bibliographies and links to
personal websites.

CONTESTS AND OTHER FUN STUFF
Advance galley giveaways, autographed
copies, and more.

THE ASPECT BUZZ
What's new, hot and upcoming from
Warner Aspect: awards news, best-
sellers, movie tie-in information . . .